Ernie Bowles watch  the restlessness she provoked made him take a more practical step to find a wife. If he couldn't have Lily he supposed someone else would do. He'd seen the lonely hearts columns in the farming magazines, had read them surreptitiously when his mother wasn't looking. He'd considered at first placing an ad there himself but had decided that that wasn't the way to go. He wanted a local girl. Someone he didn't have to travel too far to see. So he contacted an agency in Otterbridge, sent a photograph, filled in a form. And tonight he was going to meet a woman.

From an envelope that had been propped on the mantelpiece he took a photo. This was his date. She was his perfect match, the agency had said. She had chosen him from the rest of the men on their files. He read her details again, though he knew them almost by heart. Divorcée. Blond. Blue eyes.

He had arranged to meet her in the lounge bar of the Ship Hotel in Otterbridge. It was a longish way for him to go and the drinks were a bit pricey, but she hadn't said on her form if she could drive. Besides, he thought the Ship would impress her. He would buy her a meal. If they got on perhaps she would come to Mittingford next time. The real secret hope was that he would persuade her to come back with him tonight. That would show Lily Jackman.

By Ann Cleeves
Published by Fawcett Books:

The Stephen Ramsay Series
A LESSON IN DYING
MURDER IN MY BACKYARD
A DAY IN THE DEATH OF DOROTHEA CASSIDY
KILLJOY
THE HEALERS

The George and Molly Palmer-Jones Series
A BIRD IN THE HAND
COME DEATH AND HIGH WATER
MURDER IN PARADISE
A PREY TO MURDER
SEA FEVER
THE MILL ON THE SHORE

THE HEALERS

Ann Cleeves

FAWCETT GOLD MEDAL • NEW YORK

A Fawcett Gold Medal Book
Published by Ballantine Books
Copyright © 1995 by Ann Cleeves

All rights reserved under International and Pan-American Copyright Conventions. Published in the United States by Ballantine Books, a division of Random House, Inc., New York, and distributed in Canada by Random House of Canada Limited, Toronto. Originally published in Great Britain by Macmillan London in 1995.

Library of Congress Catalog Card Number: 95-90422

ISBN 0-449-14944-7

Manufactured in the United States of America

First American Edition: October 1995

10 9 8 7 6 5 4 3 2 1

1

O_n Saturday they went for a ride into the country. Like an old married couple, although marriage had never been discussed, never even been thought of as far as anyone knew. They stopped for lunch at a pub in Morpeth. There were four sorts of real ale, and in the back room drinkers were playing traditional folk music on fiddles and pipes. The musicians had between them a large number of children all brightly clothed in what seemed to be fancy dress—long velvet suits and silk waistcoats. The children danced between the tables and ate crisps by the handful but caused no real bother. Ramsay was driving and only took two halves of Gladiator, but Prue tried all the varieties of beer and after the meal felt quite tipsy. Since being a student, she'd always liked beer, but it went straight to her head.

"Where now?" Ramsay asked as they stepped out into the street. It was a warm blustery day in early May. A group of old men walked jauntily down the drive from St. George's, the big psychiatric hospital, now on the verge of closure. A sudden gust of wind blew a shower of blossoms from one of the trees along the drive and covered them in small pink flakes. The men stood still for a moment and then began to laugh, turning slowly round and round so the blossoms fell to the ground.

"Where now?" Ramsay said again, not impatiently. He regarded Prue's drunkenness indulgently. Diana, his ex-wife,

1

had always become aggressive after drinking, but Prue got giggly. And amorous.

"Home?" he suggested hopefully. "Yours or mine?"

"Neither," she said firmly. They seldom got out together and she was going to make the most of it. "A walk up Billy's Crag and then back to Mittingford for tea and cakes. And I can stock up from the health-food shop while I'm there."

Mittingford was in the middle of nowhere, close to the Scottish border, strangely out of place. It was a pretty little town, maintaining a prim Victorian gentility despite the bleakness of the moors which surrounded it. An oasis, almost, of civilization. The houses were turned in to a cobbled square and a wide main street with a culverted stream running along one side of it. Even from the middle of the town you could hear the sheep crying on the hills. Despite the flowers which had been planted in gardens, tubs, and window boxes—Mittingford regularly won best small town in the Northumberland in Bloom competition—the grey stone houses and the surrounding high crags gave the impression that it was always in shadow.

The health-food shop was in what had once been a large chapel, facing grandly onto the square with steps and pillars. Ten years previously the Methodists had built a modern church, easier to heat, and a collection of small business people had taken over the chapel and run it as a cooperative. Hippies, the locals called them, but they weren't all sixties dropouts with long hair and sandals. Some were very canny businessmen and the local shopkeepers saw the Old Chapel as dangerous competition.

Ramsay had never been there before, but Prue was an old hand. Inside, the space had been separated into small shops and craft workshops, which ran along the walls. The centre was a café with a stone floor and stripped pine tables and chairs. There they ate tea and cakes surrounded by a group of old ladies who were on a coach tour and had been allowed a twenty-minute refreshment stop. The morning, he learned as he automatically eavesdropped, had been spent in Edinburgh and there would be just time to visit the Roman fort on Hadrian's Wall before dinner in Hexham. Tomorrow would be York. The women were indefatigable, fit and lithe almost to the point of scrawniness. One of them looked at her watch, there was a sound of chairs scraping against the stone floor, and they all marched back to their bus.

The health-food shop was at the end of the chapel where the altar must have stood. If there had been an altar. Did Methodists have them? Ramsay wondered now, and found that he could not remember. As a child he had been sent to Sunday school by his devout mother, but that had been in a cold and draughty hall. He had a crush on his teacher, Miss Pearson, and there had been pictures to colour. Presumably at some point they must have been taken into the chapel to participate in the service. He tried to picture a likely occasion—Christmas perhaps or Harvest Festival—but the memory eluded him and he realised, suddenly, that Prue was speaking.

"Sorry?" he said. "I was miles away. What did you say?"

"They've converted the first floor, beyond the gallery, into an Alternative Therapy Centre. You know—acupuncture, homoeopathy, rebirthing."

What on earth, he wondered, was rebirthing? But he did not ask. Prue would have told him in far too much detail.

"Maddy's been there," she said. "For her hay fever. She swears by it. She even went away with them on a sort of weekend retreat." Maddy was her friend, a solicitor, given, Ramsay thought, to weird fads and enthusiasms which seldom lasted. Still he said nothing. He had learned, during his life with Diana, the value of strategic silence.

Prue pushed open the door into the health-food shop. Late-afternoon sunlight slanted through a stained-glass window onto sacks of grains and pulses. There was a display of organic vegetables—misshapen carrots and potatoes still covered in soil—and shelves of spices. Prue shopped enthusiastically, asking occasionally for things he had never heard of, topping off her order with whole-meal flour, free-range duck eggs, and yoghurt made from goat's milk.

"What about you?" she asked. "Isn't there anything you

3

need?" He shook his head. He did his shopping at Sainsbury's, and though he ate well enough, convenience mattered more than the way the food had been grown. He looked around the shop wondering why he found this temple to culinary correctness so depressing. Perhaps it was because the two members of staff seemed so unhealthy. There was an obese woman whose weight seemed pulled by gravity to the lower half of her body: her head was a normal size but her buttocks and legs were enormous. She presided over the bread and carrot cake. And there was a weedily malnourished young man with staring eyes and a shaved head.

Then another assistant appeared. She must have been reaching to fetch something from behind her counter. She walked out into the central space and stood, caught for a moment in the multicoloured light, almost posing. As if to prove to Ramsay the benefits of healthy eating. She had dark hair, pulled back into a smooth plait, and olive skin. She was tall and strong, and though he knew he was staring, he could not take his eyes off her. As bad as Hunter, he thought. Hunter, his assistant, insensitive, prejudiced, and lucky not to have a disciplinary charge for sexual harassment on his record.

"Isn't she a beauty?" Prue whispered, and he gave a little cough, as if he had hardly noticed.

Then he watched as she stretched up to reach a jar of coriander seeds from a high shelf. She was wearing a loose T-shirt with wide sleeves, and as she stretched, the sleeve fell back to show a bare, brown shoulder. Still he could not turn away. She walked back to her counter and he saw that she was wearing sandals with leather thongs across her toes and her feet were very long. She weighed a small amount of the spice on old-fashioned scales, tipped it into a brown paper bag, and handed it to a customer without a smile or a word.

Ramsay turned his back on her, deliberately. He opened his arms to take the bags and sacks piled on the counter beside Prue. That night he went home with Prue. He allowed her to cook a vegetarian meal for him, and even admitted that he had enjoyed it.

* * *

When she finished work at the Old Chapel, Lily pushed her bike out of the storeroom at the back of the building and began the ride home. She was angry. Sometimes she thought she was born angry. The lingering memory of her childhood was of an impotent rage, released occasionally in temper tantrums. A five-mile bike ride was the last thing she needed after a day on her feet, and her fury was directed temporarily against Sean. He should get off his backside and earn some money. Then perhaps they could afford a car. Then perhaps they could move away from Laverock Farm and find a place of their own.

The road was steep and narrow with overgrown verges, and for several minutes she thought of nothing but keeping the bike upright and getting to the top of the hill. She had to get off there to let a tractor pass in the opposite direction. She feared that Ernie Bowles might be the driver, then saw that the tractor was spanking new and the man in the cab was young, with a Walkman plugged into his ears. Peter Richardson from Long Edge Farm. Thinking about Ernie Bowles made her angry again. Her face was flushed from all the exercise and she realized that hot tears were scalding her cheeks.

Bloody Ernie Bowles, she thought. What a bastard that man is!

The farm was up a track, so potholed that she had to walk it. She wondered sometimes how he made a living. Did he have any regular income apart from the rent they paid for the caravan? When they'd first arrived they had thought the place was magical, old-fashioned, like something out of a child's storybook. No factory farming here. There were hens scratching around the yard, pigs in a sty, cows waiting patiently to be milked. They had thought Ernie had taken a moral stand against intensive farming. But it was laziness not morality which had motivated him.

Why couldn't we see what he was like then, that first time? she thought. Were we so blind?

Daniel had always said that it was Ernie's mother who had done all the work round the place. When she died the place

5

began to collapse around him. And so it had seemed to Lily, observing from the caravan. Animals sent to market were not replaced, machines which broke down were left to rot where they stood.

He'll go bust, she thought, now pushing the bike defiantly through the mucky farmyard. Then what'll become of us?

The caravan stood in the corner of a small meadow. It was painted green, but even from here she could see the rust around the door. The mild spring and the rain had made the grass come on suddenly and in places the cow parsley was almost waist-high. She left her bike by the gate and pushed a path through the grass. They had seen the caravan first in full summer with the meadow dry and the hay mixed with poppies. They had thought how lovely it was and had not considered practicalities like lugging Calor Gas cylinders from the track, or wet feet.

There was no sign of Sean, but that did not surprise her. When they had first moved to the caravan, he had spent most of the day there, in front of the portable typewriter which was the only material possession he would allow himself to get attached to. He had impressed her when they had first met by calling himself a writer and showing her a few things he'd had published in alternative magazines. That had been two years ago. There'd been a gang of them then, all travelling together, moving from festival to festival. She'd joined up with them somewhere in Mid Wales. Montgomery, was it? Newtown? Kerry? They'd been moved on so often that she couldn't quite remember.

The group had let her tag along. Sean had a pink Ford van with flowers painted on the bonnet and a sleeping bag and the typewriter in the back. Very hip. Very sixties. But she'd loved it all the same. The group were her family and it was her home. There'd been a London taxi and a purple hearse in the convoy, too, but when the weather turned cold its owners had drifted off to a squat in Cardiff and Sean and Lily had been left on the road, still in the pink van in those days, sleeping in the back even when it snowed. When the

Mittingford pigs had considered it as unroadworthy and they'd sold it as scrap, she'd been heartbroken.

When they first came to the caravan Sean had talked about writing a novel, *the* New Age novel, and had bashed away at it day and night. But recently he'd taken to disappearing during the day, evading her questions when she asked what he got up to. He seemed to have shrunk since she had first met him, to be thinner, quieter, altogether different. She worried about him occasionally, but she thought he'd always been better than her at coping, and when he said he was all right, she supposed she would have to believe him.

Just moody, she thought. Then she said out loud, her anger returning, "Bloody men!"

Why should I stay? she thought suddenly, and was immediately surprised that she had not asked the question before. What's keeping me here after all? Sean? What bloody good's he ever done me? I could leave now, cycle back to town. Someone in Mittingford would put me up. Win and Daniel. Or Magda. She'd understand.

But she stood, looking out of the open door of the caravan and she did not move. Sean had rescued her. She felt a kind of loyalty. Instead she turned her back on the meadow and the open door. She filled a kettle from the water container under the sink and lit the Calor to make some tea.

2

From behind grey net curtains Ernie Bowles watched Lily Jackman cross the yard. He always seemed to know what time she would arrive back from work. It had become his habit to be in the house to watch her. Sometimes she wore shorts, so he could see her long brown legs, and a sleeveless T-shirt which left nothing to the imagination. Today it was a skirt and a loose, shapeless top, which was disappointing. Still the glimpse of her, bent over the bicycle, excited him. He watched her through the gate and into the meadow.

It was his dream, a fantasy so delicious that he could hardly acknowledge it himself, that she would give Sean the push and move in with him. The possibility lurked on the edge of his consciousness and made him restless. It wasn't that he would take advantage of her. Marriage was at the heart of his vague, barely formed plans. Marriage had been on his mind a lot lately.

He hadn't thought much about it while his mother was alive. No one could match up to her and he couldn't imagine two women in the house. Even toward the end, when she was crippled with arthritis and nothing seemed to ease the pain, his mother had kept him straight and organised. He wasn't lazy, whatever people thought. He didn't mind work. He'd done all that needed seeing to on the farm. But his mother had told him what to do. Every morning at breakfast she'd set it out for him:

"Those lambs'll need dipping," she'd say. Or: "You won't forget that the tanker will be early today."

And she'd come out and look at what he was doing, pulling herself along on that Zimmer frame she'd got from the hospital. She would check that it was all in order. It had never really occurred to him that she might die. Not so soon. Whoever heard of arthritis killing someone?

He'd thought at first that it would be all right on his own. No one to boss him. No one waiting up when he got in late from the town to tell him that drink belonged to the devil and if he spent any more time in the Sheep's Head, he'd go to hell. No one to drag him to chapel on a Sunday to repent. But he couldn't see to everything on his own; that soon became clear. Not the house and the farm. And he deserved some comfort, a meal in his belly after a day in the fields, clean sheets on his bed once in a while.

So he watched Lily and dreamed. Then the restlessness she provoked made him take a more practical step to find a wife. If he couldn't have Lily, he supposed someone else would do. He'd seen the lonely hearts columns in the farming magazines, had read them surreptitiously when his mother wasn't looking. He'd considered at first placing an advert there himself but had decided that that wasn't the way to go on. He wanted a local girl. Someone he didn't have to travel too far to see. So he contacted an agency in Otterbridge, sent a photograph, filled in a form. And tonight he was going to meet a woman.

Lily had long since disappeared from sight and he turned back to the room. It was tidy enough. He liked to keep things tidy. If he'd known the word, he'd have called it an obsession. During his National Service he'd been an officer's batman. He knew about standards. But he didn't seem to be able to keep it clean. A film of fine ash dust from the boiler covered the surfaces, and the lino beneath his feet was tacky with spilled food. He needed a wife to look after him, he thought, like every other man he knew. It was what he deserved.

From an envelope which had been propped on the mantelpiece he took a photo. This was his date. She was his perfect match, the agency had said. She had chosen him from the rest of the men on their files. He read again her details, though he knew them almost by heart. Jane Symons. Divorcée. Blond. Blue eyes. Forty-four years old. She was, she had written, manageress of a high-class shoe store. He wondered briefly if he would get shoes at a discount. He could do with a new pair of boots. The photo was small, the kind you can have taken in a machine, just a head shot. When he looked at it he couldn't connect it with a real person, with the blond-haired, blue-eyed divorcée of his imagination.

He had arranged to meet her in the lounge bar of the Ship Hotel in Otterbridge. It was a longish way for him to go and the drinks were a bit pricey, but she hadn't said on her form if she could drive. Besides, he thought the Ship would impress her. He would buy her a meal. If they got on, perhaps she would come over to Mittingford next time. The real secret hope was that he would persuade her to come back with him tonight. That would show Lily Jackman.

In the depths of the house his mother's clock chimed the half hour. Half past six. For some reason it had kept better time since the old lady had died. Not like the one in the song. If he was going to meet Jane at eight, he'd have to get a move on. Jane. He said the word out loud, practising.

No time for a bath, he thought, without much regret. He hadn't lit the boiler this morning, and if he waited for the immersion to heat the water, he'd be there all night. He'd put a kettle on and have a wash at the kitchen sink as he had when he was a lad.

When he was ready he thought he was smart enough for any woman. He'd bought a shirt for the occasion from the small gent's outfitters in Mittingford and there was the suit his mother had made him get for his uncle's funeral. He cleaned his shoes, spitting on them as he'd been taught during National Service.

Jane, he thought again, pushing thoughts of Lily Jackman to the back of his mind. Likes: the countryside, classical music, walking. She had left the dislikes space on the form blank. He hoped that meant she was an easy and accommodating person. A gay divorcée, he thought. Meaning laughter, sex.

The grandfather clock struck seven. At least half an hour to get to Otterbridge and park, and then he'd need a couple of drinks for Dutch courage before she arrived. He locked the farmhouse door behind him. When Mother was alive he'd never bothered. She'd be more than a match for any burglar. But he didn't trust Sean any further than he could throw him.

He crossed the yard gingerly, trying to avoid getting his shoes too mucky. From the Land Rover he could see over the wall into the meadow. Sean was sitting on the caravan steps with his head in his hands. He must have heard the Land Rover starting up—it was a diesel engine and it needed a service—but he did not look up at the sound. Ernie wondered wistfully if they'd had a row.

The fantasy returned of Lily in his kitchen, cooking his meals, and in his bed smoothing away the pains of the day with her long, brown fingers. But, he told himself sternly, there were other women in his life now. He had other fish to fry. He drove off.

On Saturday night Val McDougal, too, was preparing to go out. At that point it was all she had in common with Ernie Bowles. Later their names would be linked together, but they had never met.

Val's husband, Charles, was surprised that she had arranged to go out. They had developed a ritual to Saturdays. To relieve the stress, he said, after a week at the grindstone. He worked in the university. Sociology was his subject, though these days, he said, it was hardly a thing you owned up to. Better tell the man in the Clapham omnibus that you were a serial killer than a sociologist. Val, who had never known him to travel anywhere by bus and had heard it all before, usually managed to contain her irritation. She taught basic literacy and numeracy skills in a further education college, and secretly she thought sociology was a waste of time, too.

On Saturday they got up late. Only one of their sons was still at home: James, who was in the upper sixth and preparing to take A Levels. He was a placid, amenable boy who fitted in with them. At least he did his own thing and made no demands. He did not play music late at night or throw up in the garden after an all-night party. Richard, their elder son, had done both these things. Luckily he was now away at university.

The three of them would have a late and lazy breakfast: croissants bought fresh by Charles from a local bakery and lots of coffee. At midday Val and Charles would walk into the town to a pub by the river where they'd meet a group of friends. The friends were mostly Charles's. They had clear, loud voices and told jokes about the sociology professor who spent more time talking on Radio 4 than to his staff. The same jokes were told week after week. Charles would drink beer and Val white wine and soda for most of the afternoon, then they would emerge into the town centre to go shopping.

This wasn't boring shopping. They didn't buy toilet rolls or bleach or cat food. Val would get all that from the supermarket on the way back from college on her early night. This was quite different. Late in their married life Charles had taken to cooking, and indeed he was very good. At first Val had been grateful. These Saturday-night extravagances were something of a treat and she had enjoyed wandering round Otterbridge with him looking for the special ingredients he needed. But lately the novelty had begun to wear off. His creations were always elaborate and took most of the evening to prepare. He used every utensil they possessed. And because he had cooked, she felt obliged to clear up the chaos and load the dishwasher afterwards, though she noticed that he never felt the same obligation after her weekday stews and spaghetti Bolognese.

12

At breakfast on that Saturday he had asked, as he always did:

"Well, what shall we eat tonight?"

She had answered, as casually as she could. "Well, actually, I won't be here. I'll be going out."

"Where?" he asked petulantly.

"Just to a friend's for supper."

"You didn't say." His voice was accusing.

No, she thought. I was frightened. I didn't have the nerve.

"We fixed it up at the last moment," she said, "and I thought it would be quite nice for a change."

She realised how lame that sounded, saw that her hands were shaking, wondered even if she would have one of those panic attacks which she seemed to have been controlling better lately, despite Charles's scorn. He was right, of course. She was quite feeble. But he had a frightening temper and she never liked to upset him.

"Who is this friend?" he demanded. "Someone from college?"

"No," she said vaguely. "I met her on that weekend away at the Lakes. I told you we'd kept in touch."

"Did you? I don't remember."

He thinks I'm lying, she thought with astonishment. Perhaps he thinks I'm having a wild affair with a secret lover. She smiled to herself and saw him become even more suspicious. She enjoyed his uncertainty. It served him right. She was certain that he'd been having a fling with a bright, postgraduate student called Heather for more than a term.

"I shouldn't be late," she said. "Not very late."

She could hardly tell him that he bored her to the point where she had been physically ill, and that if she didn't have an evening away from him, she would do something desperate.

3

Although the Old Chapel opened on Sundays, Lily Jackman had the day off. Yet she woke early, was suddenly wide-awake, and realised that Sean was not there. The night before he had arrived back at the caravan soon after her. He had eaten a tin of beans and gone away again. Just for a walk, he said, and she knew better than to ask where he was going. Now it seemed he had not come back all night. He had never done that before.

She opened the caravan door and looked out at Laverock Farm. Everything was very still. There was no smoke coming from the chimney, no clatter of machinery. Only a dog barking furiously and that bloody cockerel which had probably woken her in the first place.

Then she saw Sean, walking across the farmyard. He bent to slide between the struts of the five-barred gate, as if he were too tired to push it open. She shouted before he was halfway across the field:

"Where the hell have you been?"

He looked up as if he were surprised by her anger. His eyes were bleary and his coat was crumpled.

"Where the hell have you been? I've been worried sick."

"I'm sorry," he said. "I thought I'd be back before you woke."

"You haven't been walking all night?"

He shook his head. "I met some people. Parked at the

gypsy transit site on the way into town. I knew them from Wales. Wes and Lorna. They had a blue Transit, still have. You must remember."

He leaned over her, strangely insistent.

"I don't know," she said. "There were so many people."

"They've got a kid now. A girl, pretty little thing. They're talking about settling down so she can go to school."

She turned away. Sean was always talking about settling down. He blamed his midnight wanderings on the fact that he was unsettled. Because she wouldn't give him a commitment that their relationship was permanent. She saw it as a sort of blackmail.

"I'm going to get ready," she said. "Are you coming to the Abbots' or do you want to stay here?"

"No," he said. "I'll come." To spy on me, she thought. To see who I talk to. He pretended that he wasn't jealous, but she could tell from the way he looked at her that he saw her as a sort of possession.

"You can go to the launderette then," she said, to punish him, "while I go to Magda's group."

On Sundays they went to the Abbots' for lunch. Every week, Daniel and Win Abbot, acupuncturist and homoeopath, the founder members of the Old Chapel Alternative Therapy Centre, had open house. Sean and Lily were always there. Lily suspected they were invited to salve the Abbots' consciences and to provide a topic of conversation. It was the Abbots who had brought them to Mittingford in the first place and then dumped them in Ernie Bowles's caravan to keep them out of the way. This Sunday, unusually, they were the only guests. Lily could tell that the Abbots had not put as much effort into the food and its presentation as when other people were present. Lunch was a scrappy affair and the couple seemed distant and rather fraught. Lily and Sean sat at the kitchen table eating macaroni and cheese as if, Lily thought, they were the deserving poor.

Otherwise it was all much as usual. Daniel spoke smugly about his work. The Natural Therapy Society in Otterbridge had invited one of his old lecturers to give a talk, he said,

15

and he'd been asked to do the introduction. Win fussed over the children. Lily was reminded of Sunday lunch in the large and gloomy house in Clifton where she had spent her childhood. Occasionally her mother returned from London to join them and there was an attempt at gaiety, at real family life. Lily had known that it was all pretence and had the same sense now. Perhaps the Abbots weren't the model couple everyone thought them to be. She would have liked to believe in them and the idea depressed her. Sean was no help. He seemed more dazed than usual, shovelling food into his mouth with a fork, his eyes on his plate.

When she had first met them Lily had thought Win and Daniel the most together couple she had ever seen— organised, hardworking, still idealistic. Not a bundle of laughs, she'd had to admit from the beginning. Not exactly fun to be with. They took themselves and everything they did too seriously for that. But successful in every way. Now she wasn't so sure. Something about Daniel gave her the creeps and Win never seemed happy.

Lily supposed that professionally they were doing well for themselves. They had that in common. She had heard the story of their conversion to alternative medicine many times. Both, for different reasons, had been interested in health since childhood. Daniel's father had been a consultant neurologist and Daniel had enjoyed the reflected glory, the status, the power. He had applied to medical school himself but had been turned down. These days nepotism could not overcome mediocre exam results. At the interview it had been suggested that he go in for nursing, but that would hardly have provided the same rewards. He'd drifted for a while after that, travelled. Subsidised by affluent and indulgent parents, he'd made it out to India, joined second-generation hippies seeking enlightenment, had his consciousness raised. Or so he claimed. Came across the idea of natural therapy, took to acupuncture like a duck to water. It was logical, he said. It made sense. And it made him feel useful.

His parents were sceptical but determined to be liberal. He was their only son. They funded his training at the Traditional Acupuncture College at Leamington Spa. When he set up in his original practice, they paid the first six months' rent, and when he and Win moved to Mittingford, they paid the deposit on the house. The venture at the Old Chapel soon flourished. He was everything his patients required in a practitioner—grave, calm, and authoritative. He wore a white coat and they treated him as an old-fashioned family doctor. He encouraged them in the belief that he was infallible.

Win's childhood encounter with medicine had been as a consumer. Her father had died, when she was a baby, of one of those strange genetic disorders for which there is no cure. She had suffered dreadfully from asthma and eczema. In the playground she wheezed and scratched and was picked on by other children. Her mother was a remarkable woman who had survived bereavement without bitterness, but she was determined not to lose her child, too. Win was dragged along to a variety of doctors, all of whom diagnosed her illness as psychosomatic. Only after she consulted a homoeopath did the condition improve. Both mother and daughter were instantly converted to the benefits of complementary medicine. The mother, as she admitted wryly later, rather went overboard. She went on numerous courses, took up strange diets, and settled for a while on reflexology as her preferred method of healing. Throughout Win's adolescence their house was filled with unfamiliar people who exposed their feet to her mother's gaze. It was quite natural for Win to follow in the same path. She had never been a natural rebel. She believed, quite literally, her mother's assertion that homoeopathy had saved her life, and saw it as her mission in life to spread the word to others.

In time Win's mother had moved on from reflexology to rebirthing. Now she was an establishment figure in the movement, an old hand, regarded as a guru and a leader by the younger people who followed her. She had written widely and had been featured in the national press. THE ACCEPTABLE FACE OF QUACKERY, one of the headlines had said. She gave advice on childbirth, relationships, and her photogenic face made her one of the strong women loved by the

17

colour supplements. Her fame gave her a special mystique. She had a reputation among her young disciples for wisdom, though they never defined what that meant. She set up a clinic in a house in Hampstead and had politicians and rock stars among her clients.

Then Daniel had persuaded her to join them at the Old Chapel. It was a great coup. Everyone admitted that and wondered how he had managed to pull it off. Perhaps all the publicity in the capital had frightened her away. She did talk occasionally about needing to return to the simple life, and she seemed quite content in the little flat next to the Alternative Therapy Centre, under the roof of the Old Chapel. She had sold the big house in Hampstead and there was considerable speculation about what had happened to the money. Lily was occasionally tempted to ask her, but had never quite found the nerve. Magda didn't encourage idle conversation.

But Magda Pocock had definitely brought success, Lily thought, looking round the Abbots' stylish house. The Alternative Therapy Centre must be a thriving business now. Then she was ashamed that financial calculations had entered her thoughts, because Magda had become a guru to her, too, besides a surrogate mother and role model.

"Are you going to Magda's group this afternoon?" Lily asked. Win was pouring coffee into hand-thrown mugs. She looked haggard, tired, undernourished. Not a brilliant advert for homoeopathy, Lily thought, but perhaps that was what motherhood did to you. Win had given birth to two boys, only a year apart, as if she wanted to get the mucky business over with as soon as possible.

"No," Win said. "Not this afternoon." She offered no excuse.

On Sunday afternoons Magda ran what she called her Insight Group, a nineties version of the encounter group.

"We're doing Voice Dialogue," Lily said.

"What about you, Daniel?" she added. But Daniel obviously thought he had no need of insight. He led workshops but seldom participated in them. He shook his head, smiling slightly.

18

"I suppose baby-sitting must be a problem," Lily said. "Now Faye's not around anymore." She saw Win turn away and realised she'd put her foot in it. She went on, to make amends: "You know I'd always baby-sit if you're stuck."

"Would you?" Win turned to Daniel. "Perhaps Lily could baby-sit tomorrow night. So I could come to the lecture with you."

"Why not?" Daniel said, but his response was halfhearted, and Lily had the impression that he would have preferred to go alone.

"Sure," Lily said. "I'll come straight from work. Daniel can give me a lift home after, if he doesn't mind."

She was pleased with the arrangement. At least she would have an evening away from the caravan and Laverock Farm. She did wonder, briefly, what Daniel could be up to.

That Sunday afternoon, in a small terraced house in Wallsend, a dozen misfits and loners crammed into the tiny front room to sing rousing choruses to praise the Lord. Despite the heat the men wore dark suits and ties and the women gloves and mushroom-shaped fluffy hats. There was a squeaky harmonium. After the songs and some prayers they sat, excitingly crushed together on the settee or on dining chairs brought in for the purpose, to listen to Ron Irving giving the address.

Brother Ron prided himself on his topical sermons. He was a small, dark man given, some of them knew, to violent tempers and secret drinking, but he was a skilled speaker. In the previous week the newspapers and television had focused on an illegal New Age festival, held on some common land in Gloucestershire, a precursor to the solstice assault on Stonehenge. Ron took up the subject again, with delight.

"You must not think of these followers of the New Age as being simply misguided seekers of the truth," he boomed. In the house next door the television was switched up louder in compensation. "Oh no! Most have had a way to the word of the Lord and have turned away from it. They have joined the

19

path to sorcery, witchcraft, and the devil. Through choice and deliberate wickedness."

There was a shuffling of seats in anticipation. They liked to hear Ron talk about the devil. It was better than a good horror film any day. But they were disappointed. His tone changed.

"That path always leads to misery and disaster," he said, so quietly that they could hear the football commentary through the wall. "We know that, don't we? We've seen it in our own congregation. Our own little Faye, my stepdaughter, Joan's beloved baby, turned her back on righteousness and paid the ultimate price for her sin."

Magda Pocock was a striking woman. Her background was mixed—Eastern European and minor English gentry. When she was younger her features had been too large to make her attractive, but she seemed to have grown into them. The high cheekbones, the heavy eyebrows gave an impression of gravity and power, of someone at least who should be taken seriously. "The Germaine Greer of the New Age," one of the Sundays had called her. She had laughed at that but taken it as a compliment; looking at herself in the mirror, she had understood what was meant.

They had cleared all the furniture from the reception area in the Alternative Therapy Centre. It was still cramped but it was the best she could do, better at least than using a draughty church hall or a school gymnasium smelling of cabbage and sweaty children. The group were sitting on the floor, chanting. Not choruses to the glory of God but a low, communal tone. Magda always started her session that way. A deep breath into the pit of the stomach, then an exhalation which became vocalised, relieving tension, making new members feel part of the group. Lily, sitting cross-legged, shut her eyes and felt herself relax for the first time that day. Magda looked round the circle to see who was there. She saw a couple of new faces but mostly the old crowd: Lily Jackman, Val McDougal.

"Get into pairs," she said. Lily and Val moved together.

Lily looked towards Magda, expecting her to separate them so their experience could be shared, but she must have decided not to make an issue of it. Lily was pleased. She did not have the energy today to work with a stranger.

"Just a few exercises to help us feel at ease with each other," Magda said, and got them to shut their eyes and explore each other's faces with their fingertips. Her voice, compelling, still slightly foreign, allowed no awkwardness. Lily, feeling Val's hands on her neck and forehead, felt like crying.

"Now stand facing each other. Imagine one of you is the mirror image of the other. As one moves, so must the other. But let no one be the leader. Be so aware of each other that you move together, almost instinctively."

She walked among them, encouraging them. Then told them to sit again while she explained about Voice Dialogue. "Each of us has different subpersonalities within us," she said. "Each with its own voice clamouring to be heard: the submissive child, the critic, the pleaser, the pusher, the rulemaker, the playful child, and many others. Some of these subpersonalities we are conscious of, some we identify with very strongly, some we disown, not wanting to admit even to ourselves that these energies belong to us. Others we are yet to discover. By giving expression to the different voices inside us, each pulling us in its own direction, we can begin to be more aware of our complexity, more aware of balance, of what is best for us as a whole."

In their pairs they should explore these different voices, Magda said. They should speak with them. Move to different chairs or cushions as they gave expression to the different facets of their own personality. Starting with the 'primary self'; the subpersonality they identified most with. It would not do, Magda said, to blame their background or upbringing for weakness or lack of confidence. They could take responsibility for their own emotional well-being. Voice Dialogue could help them to do that.

4

News of the murder came to Stephen Ramsay early on Monday morning. He was in a meeting, one of the endless meetings the chief superintendent regularly called. The superintendent was a new appointee. He had been on management courses, spent a secondment in industry. Ramsay supposed the new Home Office plans for accountability and professional appraisal would attract others like him, grey men whose idea of effective management was more memos, more meetings. The talk was of limited resourcing, cuts. Ramsay found it hard to concentrate. The summons from Hunter came as a relief.

They stood together in the corridor outside the conference room.

"Definitely murder," Hunter said. He tried unsuccessfully to contain his relish.

"Where?"

"A place called Laverock Farm. In the wilds beyond Mittingford."

"Not a bad day for a trip into the countryside," Ramsay said, and Hunter thought his boss was almost human these days. Almost. It was getting his end away after all this time. Ramsay never talked about Prue Bennett at work, but everyone knew what was going on. You couldn't hide an affair like that in a place as small as Otterbridge.

"Who's the victim?" Ramsay asked.

"An old bloke. A farmer called Bowles. Strangled."

"I was only up that way at the weekend," Ramsay said.

With your fancy woman, Hunter thought, but did not say. He was changing, too. Learning some tact with the years. Ramsay heard the silence and was grateful. He and Hunter were rubbing along better now than at any time since they had started working together.

It's time he settled down, Ramsay thought. He should find himself a good woman. Recognising the evangelical zeal of the newly converted, he smiled to himself.

Look at him! Hunter thought with a trace of envy. Like the cat that's got the bloody cream.

The isolation of Laverock Farm was a complication. There was a worry that the scene-of-crime officers, the photographer, the pathologist might not find it. Ramsay ordered the fax of Ordnance Survey maps. He talked to an inspector in charge of the northern division about using the old police station in Mittingford as a base. When he and Hunter left Otterbridge almost an hour later, he saw, with satisfaction, that the budget meeting was still in progress.

They found Ernie Bowles in the farmhouse kitchen, lying on the floor.

"Not a pretty sight," Hunter said. "But then he wouldn't have been that when he was alive." He saw a squat plump man in his late fifties. A paunch bulged over the belt of his trousers. He was wearing a suit of sorts, shiny at the elbows with a stain down one lapel. Hunter was cared for by a doting mother and was prepared to spend half a week's wage on a designer shirt.

"He must have lived on his own," he said. "No woman would have let him out looking like that."

Hunter had definite views on the role of women.

Ramsay said nothing. Hunter's prejudices dismayed him, but he did not want to break the fragile peace between them. He was surprised by the shabby discomfort of the kitchen. In his experience farmers, despite their pleas of poverty, still had a reasonable standard of living. They drove big cars, perhaps not replaced every August now, but seldom more than a couple of years old. His ex-wife Diana knew girls who had married into farming families and he had been taken occasionally to visit. They had drunk good red wine in farmhouse kitchens, equipped with an expensive new Aga and a dishwasher and Liberty print curtains. There had been many good years, after all, before the recession. Then it occurred to him that any girl who had been a friend of Diana's probably had a private income. Perhaps this was more typical. No money had been spent on this place for a quarter of a century. The furniture was not new but there was nothing of quality. No family heirlooms but postwar utility and sixties mass production. The person who had furnished this house had been mean.

They had arrived at the farm before the hordes who always attended a suspicious death. The only other person present was the area's community policeman, a comfortable middle-aged man, who had been despatched before all the details of Ernie Bowles's death were known.

"He used to live here with his mam," the policeman said. "Don't want to speak ill of the dead, like, but she was a right old tartar. There weren't many round here who were sorry to see her go." He looked around him. "Mind you, at least she used to keep the place clean."

"When did she die?" Ramsay asked. This was what he enjoyed most about an investigation, the digging into the victim's background, piecing together a picture of the live individual. Hunter hated it. He thought it was a waste of time.

"A few months ago. Just before Christmas." The constable pulled a face. "I don't think this floor's been washed since then."

"So Bowles lived on his own?"

"In the house, aye. Of course there are those two hippies in the caravan."

"Oh?" Hunter was immediately interested. Ramsay saw he was preparing to indulge another prejudice. New Age travellers were social security scroungers who had never done a day's work in their lives. They should be rounded up and de-

24

ported. And they certainly could all be considered as potential murderers.

"Aye, the girl found him."

"Girl?" Ramsay asked.

"Well, young woman we'd have to call her now. She's in her twenties, I suppose. Lily Jackman. Pretty lass. She and her boyfriend have been Bowles's tenants since last summer. We've got a fair few of them round here."

"Them?" Ramsay asked, dangerously.

"You know. Hippy types. They don't do much harm. That crew at the Old Chapel in Mittingford seem to attract them. They could all do with a good wash, but apart from that . . ."

Ramsay heard the words with Prue's ears. She had her own prejudices. She thought all policemen were narrow-minded bigots.

"When did Ms. Jackman find the body?" he asked, emphasising the "Ms.," a gesture at least.

"She was on her way out to work," the constable said. "She called in at the house to tell Bowles that the Calor Gas cylinder needed changing. Knocked at the kitchen door, and when there was no reply she went in. She used Bowles's phone in the living room to call us."

"Where does she work?" Ramsay asked.

"At the Old Chapel in Mittingford. In the health-food shop."

"Is she there now?"

"No. I thought you'd want to talk to her. She's in the caravan with a WPC and that boyfriend of hers."

"Do you know anything about him?"

"Not much," the policeman said, "though I've seen him about. He seems to be a great one for wandering. He must walk miles. He doesn't have any work, not so far as I know. I think a couple of farmers took him on as casual labour at the end of the summer, but he wasn't much use. Not much of a worker, they said. A dreamer. Not quite all there. I don't think anyone bothers to ask him now, or even if he's looking. He survives on the dole, I suppose."

Hunter looked smug but said nothing.

Ramsay turned back to the body. It had the waxy pallor of a tailor's dummy.

"What about a next of kin?" he asked.

"None, so far as I know. He was certainly an only child. And he never married."

"His father's dead, too?"

"I presume so. If there ever *was* a father."

"Why, man, there must have been a father," Hunter said. "Unless you still believe in the gooseberry bush out here in the sticks."

"I meant a father living with the family," the constable replied stiffly. "For as long as I can remember, old lady Bowles and Ernie lived here on their own. Perhaps that was why they were so odd, the two of them. Even when he was a grown man she used to treat him as a child. They never mixed much with the other farming families. Reclusive, you could say. Illegitimacy mattered fifty years ago. Perhaps that's why they kept themselves so much to themselves. It might explain her obsession with religion, too. She was a great one for sin was Cissie Bowles. Saw it everywhere. I was called out to a disturbance in Mittingford once. She'd called some lass a harlot because she wore a skirt like a pelmet and walked through the town with her arm round her boyfriend."

"Bonkers," Hunter interrupted.

"I don't think she was really mad. Not loopy. You'd not get any doctor to lock her away. But she was eccentric, all right."

"Perhaps you could find out the family background," Ramsay suggested. "It's probably not relevant, but I'd be interested to know who the father was. Ask around the district. People will talk to you more freely than to us."

"Aye," the constable said, "though I don't know what use it'll be. All rumour and gossip. Lots of the kids in Mittingford were brought up to think of Cissie Bowles as some sort of witch. You'll get nothing objective."

"All the same," Ramsay said, "it'll give us something to work on."

"She used to come into town on market day," the police-man said. "To stock up for the week and pay her bills, even if she had no business. She always wore black. Great black boots like men would wear down the pit. A black coat which was too big for her and flapped around her ankles when she walked. And a black scarf round her head. Wor lass always said she looked like a Russian peasant." He paused for a moment in memory. "While she was alive everything was paid for in cash. The story was that she wouldn't trust banks. When they bought the Land Rover even that was paid for in cash. So the story went."

"I suppose that provides some sort of motive," Ramsay said.

"From what I hear Ernie Bowles didn't make enough to have piles of money around the house. And he'd surely have opened a bank account by now."

"It wouldn't really matter, would it?" Ramsay said. "If the murderer believed that there was a secret hoard of cash in the house, that would be motive enough. For breaking in at least. Ernie could have surprised the thief."

Hunter was dismissive. He had two credit cards and a per-manent overdraft. In the modern world that was how things were done. He wasn't going to be taken in by a fairy story about a wicked witch and a pot of gold. "There's no sign of a search here," he said. "It's all pretty mucky, but nothing's been disturbed."

"And we'll keep it that way until the SOCO and forensic have been in," Ramsay said. Most murders were simple: an explosion of family pressure, the loss of control in a fight. Most were aggravated by alcohol and macho self-delusion. But this wouldn't be simple. He'd need all the help he could get. He turned back to the policeman.

"You've spoken a lot about Cissie Bowles," he said. "I've got a clear picture of her. But you've not told us much about the victim. What was he like?"

The policeman paused. "He was in the old lady's shadow. He wouldn't fart without asking her first. He didn't have any personality of his own."

27

"But when she died, what impression did you have of him then?"

"There was something creepy about him," the policeman replied.

"Something you couldn't put your finger on." He smiled awkwardly. "Wor lass always said he was like something that had crawled out from under a stone."

"So he wasn't a pleasant man," Ramsay said.

"No," the constable assured him, "he certainly wasn't that."

"The sort of man to make enemies?"

"I wouldn't have put it as strong as that. But the sort of man to get up your nose."

They stood for a moment looking down at the body. It wasn't much of an epitaph, Ramsay thought. Not the sort of thing you'd want inscribed on your headstone.

"And whose nose, specifically, did he get up?" he asked.

There was a pause. "It was all something and nothing," the constable said at last.

"But?"

"There was a bit of a scrap in the pub a few weeks ago. Peter Richardson's a local lad. Finished at agricultural college last year. His dad farms the land next to Laverock and they've never been friendly. Peter's always been a hothead, and he'd had too much to drink and not enough sense to be quiet. He started throwing a few punches."

"Why?"

The constable shrugged. "No charges were brought in the end, but the story goes that he didn't like the way Ernie was looking at his lass."

Hardly a motive for murder, Ramsay thought, not after all this time, but all the same the boy would have to be seen.

"We'll take a statement," he said easily, "along with everyone else." He recognised the policeman's divided loyalties. "Would you mind staying here and waiting for the scientists? We'll go to the caravan and talk to the woman who found the body."

5

In the yard there was a smell of muck, coming from a heap of manure and straw in one corner. A couple of scrawny hens scrambled out from behind a pile of weeds and began to peck at their ankles. Ramsay saw with amusement that Hunter was ridiculously put out by the birds.

"Don't be scared, Sergeant," he said. "They'll not hurt you."

"Aren't they all supposed to be kept in batteries these days?" Hunter said. "It doesn't seem very hygienic letting them scrabble around in this filth."

Ramsay thought that the livestock at Laverock would cause him another headache. Someone would have to look after the animals or he'd have the RSPCA on his back for neglect. Perhaps the hippy couple would take responsibility for the place until he could sort out something more permanent. Or perhaps he should ask someone more competent, like a neighbouring farmer. Peter Richardson's father?

From the corner of his eye he watched Hunter surreptitiously kick out at the bantams.

The farmyard was bounded on one side by the house and garden, with a track to the road and the rest of the land. Two others were made up of barns and outbuildings. The fourth, and shortest side, had a stone wall and a five-barred gate leading to a field. The gate had sunk on its hinges and they had to lift it.

29

In the night there had been rain and the grass was still wet. By the time they reached the caravan their trousers, socks, and shoes were soaking. A pale-skinned young man with thin hair pulled back in a ponytail was sitting on the caravan steps. At first it seemed to Ramsay that Sean was watching their progress through the cow parsley with enjoyment, but as they got closer he said, vaguely, almost apologetically:

"I'm sorry about that. I keep meaning to cut a path. . . ."

He stood up and opened the door for them to go inside.

When Ramsay saw that Lily Jackman was the attractive girl from the health-food shop, he was not surprised. He had known, somehow, that she would be. Behind him he heard Hunter mutter something appreciative under his breath and turned to warn him. Lily looked up and stared at the two men but did not recognise Ramsay. She was sitting listlessly on the padded bench which ran against one wall and which, presumably, they pulled out each night to make a bed. In the confined space he felt clumsy and awkward. A WPC was sitting impassively and unsympathetically on an identical bench beyond a pull-down table. She, too, it seemed, did not care for travellers. Ramsay sent her back to the farm. "We can manage now," he said. "Thank you." She stood up sulkily and went out without a word.

"Miserable cow," Lily said, under her breath. Ramsay pretended not to hear.

Sean slid in beside Lily and Ramsay and Hunter took the opposite bench. It was very cramped and their knees were almost touching under the table. Ramsay was aware of Hunter staring at Lily, but she seemed not to notice. Perhaps she was used to it. He introduced himself, briefly.

"I'll have to ask some questions," he said, trying to be gentle, remembering that she had probably never seen a body before. "Mr. Bowles was murdered, you see. Perhaps you realised. There'll be a police investigation."

Lily stared back at them blankly. Hunter lowered his eyes.

"Yeah," Sean said. "Right. Of course." He took her hand.

"We didn't have anything to do with it," Lily said, suddenly. "You can't pin it on us."

"It's not my job to pin it on anyone," Ramsay said. "My job is to find out what happened."

He spoke briskly, with what Prue called his schoolmaster voice, and he realised he must have sounded pompous.

But Lily blushed. "Yes," she said. "I'm sorry. It's just that people like us always seem to get the blame. We're natural scapegoats." She took a tobacco tin from her pocket and began to roll a very thin cigarette.

"People like who?"

"Unconventional people, travellers." She paused and added mockingly: "Hippies."

"But you haven't done much travelling recently," Ramsay said. "Have you? I understand that you've been living here since last summer."

He couldn't place her social background. Her voice was without accent, deep, rather throaty. An actress's voice, he thought, then wondered if the huskiness was caused by cigarettes, not a desire for effect. Perhaps he was being unfair to her.

"You have been living here since last summer?" he repeated.

"Yes," she said bitterly. "Nine bloody months."

"Haven't you been happy here?"

"Would you be?" she snapped back, then seemed to regret her rudeness. "Look," she said, "we were glad to move in. It seemed perfect. Right out in the country. You know."

"But not so much fun in the winter," Ramsay said easily.

"Bloody freezing," she agreed. "But it wasn't only that. . . ." She paused.

"What is it, then? The inconvenience?" Hunter spoke for the first time and she looked him up and down before answering, sarcastically:

"Yes, the inconvenience."

Of course it was more than that, Ramsay thought. He waited, hoping she would explain why she really disliked the place so intensely.

"It isn't that bad here," Sean said awkwardly. "Not really. I've lived in worse places."

"You're just soft," she said. "I think you'd be happy anywhere."

"I would," he said. "Anywhere living with you." The words were so sentimental that Ramsay thought he was teasing, but he was quite serious. Lily seemed infuriated by the remark.

"Then you're a bloody fool," she said.

"You could have moved on," Ramsay said. "Couldn't you?" He directed the question at Lily, sensing that she was the one who took all the decisions.

"Yes," she said. "I suppose we could."

"Why didn't you?"

She shrugged. "Partly money," she said. "I work in the health-food shop in Mittingford. It only pays peanuts, but it's too much for Sean to be eligible for benefit. We're stuck in the poverty trap. Isn't that what they call it? That's what it feels like. We'd need some money to move on, to buy a van or a truck and do it up."

"But it isn't just money," Ramsay said.

"No," she said, "it isn't just that." She leaned forward, stubbing out the cigarette on the lid of the tobacco tin. "We've made friends around here. There are people we'd miss. Wouldn't we, Sean?"

"Yeah," Sean said. "That's right." But Ramsay thought the only person he cared about was Lily.

"Was Ernie Bowles one of those people?" Hunter asked abruptly.

"What?" She was startled, uncomprehending.

"Was Mr. Bowles one of the people you'd miss?"

"Good God, no," she said. "He was why we wanted to leave."

"Why?"

"Because he was hassle," she said. "We should have realised. I don't know how we didn't see it when we first looked round."

"In what way was he hassle?"

She turned to Sean. "You explain."

"He was sort of strange," Sean said. "Weird. You know."

32

"How did that affect you?"

"When we moved in he was really helpful. Nothing was too much trouble. You know. He said he liked having us here, he wanted to meet our friends. That sort of thing. He used to drop in some evenings. We didn't know what he wanted. I suppose we thought he was lonely. Then he seemed kind of disappointed and everything went sour. If we were a day late with the rent, he was up here causing a scene. He even tried to start charging for bringing the Calor cylinders back from Mittingford."

"What do you mean," Ramsay said, "disappointed?"

This time Lily answered.

"He was a smutty old man," she said. "He'd imagined all sorts going on here. . . ."

"What sort of things?"

"He'd read the tabloid press," she said impatiently. "He'd been young in the sixties, hadn't he? Well, youngish. But his mother had kept him on a tight rein. He thought we'd be like a sixties commune: free love, orgies, you know."

"Ah." Ramsay, too, had been young in the sixties. He, too, had felt that he'd missed out. "I see."

"We're not like that," Lily said. "Even when we were on the road we kept ourselves to ourselves." Then in a brave attempt at a joke: "Besides, there's not a whole heap of room in here for all-night parties."

"Did he bother you?" Hunter asked sharply. "Personally?"

There was a pause and then she shook her head. "No," she replied at last. "He wouldn't have had the guts. Like Sean said, he was just weird."

She stared out of the window.

"So how did you come to live here?" Ramsay asked.

"We were desperate," she said. "We must have been."

"Did Mr. Bowles advertise the caravan for let?"

"No," she said. "I don't think so. We heard about it through a friend. We were still dossing in Sean's van then, but we kept getting moved on. And it was clapped out anyway. I'd been offered a job in the health shop. We both like

Northumberland. The caravan seemed like the answer to our dreams. Didn't it, Sean?"

Sean looked up at her. He had very fine eyelashes, barely visible, which gave his eyes a staring quality.

"That's right," he said. "We were looking for a chance to settle down. Be a proper family. I even thought we might have a kid one day. . . ."

"Dream on!" Lily spat at him, under her breath.

He turned away from her as if he'd been hit.

There was a silence. Ramsay looked at Hunter, thinking he might want to take over the questioning, but he shook his head.

"When did you last see Mr. Bowles alive?" he asked formally.

"Saturday evening after work," she said. "He was ogling me through the kitchen window. Dirty bastard. He thought I didn't know he was there, but you could almost hear the heavy breathing across the farmyard." She caught her breath. "I'm sorry. I'd almost forgotten he was dead. I don't suppose he was so bad really. Just lonely and screwed up."

"I saw him later than that," Sean said.

"Did you?" She was still resentful.

"Yeah, don't you remember? I was sitting outside and I called you to come and look. He was all dressed up and he drove off in the Land Rover. We laughed. You said he must have found a woman at last."

"Yes," she said sombrely. "I do remember."

"Did you hear the Land Rover come back?"

"I didn't," Sean said. "I was out all evening."

"Where did you go?"

"I went for a walk. I do a lot of walking. And thinking."

"Communing with nature?" Hunter said unpleasantly.

"Yes actually," Sean said. "Something like that."

"What time did you get back?" Hunter asked.

There was a pause. Sean looked helplessly at Lily.

"Seven-thirty on Sunday morning."

"By man, that was a long walk," Hunter said, scenting blood. It would all be over by the end of the day.

"I met some friends."

"Just bumped into them, did you, out on the lanes?"

"It was a bit like that," Sean said. "They were parked in the gypsy transit site."

"And what were they called, these friends of yours? Just in case we want to check your story."

"Wes and Lorna," Sean said. "They've got a little girl called Briony."

"Surnames?" asked Hunter.

"I'm not sure," Sean said. "I don't think I ever knew." He looked at Lily again.

"Don't ask me," she said, "I never met them."

"Will they still be at the transit site?" Ramsay asked quietly.

Sean shook his head sadly. "They were moving on yesterday. They dropped me off on the way."

"What vehicle were they driving?"

"A blue Transit."

"Registration number?"

"How would I know?" He was starting to get rattled.

"I don't suppose you know where they were going either?" Hunter said.

"No, they didn't say."

He stared ahead with his blank eyes.

Ramsay was intrigued by the midnight wanderings and would have liked to ask more, but knew this wasn't the time. He turned his attention to Lily.

"Did you go out on Saturday night?"

"No," she said angrily. "I was too bloody tired after a day at work."

"Did you hear the Land Rover return?"

"Yes," she said. "I was surprised because he came back earlier than I'd expected. Tennish. Before the pubs had closed anyway."

"Did Mr. Bowles have anyone with him?" Ramsay asked. "Perhaps you heard voices."

She shook her head. "But that doesn't mean that he didn't bring someone back with him. You can hear the Land Rover a mile away—I think the exhaust must have gone. I'm sure I'd not have heard people talking in the yard. The windows were closed and I was listening to the radio."

"Had you talked to Mr. Bowles earlier in the day? Did he mention where he might be going?"

"No. Like I said, recently we've tried to keep out of his way."

"And neither of you saw him at all yesterday?"

They shook their heads.

"Didn't that strike you as odd?"

"No," Lily said dismissively. "He was a heavy drinker. I suppose I thought he was sleeping off the effects of the night before. That wouldn't have been unusual. When Cissie was alive she used to drag him off to the chapel, but I don't think he's been near the place since her funeral."

"Were there any visitors to the farm?"

"I didn't see anyone, but I was out all afternoon."

"How did you spend Sunday?"

"We walked into Mittingford to have lunch with friends. The Abbots. They work at the Old Chapel, too. And to use their shower. You need friends when you live like this."

"Did you both go?"

"Yes," she said with irritation. "You can check if you like."

"Oh yes, Ms. Jackman," Ramsay said, "you can be sure that we will."

6

They were at Laverock Farm until mid-afternoon, mostly hanging about, waiting for the experts to finish, for reinforcements from the Otterbridge team. Then Ramsay sent Hunter back to Mittingford to supervise the setting up of the incident room. Hunter, at least, knew how he liked things.

"I'll go to talk to the neighbour," Ramsay said. "Richardson. The one whose lad had a go at Ernie Bowles in the pub. We'll need someone to manage the livestock until a sale can be arranged. Besides, I'm interested to meet the boy."

Hunter nodded, but he thought Ramsay was wasting his time. He had Sean Slater down for the murder. There was something odd about him: the glazed expression, the way he looked at the girl, the improbable alibi. He was on the point of betting Ramsay a tenner that they'd have Slater for it in the end, but thought better of it. You could never tell how he'd take things like that.

The Richardson farm straddled the lane, with the house on one side, a large open barn on the other, and lots of mud on the road between. To the south of the house the land fell away to low fields and a burn. Beyond that there was hill and heather moorland. Next to the barn a row of outhouses had been converted into neat cottages, each with its own small front garden. In one a middle-aged couple were sitting, eating a late picnic lunch, drinking red wine. They took no notice of Ramsay.

The farmhouse was in full sunlight. The door was wide-open. Ramsay knocked and, when there was no reply, called in. A woman hurried out of one of the inside doors and into the hall. She was perhaps fifty, smartly dressed in a rather unconventional way with a brightly striped loose-weave skirt and jacket. She collected items as she moved—a large hand-bag retrieved from the bottom of the stairs was slung across her shoulder and shoes were stepped into, almost without stopping. She gave the impression of relentless energy and enthusiasm. She had not been aware of Ramsay's presence, and when she saw him she stopped briefly in her tracks.

"You'll want my husband," she said breathlessly, assuming, he supposed, that he was a vet or a food rep. "Round the back in the kitchen. If you're quick you might even get a cup of tea."

And she was gone. He stood on the step and watched while she got into her new Fiesta and drove away.

He walked around the outside of the house. The windows were low and he could see into a large living room with a chintz sofa and chairs, a grand piano. It was very different from Laverock Farm. The kitchen door was at the side of the house, slightly open. There were two pairs of Wellingtons on the step, and inside, people were talking. He tapped on the door.

"Yes?" said an impatient voice with a strong local accent. "What is it?"

Ramsay pushed open the door.

The speaker was a squat bull terrier of a man with wild grey hair and bushy eyebrows. He sat in a wicker basket chair cupping a mug of tea in his hand. As he moved, the wicker creaked. A younger man stood by the table, leaning against it. The kitchen looked as if it had come out of a magazine for townies aspiring to country living. The red quarry tile floor matched the red Aga. There were earthenware crocks, gleaming pans, drying herbs. The men in their stock-inged feet and overalls seemed strangely out of place.

"Mr. Richardson?" Ramsay said.

The older man stood up and looked at him. "Aye. And who the hell are you?" It was, Ramsay felt, his standard greeting. He introduced himself.

"You'll be here about Ernie Bowles. You'd best come in, then."

"You know about Mr. Bowles?"

"You don't think you could keep a thing like that quiet. Your chaps turned away the post van this morning and the postman came straight on here. It'll be all over the county by now."

"Yes," Ramsay said. "I suppose it will."

"How can I help you then?"

"I'm worried about Bowles's stock," Ramsay said.

"I don't know why. He never bothered much."

"Someone needs to look after things. I was wondering if you could come to an arrangement with his solicitor. It shouldn't take me long to find out who that is."

"No need for that," Richardson said. "It's Johnny Wright in Mittingford. I should know. I've had enough solicitor's letters from him." He paused. "You can leave it to me. I'll keep an eye on things until the place goes up for sale." And it occurred to Ramsay that Richardson had already thought things through, that he was considering Laverock Farm for himself. And then, sensing the younger man's interest, he thought: No, he intends buying it for his son.

"What were the solicitor's letters about?" Ramsay asked.

"Planning matters," Richardson said shortly.

"What sort of planning matters?"

"We were trying to make a living," Richardson said. "Not easy for farmers at the moment."

There was a silence which Ramsay did not fill and he felt forced to continue.

"My wife's always taken in a few guests for bed and breakfast. She was in catering before we married. It's what she knows. She didn't make much, but she enjoyed it. Said it was keeping her hand in, like." He spoke of his wife with a mixture of awe, admiration, and incomprehension. "It was her idea to expand that side of the business. The first year we had a few campers and caravanners on the bottom field. Then we decided to convert some of the outhouses into holiday cottages. She saw to all that. She talked to the architects, worked out a business plan, got the finance. A couple of months ago we got an award from the Tourist Board. She's planning to expand again, talking about opening a restaurant. That's where she's off to today. To talk to the bank manager."

"And Mr. Bowles objected to all these plans?"

"Cissie started it. Said she didn't want strangers trespassing all over her land. Ernie just took over when she died."

"But you went ahead all the same?"

"Of course. He had no real grounds for objection. There was no way our guests could stray over to Laverock Farm. It was just spite." He walked stiffly to the table to pour more tea, turned to Ramsay, and asked grudgingly, "Do you want a cup?"

Ramsay shook his head.

"And then he had the bloody nerve to tell me that he was going into the same line of business himself."

"In what way?"

"You know he's got those hippies living there?"

"Yes."

"Apparently that was only the start. He said he'd decided to open up Laverock Farm for a weekend for one of those festivals. You know, the New Age things that they show on the television. Convoys of travellers descending on an area, doing God knows what damage. Loud music all night. Drugs. And no way of knowing when they're going to move on or where they're going to end up next."

He paused for breath.

"When was this festival going to take place?"

"June," Bowles said. "The summer solstice."

"Was he serious?"

"No!" Peter Richardson interrupted with a sneer. "It was just a wind-up."

"How was I to know?" the father demanded angrily. "That man was capable of anything."

"You objected to the plan? Formally?"

"Of course I bloody objected. We run a classy operation, upmarket. Sue sees to that. I didn't want my punters frightened off by a load of drug-crazed morons."

"Yes," Ramsay said. "I understand."

"Do you?" Richardson was almost shouting. "It's only the holiday side of the business that's stopped us from going bankrupt."

He stopped abruptly.

Ramsay turned to Peter, the son, who had been watching the exchange with an amused detachment. He seemed untroubled by the prospect of bankruptcy, or perhaps his father had made the threat so many times that he no longer believed it. He was full of himself. Ramsay could see that. Too cocky by half. If he'd been brought up on an inner-city estate, he'd have been a delinquent, a stealer of flash cars, the sort of lad who didn't mind a prison sentence because it gave him the reputation for being hard. Here in the country Ramsay suspected he would have the same reputation, but with less effort. He'd be a heavy drinker, known for screwing his suppliers for the best possible deal, a jack the lad to be rather admired.

"Is that what your argument with Mr. Bowles was about?" Ramsay asked.

"What do you mean?" Peter Richardson spoke incidentally.

"I understand there was a fight in a Mittingford pub."

"That?" The boy laughed. "That wasn't a fight. He'd have been in hospital if he tried to mess with me. He tripped, that was all. I wouldn't waste my time on him."

"But there was an argument. What was that about?"

"He needed teaching a lesson," Peter said, contradicting himself. "He was a mucky old sod."

Ramsay saw his father flash him a look of warning, but he took no notice.

"So you decided to teach him a lesson," Ramsay said. "Why that night?"

"He was annoying my girl. She didn't like it and I wasn't going to stand for it. Sexual harassment, that's what it was. Leering across the bar at her, suggesting all sorts. It's an offence these days, isn't it? I was doing your job for you, that's all."

"You didn't have any other occasions to teach him a lesson?" Ramsay asked. His voice was dangerously quiet.

At last the boy seemed to recognise the need for caution.

"No!" he said. "I've told you. He wasn't worth bothering about. I just kept out of his way."

"When was the last time you saw Mr. Bowles?"

Peter Richardson shook his head. "Don't know. Probably not since that time in the pub." He gave a little triumphant laugh. "He probably kept out of my way after that."

Ramsay turned to the father. "And you, Mr. Richardson?"

"I've not seen him to speak to since he was up here with that plan for the New Age festival. I'd only lose my temper. I've passed him sometimes in the lane when he was driving that Land Rover of his—"

"Did you see the Land Rover this weekend?"

Richardson shook his head.

"You didn't notice any strange cars on the land?"

"Not 'specially. But this time of the year lots of people come out from town for a ride in the country. That's why Sue thinks she could make a go of a restaurant."

Sue, it seemed, was some kind of oracle.

"What about a blue Transit van, early Sunday morning, coming from the Mittingford direction?"

"No." He turned to his son. "You were out shooting yesterday morning. Did you see anything?"

"No." But the reply was automatic. He could not be bothered to remember.

"Where were you shooting?" Ramsay asked.

"On our land. Nowhere near a footpath. No law against that, is there?"

"Could you have seen the road from where you were?"

"No."

"What about Laverock Farm?"

"Yeah, I was over that way. I had a view down on the farm."

"Did you see anyone about?"

"Only that hippy couple. They walked down the track and onto the road. They started walking towards town, hitching."

"Did anyone give them a lift?"

"Not that I saw."

They would be on their way into Mittingford to have lunch with their friends. That part of the story fitted in.

"Have you had any dealings with Miss Jackman and Mr. Slater?" he asked the older man.

"The travellers? No. He came round asking for work when he first arrived, but I told him we had nothing. Not that I'd have taken him on anyway."

"Why?"

Richardson seemed not to think that worth answering.

"You didn't ever meet them socially?"

"No. They seem an unfriendly pair. Keep themselves to themselves."

That, Ramsay thought, was hardly surprising.

"You see the lad about, though. Walking. All times of day and night. I don't think he's quite all right in the head." He paused, before adding reluctantly, "Never caused any bother, though. Keeps to the footpaths."

"Did you see him on your land over the weekend?"

There was a pause. "I can't remember," Richardson said at last. "He's around so often that I don't notice him anymore, if you know what I mean. You take him for granted."

7

Mittingford police station was built in the same overblown style as the Old Chapel and stood close to it in the High Street with a view from the back down to the river. It, too, had the air of a building which had become redundant. Now it was only manned at all as a gesture to rural policing. Everyone knew it was being run down in preparation for closure. Stone steps led to a grand doorway, but inside it was shabby, gloomy, and overheated.

Hunter was lording it in the incident room, irritating his colleagues on the team and putting up the backs of the locals.

"They say we can use this. . . ." he told Ramsay, looking around him disparagingly. "I suppose it's better than nowt. Just."

It had been some sort of storeroom and a line of men in shirtsleeves were carrying out boxes, piles of rubbish. In time it would be transformed into a modern incident room, with computer terminals and phone lines. Now it was dusty and depressing. Hunter was perched on the windowsill, supervising. He was in his element.

"I've sent Sal Wedderburn to check the hippies' alibi for Sunday," Hunter said. "The Abbots both work at the Alternative Therapy Centre at the Old Chapel. She's gone to talk to them there. It's not really relevant now, though. The pathologist's just phoned with his first impressions. Bowles was killed between eight P.M. Saturday evening and eight A.M.

Sunday morning. He'll try to narrow it down, but he's quite certain that the old man was dead by the time Jackman and Slater went off for their Sunday lunch."

"Yes," Ramsay said absentmindedly. "Thanks." So Bowles had had a visitor on Saturday night. He'd either brought a companion back with him in the Land Rover at ten o'clock or someone had called to the farm later. Surely not on foot at that time. He should have asked Lily if she'd heard another vehicle. It was a blow that the farmyard wasn't visible from the road. They'd have been able to ask passing motorists if they'd seen a strange car parked there.

"We'll need to find somewhere to stay," he said. "Somewhere big enough to take the whole team."

"I've phoned around," Hunter said. "The pub seems the best bet. The Blue Bell."

In Hunter's opinion the pub usually was the best bet.

"Isn't that where Bowles had his scrap with the Richardson lad?" Ramsay asked. "We'll need to find witnesses of that."

"How did you get on with the Richardsons?"

Ramsay shrugged. "No love lost between them and Bowles," he said. "Apparently Ernie was threatening to have a New Age festival on his land. Richardson takes in well-heeled paying guests and wasn't best pleased."

"Can't bloody blame him either," Hunter said. "Strange that Jackman and Slater didn't mention it. . . ."

"Perhaps they didn't know. I had the impression that Bowles only dreamed up the idea to annoy his neighbours."

In a corner a telephone rang. The middle-aged constable they had met at the farm was staggering under the weight of a manual typewriter which might have been there before the war. He rested the typewriter against a scratched filing cabinet to take the call.

"There's been a message for you from Otterbridge," he said. "Can you call them back? As soon as you can?"

He took the strain of the typewriter again, swore under his breath, and went on down the corridor without a word.

"By, he's a happy soul, isn't he?" Hunter said. "You'd

think he'd be glad of the excitement. Make a change from sheep rustling and incest."

"I don't suppose he joined the force to be a removal man," Ramsay said mildly.

"I'll make that phone call then, shall I?" Hunter said. "Find out what the panic is. I'll try and find a phone away from all this bloody noise."

He wandered off. Ramsay stared in at the chaos and wondered if all this effort would be unnecessary in the end. Perhaps the forensic team would find fingerprints of some local villains, kids perhaps, misled by the rumours of Cissie Bowles's money. A robbery that had gone wrong and turned into murder when Ernie got home early and disturbed them. But he didn't think it would work out like that. There'd been no sign of a break-in and kids wouldn't strangle. They'd lash out with a knife or a heavy object, might even have got hold of a gun. Plenty of shotguns out here in the wilds. But they wouldn't get close enough to strangle.

No, Ramsay thought, this wouldn't be over quickly. There'd be time enough for his team to make themselves at home here. They'd bring a kettle and jars of coffee and powdered milk. Someone would start a tea fund. By the end of the investigation there'd probably be potted plants on the windowsills and posters on the walls. If there ever was a successful end.

Hunter bounced in, full of himself and his news.

"There's been a development," he said. "We know where Bowles was on Saturday night." He paused. Ramsay waited patiently. Hunter would make the most of the drama. "He met a woman, in the Ship in Otterbridge. She saw the report of his death on the teatime news and she got in touch."

"Who is she?"

"Name of Jane Symons," Hunter said. "A divorcée." He made the word sound almost pornographic.

"Were they having an affair?" Because that was what Hunter was suggesting.

"I haven't got the details," Hunter admitted. "The lads at Otterbridge took a statement. They'd have sent it by fax, but there's no machine here yet. I've got her address, though, if you want to see her." *He* certainly wanted to see her. His imagination was working overtime.

"Where does she live?"

"Otterbridge. The Orchard Park estate. You never know what goes on behind those net curtains, do you?" The Orchard Park was a respectable, middle-class development on the edge of the town.

Ramsay looked at his watch. It was six-thirty. He still hadn't phoned Prue to cancel their evening out. He realised suddenly that he hadn't eaten all day. He found this new development frustrating. He felt that it was a distraction and that the root of the evidence against Ernie Bowles lay here, in the hills. He hesitated, wondering if he could send Hunter on his own, came to the conclusion that that would be a mistake.

"Give me half an hour," he said. "You can confirm the arrangements at the pub if you like. We'll come back here tonight so we can make an early start in the morning." And get a feel for the place, he thought. Listen to the gossip. Find out who else hated Ernie Bowles.

When he phoned Prue she was disappointed but understanding, which was more than he could have hoped for.

"I expect I'll be here for a few days," he said. "At least. I'll phone you."

"I suppose I'll get used to your sudden disappearances," she said, and he experienced the warmth he always felt when she spoke of them having a future together. He never took that for granted. "But don't think I like it."

He told her that he didn't like it either.

DC Sally Wedderburn decided that Gordon Hunter got right up her nose. Dishing out the orders as if he was the boss. Arrogant sod. He was good-looking, she supposed, if you liked that rather greasy Mediterranean type, and she had to admit he had a nice arse, but it was about time someone put him in his place.

In contrast Daniel Abbot was charming. When she arrived

47

at the Old Chapel he had just finished with his last patient. He took her into his room and asked his receptionist to make them tea. He was still wearing his white coat and she realised she'd always fancied medical men.

"I'll need a statement," she said. "Just a formality. You had heard about Mr. Bowles?"

"Yes. One of my patients told me. . . ."

"Miss Jackman and Mr. Slater have told us that they spent Sunday with you."

"Well, not all Sunday. They arrived in time for lunch. Later Lily went to Magda's group. I suppose Sean went straight home."

"Magda's group?"

"Magda Pocock. My mother-in-law. You may have heard of her."

Sally shook her head and he seemed disappointed by her ignorance.

"She's a great practitioner. A wonderful woman." Sally had the impression the epitaphs came automatically. "She runs a workshop for some of her clients here at the centre on Sunday afternoons. Lily was definitely at that. Magda mentioned it later."

Sally prepared a short statement, which he signed a little impatiently. "I'm sorry to hurry you," he said, "but I've an appointment tonight. I have to be in Otterbridge by seventhirty. There's a lecture by an old teacher of mine at the college. It would be unforgivable to be late." Even at the time it seemed strange to her that Daniel Abbot felt the need to give her so many details of his evening out. Later, it would become positively suspicious.

8

M_{rs}. Symons was embarrassed. That was clear from the moment she opened the double-glazed door of her smart little semi. She looked down the street to check that none of her neighbours could see she had gentlemen callers. Throughout the interview her face was flushed. She was hating every minute of it. At first Ramsay wondered why she had come forward so promptly. If she had kept quiet, they would never have tracked her down. Then he realised she was a good woman. She would do what she considered right.

"It was a terrible mistake," she said as she showed them into her living room. "Really. I don't know what came over me."

Ramsay had stopped in Otterbridge to read her statement and understood a little of what she meant.

"The dating agency?" he asked gently.

She nodded, horrified.

"Why don't you explain?"

"My husband left me ten years ago," she said, as if that, too, was a matter of shame. "For his nurse." Then, seeing that they were confused: "He's a dentist with a practice in the town centre. Symons and Miller."

Ramsay nodded encouragingly.

"It was a shock," she said. She was a little, small-featured

49

woman, attractive in a neat, contained way. "Unexpected. I had thought we were settled. Happy even."

Ramsay nodded again. She continued, gaining in confidence.

"I'd never worked. We married early before I'd decided, really, on a career. I had O Levels, of course, and one A Level but no training, nothing useful in the way of skills. I'd thought marriage would be enough. Marriage and children." She paused, then continued in a rush: "There was one baby. A little girl. Helen. But she died. A cot death, you know. She'd be a teenager now. There weren't any more."

She stared blankly ahead of her.

Hunter had been expecting quite a different sort of woman, someone blowsy and sexy, like his favourite barmaid, but even he was moved. Almost to tears. Christ, he thought, I must be getting soft in my old age.

She went on matter-of-factly: "When Russel left I knew I'd have to get a job of some sort. To support myself. His new wife very soon had a baby and I couldn't expect him to give me money when they had financial commitments of their own. But I wasn't qualified for anything and I'd lost any self-esteem I'd had with the divorce. So I went for shop work. I didn't think that would be too demanding. I got taken on by Hawkins." Ramsay nodded. He recognised the name. Hawkins was an old-fashioned, family-run department store. "I enjoyed it. I progressed through the business and became a supervisor. Then I was approached by Mr. Jones, who has the shoe shop in the square. He wanted to retire and he needed a manager. He thought I'd do. It was rather flattering to be asked. And the money was good. A commission on top of the salary. I built up the business and did rather well." She paused again. "I'm sorry," she said. "None of this is relevant to your enquiry. I'm afraid I'm wasting your time. But I'm trying to explain how I went to the agency."

"The work had given you confidence," Ramsay said.

"Yes," she said, pleased that he knew what she meant. "And I thought: if I can be quite successful in work, why not

50

in my private life? It wasn't so much that I felt lonely. But incomplete. I don't suppose you understand. . . ."

Ramsay understood very well.

"I never met men," she explained. "Except in the shop, and that was no good. I tried the usual things—evening classes, clubs. That got me out of the house, but I only met other women, or occasionally a happily married man. I had the feeling that time was running out. It sounds awful, but I thought: soon I'll be in competition not only with spinsters and divorcées but with widows, too. I suppose I was getting desperate."

"So you decided to try a more direct approach?"

She nodded. "One of my regular customers had been to the agency. She didn't hide it. She even turned it into a joke. And suddenly she seemed so well and alive. She'd met such a nice man, older than her, a retired bank clerk, a widower."

She stopped short. "I'm losing track," she said. "You don't want to hear all this. I don't very often have the opportunity to talk about myself."

"Go on," Ramsay said. "We're in no hurry."

Speak for yourself, Hunter thought. He wanted his tea and a few pints before closing time.

"So I plucked up courage and thought: why not? Why not give it a go at least? To see if I could find someone nice like my customer. Perhaps it sounds ridiculous at my age, but I wanted that excitement, you know, of falling in love. Just once more."

"You went to the agency in person?"

"Yes," she said. "I made a telephone appointment first and then I went. I'd been expecting an office, something official, but it was run by a young woman, a young mother actually, who couldn't get out to work, from her own home."

"And she introduced you to Mr. Bowles?"

"Not directly. She showed me a file of application forms. I read through them and chose three, put them in order of preference. Mr. Bowles was my first choice." Her voice was flat.

"Had the manager of the agency met him?"

"I'm not sure," she said. "I don't think she can have done." She shivered slightly. "She seemed a very *honest* woman. I don't think she would have recommended him if she'd met him."

Ramsay let that go. They would come to Mrs. Symons's meeting with Ernie Bowles in time.

"Were you the first woman to be introduced to Mr. Bowles?" he asked.

"Yes," she said. "I rather think I was."

"What was it about Mr. Bowles's application form which led you to choose him?"

She paused, considered. "To be honest I expect it was wishful thinking," she said. "The form wasn't very well written, you know, and at the time I even saw that in a positive light. Russel, my husband, had always been very superior about his education. It was the farming, I suppose, which attracted me, and the fact that he'd never been married. I've always been a fan of Thomas Hardy and I imagined Mr. Bowles as one of his heroes: uneducated perhaps and shy, but close to nature, gentle."

"And Mr. Bowles didn't live up to those expectations?"

"No," she said. "But to be honest, no one would. I see that now."

"How did you arrange to meet?"

"The agency gave him my telephone number. He phoned me up."

"When was that?"

"At the beginning of the week. Monday morning."

"You weren't put off by his phone call?"

"No," she said. "He sounded a little . . . rough, but I'd expected that. I've never been a snob, Inspector."

Hardy again, Ramsay thought. Hunter, who'd never heard of Thomas Hardy, thought she'd been turned on by the idea of doing it with one of the working class.

"Tell me about Saturday night," Ramsay said. "What happened?"

"We arranged to meet in the lounge of the Ship. He said he would buy me dinner."

"He was there when you got there?"

"Yes," she said. "He may have been there for some time. He'd certainly had a couple of drinks."

"He was drunk?"

"No. Not really drunk."

"Could you give me your first impressions of him?"

She hesitated, surprised by the question.

"He was short, thickset. He'd obviously made some effort to get ready to meet me, but it hadn't quite come off. I suppose I should have found that touching."

"But you didn't?"

"No," she said. "I'm finding this hard to explain, Inspector, but there was something about him which disturbed me. Nothing concrete. A way of looking at me. Perhaps that's it."

"One witness has described him as 'creepy,'" Ramsay said.

"Yes," she said gratefully. "That's just it. I thought I was overreacting." She gave a sudden smile, self-mocking. "But I don't think I lived up to his expectations either. We were both disappointed."

"Yet you went through with the dinner?"

"I wasn't sure how to get out of it. He was quite insistent and I didn't want to make a scene. I might not have been the sort of woman he imagined, but I had the impression that he considered me better than nothing. I really think he believed I was grateful for his attentions."

There was a silence.

"We ordered a meal," she said. "I tried to talk to him, find out about his life on the farm. I thought that would be safe ground."

"What did he say about the farm?"

"It was rather a litany of complaint. About how much work there was for one man, how little money it brought in, how lonely he was. I stopped being frightened of him then. He just seemed very pathetic. That's when I decided to leave. I told him I had to go to the ladies' cloakroom and walked out through the back door. I suppose it was a very cowardly thing to do, just to leave him sitting there. And rather unkind. But I didn't want to spend any more time with him, and I didn't see why I should."

The words were defiant. It would have come hard to her to walk out, Ramsay thought, after years of always doing the decent thing.

"I stood in the backyard of the Ship with all the empty barrels and I burst into tears. It wasn't so much that Mr. Bowles had upset me. It was disappointment, I suppose. Injured pride."

"Did anyone see you there?" Ramsay asked.

"Sorry?"

"Did anyone see you in the yard?"

"I don't know," she said. "The kitchen's at the back of the hotel. Perhaps one of the staff would have seen me. Why?"

"You were one of the last people to see Mr. Bowles alive," Ramsay said gently. "You do see that we have to corroborate your story."

"Oh yes! Of course. I should have realised." She thought again. "When I pulled myself together I walked round the side of the hotel and into the street. I met Mr. Jones there, my boss. He asked me if I was all right. I suppose I looked upset. I said I was fine, but I let him walk me to my car. I thought Mr. Bowles might come chasing after me."

"But he didn't? You never saw him again?"

"No."

"During the time you spent with Mr. Bowles, did he mention that he'd arranged to meet anyone else later that evening?"

"Oh no," she said. "Definitely not." She blushed a deeper shade of scarlet. "I had the impression, you see, that he'd expected to spend the night with me."

"Did he talk about friends, business acquaintances? Anyone he'd had a row with?"

"No," she said. "There was nothing like that."

"What about his tenants? Sean and Lily. Did he mention them?"

She shook her head.

"Well, what *did* he talk about?" Hunter demanded, losing patience. "Apart from the farm."

"His mother," she said. "He talked about his mother."

"What did he say about her?"

"Nothing really. Nothing specific. He just wanted to talk about her. For me to know how important she'd been to him. I think that was it."

They stood for a moment on the pavement. It was dusk. In the little house Jane Symons turned on the light and drew the curtains.

"That doesn't get us much further forward, then, does it?" Hunter said. He was disappointed, felt the interview had been an anticlimax. Then he reconsidered, brightened. "If anything, it points more to Slater. We know now that Bowles went home alone."

"Not exactly," Ramsay said. "We know he was alone when Mrs. Symons left him. That's all."

Ernie Bowles would have been furious, Ramsay thought. And frustrated. He'd made all that effort, only to be stood up. What would he have done to try to mend his hurt pride? Find another woman, surely. And the fact that he'd arrived at the farm at ten o'clock made it seem that he'd found one quickly.

"Tomorrow I want all the pubs in Otterbridge checked," Ramsay said. "Especially the ones where women hang out on their own. And in Mittingford. He might have gone back there when he was stood up. Find out if anyone saw the Land Rover. And I want to know if anyone was hitchhiking along the road he'd have taken. He might have picked someone up."

"Yeah," Hunter said. "Okay."

Ramsay had been expecting some complaint. Hunter hated that sort of routine checking. But he seemed hardly to have been listening.

Hunter had found himself suddenly thinking of Lily Jackman, and how it wouldn't be so bad coming back to a place like this, a little house in a suburban street, if she were there, waiting for him.

9

On their way back to Mittingford, Ramsay and Hunter drove past the Otterbridge College of Further Education. When it was opened in 1967 the college had won an award for its design; now it had degenerated into shabbiness. The concrete was stained with damp and the paint was peeling. Hunter regarded the place with affection. It always evoked a twinge of nostalgia. He had hated school and left as soon as he could, then went on to the college to resit O Levels and try for an A Level in technical drawing. Which he had just scraped through. While he was a student there he had passed his driving test. His mother, somehow, had found the money to buy an old Escort, and in the back of the car he had made his first sexual conquests.

That was fifteen years ago, he realised, and he wondered, as he had on the pavement at Orchard Park, whether it might be time for him to think of settling down. The interview with Jane Symons had made him uncharacteristically uneasy. To be that desperate! he thought. That old and that desperate. What if I'm like that in fifteen years' time, left with the feeling that I've missed the boat? For some reason the girl in the caravan had got under his skin. He couldn't forget her.

Deliberately, he pushed the thought away, and went on to consider the chances of getting Sally Wedderburn into bed. He'd always fancied redheads and he'd had his eye on Sally for months. She'd been going out with some slob in the serious crime squad and he'd even heard rumours of an engagement, but he'd always liked a challenge. In the hothouse atmosphere of a murder investigation, he thought, with everyone living away from home, drinking too much to relieve the stress of the day's disappointments or to celebrate small victories, in that atmosphere anything was possible.

Val McDougal would have liked to go to the acupuncture lecture in the college. Magda had announced it during the group and asked them all to give their support. Val would have done almost anything for Magda, but tonight she was working late. She always worked late on Mondays. She taught a numeracy course for mature students recruited from a nearby industrial estate. Business and Education in partnership. That was what it was all about now. Most were women and most were conscripts sent along by a couple of personnel managers who wanted to be seen to be doing something about training. Val usually enjoyed the class, but tonight she found it hard to concentrate.

At seven-thirty they had a coffee break and trooped off to the cafeteria.

"What's wrong with you tonight then, Val?" asked one woman, who still wore the white overall she used at work. "Going down with something, pet?"

"Perhaps I am," Val said. "Some sort of bug."

"We don't want you going sick on us, do we, girls? We'd miss our Monday nights. I would anyway. If school had been a bit more like this, I might have done something with my life."

"You'd have been a brain surgeon, would you?" said her friend. "Instead of a packer at Fullertons." Fullertons made toiletries for most of the big chain stores. You could always tell the women who worked there. They smelled faintly of chemicals and cheap perfume.

"You never know I might and all," said the first woman, waiting for them all to laugh. "What do you think, Val? Make a good brain surgeon, would I?"

"Why not?" Val replied, although she had only been half

57

following the conversation. They laughed again and shared round the cigarettes. They could not imagine what troubles Val might have. She lived in a big house with a husband who worked at the university and two sons you could be proud of. She didn't get letters from the Gas Board threatening to cut off the supply or the police at her door because one of the kids had got into bother again.

"Back to the grindstone, then," Val said, and led them back to the classroom on the third floor for another hour of simple fractions and decimals.

The class finished at eight-thirty, but there were always students who wanted to stay behind to chat. Usually she liked to be home by nine because there was a television programme she enjoyed watching—a thriller set in Glasgow, which Charles said was trash. Tonight she was reluctant to let them go. She had things on her mind, and if she were alone she would be forced to come to a decision. So far she had done nothing, but that, she thought as the last of the women clattered down the bare concrete steps, had been a decision of sorts.

On her way to her car she walked past the lecture hall and saw that the speaker was still on his feet. She thought there'd been a good turnout, but it was hard to tell. He'd been showing slides and the body of the hall was in darkness. She contemplated slipping into the back to watch the remainder of the speech—there was no one at home to go back to—but decided against it. She still found crowds intimidating.

In the car park she hesitated. She was sure the Abbots and Magda would have attended the lecture—Daniel Abbot was giving the introduction. Perhaps she should wait and speak to them. She scanned the row of cars briefly but did not see the Abbots' Rover or Magda's VW. It was probably just as well, she thought. Probably they were the last people she should speak to.

In the car she switched on the radio, hoping to get some local news, but there was only pop music and she turned it off. It had been a lousy weekend, she thought as she drove through the quiet suburban streets. Magda's invitation to supper had been an honour, but she should have turned it down, explained that Charles always cooked on Saturdays, made some excuse. It hadn't lived up to expectations anyway. Magda had brought up the subject of Juniper Hall again. She seemed to be probing for information. Val thought that after all this time they should let Faye Cooper rest in peace.

Sunday had been even worse. Usually she loved Magda's group. Charles had been in such a bad mood that she almost decided to skip it. She wished now that she'd stayed at home.

Perhaps it's all the lying that's getting me down, she thought as she approached her street. All the pretence. Because Charles knew nothing of her connection with the Alternative Therapy Centre. She could imagine the ridicule she'd be tormented with if he ever found out. Quacks or morons, he always said if he read an item about complementary medicine in the newspaper, directing the same scorn at them as he did at organised religion or the kids she taught. She could talk to James, of course, but it hardly seemed fair to burden her son with her problems, especially now when he was preparing for exams. He'd been through enough lately. . . .

She realised that her thoughts had been rambling and that she was home. The house was dark and empty. Charles was always back late on Monday nights. He had a meeting of sociology department staff which sometimes went on until midnight. At least that was what he told Val. She suspected that Monday was his night for Heather, his postgraduate student and occasional mistress. Val imagined them sometimes in Heather's hall of residence bedsit, making love in a single bed while the thump of other students' music came through the walls. She found it hard to picture Charles, so obsessive, so concerned about his privacy, performing in such circumstances, but perhaps these Monday nights had become part of his routine, and if Heather cancelled one, he would be as put out as he was with her missing dinner on Saturday.

Usually, on Monday nights James was waiting for her. Often he'd have cooked the supper and have a bottle of wine

59

open. He never mentioned the tension between her and Charles, but he knew how things stood.

"Come on, Mum," he'd say. "You need spoiling."

Now he was away on a week's geography field trip, roughing it in a youth hostel in Keswick. Oh well, she thought, tonight I'll have to spoil myself.

The house was not large, but it was detached and set back from the road. When they had bought it they had scarcely been able to afford the mortgage, but Charles had been determined to have it. It suited his need for privacy and reflected his self-importance. There was a small car she did not recognise parked in the road outside the house. Most of James's friends had cars and she wondered if someone had come to visit him, not realising he was away, but the driver's seat was empty and she thought no more about it. As she pulled her car into the gravel drive, the security light came on, illuminating the high holly hedge that Charles had encouraged to separate the house from the street. Although it had been Charles's choice, she had come to like the house, too. Was that why she still put up with him, she thought, because she couldn't face moving?

The front door had two locks, a Yale and a mortice, and she juggled with keys and an armful of books to get it open. Inside, she felt herself relax and made up her mind to put off any decision until later. She would not upset her prized husband-free evening with gloomy thoughts. She always enjoyed Monday evenings: the appreciation of the women from Fullertons, the sense that after all she was achieving something worthwhile at work, made her feel like celebrating and she didn't see why she should miss out on that tonight.

She dumped the exercise books on the kitchen table and wandered through to the living room to switch on the television. She must be later than usual because the serial had already started. As she drew the long curtains across the patio doors, she thought there was a movement in the back garden. The cat, she thought. The light always attracted him. She expected any minute to hear the cat-flap in the utility-room door and to feel him rubbing against her legs for food.

She left the living-room door open so she could watch the television from the kitchen. Did youth hostels have televisions these days? she wondered. James had always liked the programme, too. It occurred to her that soon he would be away to university and she realised for the first time how much she would miss him. That would be the time to break away from Charles, she thought. She'd discuss the idea with Magda. Magda would know what to do.

She did nothing elaborate for supper. Toasted cheese covered with thin strips of smoked ham, and mayonnaise to go with it. She put the plate on a tray and carried it through to the living room, then returned to the kitchen to open a bottle of wine. The thriller was twenty minutes in and the adverts had started. There was still no sign of the cat. She opened the back door and called to him, but the signature tune of the programme attracted her back. She ate the meal and drank half a bottle of wine before the ten o'clock news. The worry of the day now seemed slightly ridiculous. It was all a fuss about nothing.

She might even have started to doze because the front doorbell made her jump, although when she looked at the clock it had still only just gone ten.

Bloody Charles, she thought. That's all I need. She imagined him rejected for some reason by Heather. Frustrated. Demanding. She knew that Charles should have a key, but it was quite in character, if the key wasn't immediately at hand, to inconvenience her rather than look for it. The doorbell rang again, more insistently.

Sod you, Charles, she thought, still drowsy, stumbling from her chair.

She opened the door, not bothering to attach the chain which Charles had insisted on having fitted. Behind her, in the background, came the noise of the television news. A man's voice talked of the renewal of the Bosnian peace talks. But Val did not hear what he said. The door was pushed open from the outside against her. The babbling television voice hid the sound of her struggles and the muffled screams as the life was squeezed from her.

10

There was nothing at first to connect Val
McDougal with Ernie Bowles. They had both been strangled,
but the methods used had been altogether different. Bowles
had been killed manually. The marks of the fingers on his
neck had been quite obvious. Val had been strangled by a
piece of thin nylon rope, twisted into a noose. It had been
left behind at the scene of the crime, but it would be of little
assistance in tracing the murderer. It had been cut from a ball
which had been left outside on the McDougal's patio—Val
had been tying climbing roses on to a trellis there. All this
indicated was that the murderer had not come prepared.

Then what could the victims have in common? They were
perhaps of a similar age, but there was no indication that
they had ever met. Their backgrounds and education would
suggest that they led quite different lives. They had lived
fifty miles apart and Ernie seldom strayed beyond Mittingford. James McDougal, who might have thrown some light
on this, was in a small group on a two-day survival trek
through the fells and had not even been informed of his
mother's death.

Charles McDougal had been of so little help that at first he
was suspected of killing his wife. When he was questioned
he lied about where he had been all evening. At a university
meeting, he told the duty detective who came out early on
Tuesday morning, all bleary-eyed from being woken from

sleep. A university meeting which had dragged on. Then, when he realised that the detective did not believe him, that he was actually in danger of being arrested, he changed his story and suddenly became very helpful. He said he was sorry to have been so foolish. Shock did strange things to people. The notion that he might have appeared foolish seemed to distress him more than the death of his wife and he made a great effort then to be calm and efficient. He gave the detective Heather's name and address. She was woken just as it was getting light and confirmed his story. She said that Charles had been with her all evening. Until one in the morning, when he had gone home to find the front door still ajar and his wife's body slumped at the bottom of the stairs.

"I thought she'd fallen," he said to the policeman who was taking the statement. "I thought it was a terrible accident."

Later that day Ramsay came to ask him about possible connections with Ernie Bowles.

"I'm sorry," Charles said. "I've never heard the name before. I suppose he could have been one of her mature students."

That seemed unlikely from the beginning, and when they checked they found out that Ernie had left school at fourteen and had had no education of any sort since.

"Did your wife have any reason to go to Mittingford?" Ramsay asked.

Charles shook his head. "We used to go there when the boys were young. For family picnics, you know. To walk along the river. But we haven't been there recently. Probably not for years."

"Did anything unusual happen over the weekend?" Ramsay asked.

"Not really. She went out on Saturday night. Usually we spent that together."

"Where did she go?" It occurred to Ramsay that Val could have been a witness to the Bowles murder. Perhaps that was the connection.

"I'm not sure. Out for a meal with a friend, she said."

"And the name of the friend?"

Charles shrugged. "I'm not sure. Someone she met when she was on holiday last year."

"What did she do on Sunday?"

"I don't know. I went into the university to do some work. I think she went for a walk. She was here when I got back, helping James get ready to go away."

"And she didn't seem at all upset or distressed?"

"Of course not. She wasn't that sort at all." But Ramsay thought he would have been so wrapped up in his own affairs that he would not have noticed.

"Perhaps you could give us the names of some of her friends," Ramsay said. "People who knew her well. People she might have confided in."

"She didn't have many friends. Not of her own. Wives of my colleagues, of course, but no one she was close to. Occasionally people phoned to speak to her. Last autumn she went away for a weekend break. Somewhere in Cumbria. She'd had a heavy term and needed time to recharge her batteries. That's what she said, though her work never seemed that demanding to me. I think she got to know some people then."

"And they were the people who phoned?"

"I think so. Yes."

When Ramsay pressed him for details of the weekend trip, he could not help. His affair with Heather had been at the height of its passion then and he had been grateful just to have two days to himself.

"It was a really busy time," he told Ramsay. "The start of the academic year. You know. I expect she told me where she was staying, but really I don't remember. No. I never had the phone number of the hotel. We didn't live in each other's pockets. Someone at the college might know."

But her friends from college knew nothing about her holiday either. They remembered her going away, thought it would do her some good. She was too conscientious. Put her heart and soul into her work. She'd swapped one of her classes so she could have Friday afternoon free. But they couldn't remember where she'd been going or even if she'd said.

Perhaps she had a lover? the police probed gently. Perhaps that was why she kept the weekend away so secret.

"Val? A lover? You must be joking. She wouldn't know where to start."

They seemed to find the idea laughable and the impression grew of a reserved woman, well liked but painfully shy with everyone but her students. The sort of woman who wouldn't make waves. Certainly not the sort of woman to get herself murdered.

In the end Ramsay put the second murder down to coincidence. Though he'd never liked coincidences and kept his own copy of the interview with Charles McDougal just in case. For two days the investigations went on in tandem. Ramsay's team, based in Mittingford, were in charge of Ernie Bowles's murder and an inspector from Otterbridge set up an incident room in police headquarters and took over the Val McDougal case.

The connection with Ernie Bowles came through routine policing, the sort of detailed and repetitive work that Hunter hated. The principal of the Further Education College had cleared Val's desk and gave the contents to the police for checking before they would be released to her husband. The young detective constable given responsibility for going through the piles of papers, the year old diaries, the unmarked exercise books, was called Paul Simonsides. He was engaged, unofficially, to Sally Wedderburn, the fiery redhead of Hunter's fantasies, and made up for her absence with long, if unromantic, phone calls. Sally had been excited about her place on the Bowles investigation. She saw it as her first real chance to shine. She had talked at length about the weird New Age connections, the hippy travellers who had come to rest on Ernie Bowles's land. And Lily Jackman's work in the Old Chapel. She had mentioned that specifically. Paul Simonsides was a big man but not the slob Hunter imagined. He was a keen hill walker and a lot of their courting had been done in the hills. Like Prue and Ramsay they had often stopped off afterwards for tea and cakes in the Old Chapel café.

Paul Simonsides almost threw the evidence away. It was a small square of card used as a bookmark in a standard text on adult literacy. He glanced at it, thinking it might be a dental appointment card. It was that sort of shape with that sort of print and so creased and dog-eared that it was obviously old. In handwritten script on the printed form an appointment had been made for Mrs. McDougal for six P.M. on July 20 of the previous year. But not for a scrape and polish. The appointment was made with Daniel Abbot, acupuncturist. And it was at the Alternative Therapy Centre in the Old Chapel, Mittingford.

That was too much of a coincidence even for Ramsay's superior. The investigation became a joint enquiry, and because Ramsay had been there since the beginning of it, he took charge.

Hunter had ignored the murder of Val McDougal. He had always found it hard to concentrate on more than one thing at a time. Instead he continued with his own routine policing. He didn't usually enjoy researching into suspects' backgrounds, but this time it was different. He really wanted to know. He told himself he was interested in finding out what sort of person ended up on the road, but it was more complicated than that. He had convinced himself that Sean Slater was a murderer and wanted to prove it. About Lily Jackman he was obsessively curious.

Slater had a record for criminal damage and a number of motoring offences—taking without the owner's consent and driving without MOT or insurance. An outstanding fine remained. The criminal damage related to a farmer's property in Somerset—crops were flattened and windows in the farmhouse were broken during a confrontation following an impromptu festival on his land. Lily Jackman had also been charged with the criminal damage, then the charges had been dropped and she had been cautioned.

Hunter, who had a nose for these things, smelled funny

business and phoned the arresting officer. Although the incident had happened more than a year before, the officer still remembered it. It obviously rankled.

"Strings were pulled," he said.

"How?"

"The mother's an MP. You'll have heard of her. She sails under her maiden name—Bridget Dunn. She's got a constituency in Bristol and she's well-known round here. A good supporter of the police even in difficult times. She never asked for favours, but someone must have thought we owed her one. It was decided that the girl's offence wasn't serious enough to warrant the embarrassment which would come her mother's way if the relationship came out in the press."

"So it was all hushed up?"

"And they were shipped pretty smartly out of the district."

"To end up on our doorstep," Hunter said gloomily. "Well, they'll find it harder to hush up murder."

He wasn't surprised about Lily's background. Whatever you thought of it, he told himself, class always showed. It made her more intriguing, even more distant.

Sean Slater's background was quite ordinary. Hunter was able to dig out some biographical details but didn't feel he could understand him and certainly couldn't understand how he'd ended up with a lady like Lily Jackman. He'd been born in a new town in the West Midlands to respectable working-class parents. He'd done reasonably well at school, better at least than Hunter himself. He'd got a place to read English at one of the less glamorous universities, and then, as Hunter put it, after one term he'd flipped. Perhaps the freedom was too much for him, perhaps he'd just cracked up under the strain of academic life. In any event he'd drifted away to join a group of hippies at Stonehenge, and until he'd settled in the caravan at Laverock Farm, he'd been on the road ever since.

His parents had been frantic and had contacted the police to report him missing. They only knew that he'd disappeared from his hall of residence with twenty pounds in cash and a book of Keats's poetry. The police traced him through friends and talked to him, but they had no power to drag him back home. He was an adult and able to do as he pleased.

There was no explanation, either, of the midnight wanderings. Hunter tried to find a pattern to them. Was he working? Keeping the work secret and fiddling his benefit? Was there another woman somewhere? Hunter imagined a second caravan in the hills, with a lover, perhaps even children, a secret existence, but no evidence came to light. When he asked Richardson's farm worker, who lived in a cottage by the Mittingford Road, the man said he had seen Sean about but he couldn't remember exactly when.

"He always seems to be there," he said, "flitting up the lane or across the hill. Like a bloody ghost come to haunt you."

A similar blank was drawn on the blue Transit van in which Slater had claimed to have stayed on the night that Ernie Bowles died. Enquiries had been made all over the county, but no one had seen it. Hardly surprising, Hunter thought, as it was a figment of Slater's imagination.

On Tuesday morning he went to the health-food shop and talked to the huge woman who owned it. He was told that Lily had been working at the Old Chapel for nearly a year. She was punctual and reliable, always willing to work overtime. Yet despite the positive response to all his questions, Hunter sensed a reserve.

"What's she like, then?" he asked. "How does she get on with the rest of the staff? Friendly, is she?"

"No," the shopkeeper said, "she could not really be described as friendly. She rather kept herself to herself."

"A bit stuck-up?" Hunter prompted.

"Probably not," the shopkeeper said uncertainly, wanting to be fair. "But that's sometimes the impression that she gives."

It was the impression she gave to Hunter. He sat in the café drinking coffee and watching her, knowing that he had other work to do but unable to leave.

11

W_{ith} the knowledge that Val had consulted Daniel Abbot, Ramsay went back to Charles McDougal. The son James was home, too, and it was the boy who let him in. He called to his father then disappeared upstairs, leaving Ramsay only with the impression of intense grief—a white face and large dark-rimmed eyes. Charles McDougal wandered into the hall.

"Ah," he said. "Yes, come through. I'm just in the kitchen."

He was staring in a bemused way at the washing machine. A pile of his laundry was on the floor.

"I don't know which button to press," he said, "to get the door open."

He looked up pathetically at Ramsay, who pressed the release trigger so the door sprang open.

"Great," Charles said. "Great." And he pushed the shirts in, then looked at Ramsay again, expecting him perhaps to set the machine in operation. But Ramsay had moved away to the open kitchen door. Let the man work it out for himself.

It was early evening and the sun was still warm. From one of the neighbouring gardens came the smell of the first barbecue of the season. The garden at the back of the McDougals' house was long and narrow, and even to Ramsay's untutored eye it was loved. The lawn was neatly edged and there were already splashes of colour in the borders.

"Val's pride and joy," Charles said. He seemed to have lost interest in his washing and had joined Ramsay by the open door. There was something of a sneer in his voice, as if gardening was beneath him. "She spent all her spare time out here."

They walked together onto the roughly paved patio. "It'll be too much for me," he said. "I suppose I'll have to get someone in. If I decide to stay here."

In his mind he was already moving on, making plans for the future.

"Can I offer you something?" he asked. "Tea? A glass of wine?"

Ramsay shook his head.

"Shall we go in, then?" It was his university voice, brisk and authoritative. His domestic helplessness was set aside. "I expect you've more questions to ask."

"I'm afraid so."

He took Ramsay into a small study and sat behind the desk. It was not an attempt to intimidate but he was making a point. I'm an intelligent man, he was saying, with a position in society. I don't suppose you deal with people like me very often.

"We think we may have come across a link between your wife and Ernest Bowles," Ramsay said. "It's not an obvious link, and of course we're keeping an open mind about its importance."

He handled his dislike of Charles McDougal by being bland and polite, qualities which had irritated his wife Diana into divorce. He set the appointment card, wrapped in a clear plastic envelope, on the desk.

"We found this among your wife's possessions at college," he said. "Did you know that your wife had consulted an acupuncturist?"

"No," Charles said. He picked up the card and studied it.

"Mr. Abbot practises in Mittingford," Ramsay said. "He's

an acquaintance of Mr. Bowles's tenants. It's a tenuous link, but of course we'll have to follow it up."

"Did she keep this appointment?" Charles demanded.

"We don't know yet," Ramsay replied smoothly.

"She can't have done," he said with certainty. "She would have said. We didn't have secrets."

Except postgraduate students called Heather, Ramsay thought. Charles must have been following the same train of thought because he blushed slightly.

"Had your wife been ill?" Ramsay asked. It had occurred to him that people often turned to alternative therapies when conventional medicine failed.

"Val, ill!" Charles gave a sharp laugh. "She was as strong as a horse. I was the one that suffered. Terrible migraines."

"Perhaps then she consulted the acupuncturist on your behalf," Ramsay said.

"She would have said," Charles answered uncertainly. "Surely she would have told me." He liked the idea, though. He liked the idea that he was at the centre of her thoughts and she'd gone all the way to Mittingford to help him.

"Well," Ramsay said. "We'll talk to Mr. Abbot. He'll remember her or at least have some record of the consultation."

"Yes." Charles half got up as though he expected the interview to be over, but when Ramsay did not move he fell back into his chair. "James might know," he said. "He was very close to his mother."

"The tenants of the murdered man at Laverock Farm had once been New Age travellers," Ramsay said. "Their names are Lily Jackman and Sean Slater. Your wife never mentioned them?"

Charles shook his head. "James hung around with a group of hippies last summer," he said. "Went to the festivals. For the music first, but he got into the New Age thing for a while. Read some books. Went to lectures about discovering himself and saving the planet. It was a phase. I knew it would pass. It's A Levels now and a place at Oxford if he's lucky."

"Did he bring any of his New Age friends home?"

"Only one. A girl a bit older than him. Pretty. I can't remember her name."

"And he never talked about the Abbots?"

"I don't think so, but you must understand, Inspector, that I'm a busy man. Work's important to me. I tried to make time for the boys, but I have to admit I never always listened to them as much as I should. There was always something else demanding my attention."

Yes, Ramsay thought. A student half your age.

There was a silence and again Charles seemed to think that the interview was over. Ramsay decided not to let him off the hook.

"Why would your wife keep a visit to an acupuncturist secret from you?" he asked. "Was she frightened of you?"

"No," Charles said. "Of course not. But she'd know I'd not approve. She was rather a weak woman, Inspector. She'd do anything to avoid unpleasantries."

"Why would you disapprove so strongly of alternative therapies?"

"Because they have no basis in reason. A placebo effect, perhaps, on those who need attention and sympathy . . ."

And who could blame your wife, Ramsay thought, for wanting those?

"Thank you," Ramsay said. "You've been very helpful." Bullshit, said Diana in his head. "I wonder if I might talk to your son?"

"James? I don't see why not. His room's at the top of the stairs."

A different father would have made more effort to protect his son, insisted perhaps on being in on the interview, but Charles just seemed pleased that his own ordeal was over.

The boy was lying on his bed listening to music, something folky and Celtic which meant nothing to Ramsay but which reminded him of the fiddlers in the Morpeth pub where he had taken Prue. That seemed a long time ago. Ramsay knocked at the door, which was slightly ajar. The boy got up, switched off the music, pushed some books from

72

a swivel chair so Ramsay could sit down. He did not seem surprised to see the policeman. Ramsay thought he had been expecting, even anticipating, the visit.

"Do you want coffee?" he asked. "Or did Dad offer you some downstairs?"

"Coffee would be splendid."

"Only Nescaff," James said, spooning granules into a mug. The kettle, plugged into a point by the desk, was already full.

When I was your age, Ramsay thought, I didn't know there was any other sort.

"I suppose you want to talk about Mum," James said.

"If it wouldn't be too upsetting."

"No," James said. "I want to talk about her. No one else seems to. Friends and everyone have been sympathetic, but they don't like to mention her name. That's not fair, is it? It's as if she never existed."

His control was slipping and he turned away.

"And your father?"

"Oh," James said dismissively, "Dad and I never talk about anything important."

The kettle boiled and he made the coffee. Ramsay looked around the room. It seemed a typical teenage pit. A rucksack, with clothes spilling out from the top, stood in one corner. The walls were painted black and covered with posters. STOP THE BLOODY WHALING said one. Another, showing a bulldozer flattening a clump of primroses, read, I WAS AT TWYFORD DOWN.

"Twyford Down?" Ramsay asked.

"It's in Hampshire. The government want to build a motorway across it."

"And were you there?"

"For a week at the beginning of the summer. There was a sort of protest camp. I went with my girlfriend."

"What's your girlfriend's name?"

James answered automatically, too stunned apparently to wonder what the questions were about.

"Faye. But she's not my girlfriend anymore. She's not anyone's girlfriend."

Ramsay did not follow that up. He had wondered, when Charles said James had brought an older girl to the house, if it might have been Lily, but now he lost interest.

"We think there might be a link between your mother's death and a farmer called Ernest Bowles who was killed near Mittingford last Saturday," Ramsay said carefully. "Do you know if Mr. Bowles was a friend of your mother's?"

"She never mentioned him."

"And she would have done, wouldn't she?" Ramsay said. "If she were seeing another man, she would have told you. You were very close."

"Yes. We were very close. And there was no one else. She still felt some kind of misguided loyalty to my father."

"But she did go to Mittingford, didn't she? She consulted an acupuncturist, Daniel Abbot, at the Old Chapel. You must have known about that."

"Of course. I suggested that she went there."

"You know Mr. Abbot?"

"Not personally. But I'd heard of him, through Faye. And she dragged us along to one of his lectures."

"Why did you suggest that your mother go to see Mr. Abbot?"

"Because I hoped he would help her. She'd been really uptight for months. Dad was always putting her down, belittling her, you know, even in front of other people. He said she only taught dummies. Anyone could do that. Then he started seeing this woman at college. . . . That only seemed to make him worse. More arrogant, more full of himself, you know." He paused, drank the last of his coffee. "Mum started getting panic attacks. Rushing in her ears, palpitations. She thought she was dying. She went to her GP, who wanted to put her on tranquillizers. I said 'No way' and suggested she went to the Old Chapel."

"When was this?"

"Last summer. When I came back from Twyford she was really bad. She'd just broken up from college and she was always worse in the holidays."

74

"We found an appointment card among her things for July twentieth. Would that have been her first visit to Mr. Abbot?"

"Yeah, I think so. I'm not sure if she actually saw him again, but she got involved with other activities at the Old Chapel. That's where she was on Sunday afternoon."

"Was she?" It was more than Ramsay had hoped for. "Thank you, that's very helpful."

He paused. "We know that your mother went away for a weekend last autumn, but we can't trace where she was staying. Might she have been with friends from the Old Chapel?"

James took a long time to answer. He turned away and his eyes filled with tears.

"She was at a weekend retreat at a place called Juniper Hall in Cumbria. It was organised by the people from the Old Chapel. . . ." He paused and Ramsay thought he was going on to say more, but he fell silent, absorbed, it seemed, by memories of his own.

"Just one last question," Ramsay asked gently. "Do the names Lily Jackman and Sean Slater mean anything to you?"

James shook his head and Ramsay was not quite sure whether the gesture meant an answer no or simply that he could not face any more questions.

On the way back to Mittingford Ramsay called in at Prue Bennett's house. She lived in Otterbridge, not far from the McDougals. He wouldn't have been surprised if she'd known Val. He thought that they would have got on. But when he pulled up outside there were no lights at the windows, and though he rang the front doorbell over and over again, there was no reply.

12

Ramsay took Hunter with him to interview Daniel Abbot and wondered if he would regret the decision. Jokes about pins and needles he could do without. Access to the Alternative Therapy Centre was by some narrow stone stairs, which must once have led to the chapel's gallery, and then there was a large, pleasant space, very light, with a polished wooden floor and comfortable chairs. The practitioners' treatment rooms led off. Behind a desk sat a young and pretty receptionist, barely, it seemed to Ramsay, out of school.

"We'd like to see Mr. Abbot," he said.

"Have you got an appointment?" She seemed newly scrubbed, glowing with health and enthusiasm. She made Ramsay feel old.

"No," he said. "We're from Northumbria police. It's rather important."

"I'll just see if he's free." She pressed a button on the telephone and spoke into the receiver. "If you'd like to take a seat, he'll be out in a minute."

They sat on the comfortable seats. There was a low coffee table scattered with magazines and leaflets extolling the virtues of aroma therapy and osteopathy. Ramsay picked up a magazine and began to read an article on "Healing the Inner Child." One of the doors opened and Abbot came out.

He was not what Hunter had been expecting. He was big

for one thing, strong and fit. He looked as if he ran five miles before breakfast and lifted weights. Hunter admired physical strength. Sticking pins into people was a funny kind of job, but having seen the man, he wasn't inclined to dismiss acupuncture out of hand.

"Inspector," Abbot said, "how can I help you? I've already given a statement to your constable."

"There's been a development," Ramsay said. "Perhaps we could talk in private?"

"Of course, come into my room. It's a bit cramped, but we won't be overheard there. Rebecca, perhaps you could make us some tea. Rebecca's just started with us. She's already a great asset."

The girl blushed, gave a nervous smile, and disappeared.

"I'll ask the questions," Ramsay had said to Hunter as they'd climbed the stone stairs to the centre.

"Afraid I'll put my foot in it," Hunter had muttered, and he almost did put his foot in it. The girl came in with a tray. There was a teapot and three wide cups. No milk, no sugar, and when the tea was poured from the pot, it was transparent, yellowish. The colour of a urine sample, Hunter thought. And smelling of flowers and tasting of shite.

"What the hell is this?" he almost exclaimed, but stopped himself in time.

"Thank you, Rebecca," Abbot said. Smiling. She blushed again and left the room, closing the door carefully behind her. She had been well trained.

The room was square and functional. There was a high treatment table covered in a white sheet, a sink. Abbot sat behind his desk and Hunter and Ramsay took the moulded plastic seats which could have come from any hospital waiting room.

Ramsay drank the herb tea as if he was enjoying it, and apologised for causing any inconvenience.

"I've already told your constable," Daniel said again with a trace of impatience, "Lily and Sean were definitely with us on Sunday."

"Perhaps you could go over it again."

77

"This is rather tiresome, Inspector."

"And very important."

"They came for lunch. They often come for lunch on Sunday. They arrived at about eleven, had a shower and a coffee. We ate at one o'clock and then they left."

"Where did they go?"

"Lily came here, to the Old Chapel. I presume Sean went straight back to Laverock Farm. He seemed even more spaced-out than usual and I didn't ask. To be honest I thought I'd done my duty by feeding them and I was glad to be rid of him."

"Why did Lily come to the Old Chapel? To work?"

"No. She's a member of Magda's Insight Group. They meet here once a month."

That must have been the group which Val had attended, Ramsay thought. Another connection.

"Magda?" he asked.

"Magda Pocock, my mother-in-law. She's a rebirther. Rather famous actually."

"And is Mrs. Pocock here today?"

"No. She was speaking at a conference in Nottingham yesterday. She decided to stay overnight. We're expecting her back at lunchtime."

"Lily and Sean," Ramsay said quietly, "how did they seem on Sunday?"

"What do you mean?"

"In your work you must be skilled at picking up emotional responses. The holistic approach. Isn't that what it's called? I wondered what emotional state Lily and Sean were in when you saw them on Sunday lunchtime."

Abbot seemed taken aback. "Oh," he said, "I see. . . ." His professionalism reasserted itself. "They were a little tense, but that's quite normal, I'm afraid. I don't see that relationship as a permanent one. It's become rather destructive, especially for Lily."

"You think she'll leave him?" Hunter asked.

"Eventually, yes," Abbot said. "At the moment she feels

sorry for him. She knows he's dependent on her and she's reluctant to break the tie."

Hunter felt suddenly and unaccountably more cheerful. All the same he wished Ramsay would move on. Why didn't he ask about Val McDougal? Ramsay's trouble was that he was afraid of confrontation. Hunter always favoured the direct approach.

"Where did you first meet Lily and Sean?"

"My wife met them here, in the café downstairs. She brought them home for a meal. She's given to collecting strays." He must have realised that the words sounded bitter because he added with a forced smile, "I'm always telling her she's too softhearted."

"And they'd just turned up in Mittingford?"

"Yes, I suppose they must have done. Win would be able to tell you more about them. I think they were part of a convoy of travellers who'd pulled up on some common land on the edge of town. They came here to buy food, keep warm. Win took pity on them." There was a critical edge to his voice. "When the rest of the convoy moved on, they stayed. I could have done without it actually. Because Win had befriended them, people thought they were something to do with us, that we'd encouraged them to stay. It caused a lot of bad feeling locally, just as we were establishing a good reputation here. The farmers in the area didn't like having them camping and called the police. They were dossing in a clapped-out old van which wasn't roadworthy and didn't have any tax, so they couldn't move on. Things were starting to get really ugly when Win thought of the caravan at Laverock Farm."

"Mr. Bowles was a friend of yours?"

"Oh no, hardly." He gave a brief smile at the suggestion. Snobby bastard, Hunter thought. "Cissie Bowles, his mother, was my patient. I was treating her for arthritis. She came here to the centre first, but by the end she was almost bedridden and I went to the farm. That was how we knew about the caravan."

"It didn't work, then, did it?" Hunter couldn't help himself. He had behaved for long enough.

"What do you mean?"

"The acupuncture. It didn't work if she ended up having to take to her bed."

"It slowed the progress of the disease and helped relieve the pain." Abbot spoke slowly as if Hunter were stupid. "We don't claim to work miracles."

"I'd like to ask about another patient," Ramsay said.

Abbot was rattled, Hunter thought. He was hiding it well, but he was definitely rattled.

"But perhaps you'll be expecting that," Ramsay went on. "I'm surprised that you didn't come forward yourself."

"I'm afraid I don't know what you're talking about, Inspector."

But you do, Hunter thought. You know what we're talking about all right.

"I mean another suspicious death," Ramsay said. "Another victim connected with the Alternative Therapy Centre."

Abbot said nothing. He stared at Ramsay. Perfectly controlled but terrified.

"You must have seen the news report," Ramsay persisted. "Val McDougal. She was murdered in Otterbridge on Monday night."

Then, surprisingly, there was relief. Hunter was sure of that. A relaxation of tension.

"No," Abbot said. "I didn't know. At least I didn't realise it was Val. Someone told me a teacher had been killed in Otterbridge, but I didn't hear the name. We don't have a television and not much time for reading papers."

"But you did know Val McDougal?"

"Yes. She was a patient at the centre. She came to me originally, complaining of panic attacks. I referred her on to Magda. I saw her occasionally in reception, then she came with us to our weekend retreat in Cumbria last autumn."

"You didn't actually treat her?"

"No," Abbot said. "I did a traditional diagnosis, took the

80

pulses, blood pressure, but decided that rebirthing seemed more appropriate."

"She was killed on Monday night," Ramsay said. "Strangled like Mr. Bowles." He paused, then continued provocatively. "Could you tell me where you were on Monday evening?"

"Why?" Abbot demanded, no longer frightened but very much on his dignity.

"It's a matter of routine," Ramsay said smoothly. "Elimination. I'm sure you understand."

"Win and I were in Otterbridge, actually. At the Further Education College. An old tutor of mine was giving a lecture."

"Mrs. McDougal was working at the college on Monday evening. Did you see her?"

Abbot shook his head impatiently.

"What time did you get home?"

"Not till late. After midnight. A few of us took the lecturer out for a meal. Then I had to take Lily home."

"Lily was in Otterbridge with you?"

"No. She was here, baby-sitting. I dropped Win off and drove her back to Laverock Farm."

"Sean wasn't with her?"

"No."

There was a pause while Ramsay considered the information.

"Would Mrs. McDougal have known Lily and Sean?"

"Lily certainly. They both went to Magda's group."

"Oh yes, of course," Ramsay said. "The Insight Group. And Mr. Bowles? Would she have known him?"

"I wouldn't have thought so. Unless she went to Laverock Farm to see Lily."

"So the Old Chapel is the only link between the murders," Ramsay said. "I think that puts you in a rather uncomfortable position. . . ."

"What are you implying, Inspector?" It was an expression of injured surprise.

"I'm not implying anything," Ramsay said calmly. "It's not as if you benefit from either of the deaths."

"No," Abbot said, a little uncertainly. "At least not personally."

"What do you mean?" For the first time Ramsay's voice was sharp. "We're not playing games, Mr. Abbot."

The man leant forward across the desk in a conciliatory gesture. "Look, I'll have to explain about Cissie Bowles or you'll not understand. She came to us after a row with her GP. To pay him back, I suspect, for not giving her enough attention and not being sufficiently polite. You can hardly blame the doctor. She was a demanding and cantankerous old thing. Certainly not polite herself. Given to strange oaths of a vaguely biblical nature. I think she'd been through three GPs already before she decided to try me. I'm sure she only stuck with me because it amused her to be treated by what's known generally in the town as 'that group of hippies.' She'd never been properly accepted here, although she was brought up in Laverock Farm and went to school with most of the old crows who disapproved of her."

He paused for breath. Ramsay said nothing. He was prepared to wait to see where this was leading.

"Ernie was her only relative," Abbot went on. "Her parents were middle-aged when she was born and she was an only child. I know all this because I took a personal history when she first consulted me. Her parents died when she was in her early twenties and she took on the farm. Ran it, apparently, almost single-handed until Ernie was old enough to help. There was a hired help. He was an outsider, too, I imagine. Not immediately local anyway because he had to live in."

Ramsay raised his eyebrows. "Ernie's father?"

"Yes," Abbot said. "Ernie's father. She fired him as soon as she discovered she was pregnant and made do after that with casual labour from the town—"

"This is very interesting," Ramsay interrupted, "but I don't see how you come to benefit from Mr. Bowles's death." He suspected that Daniel Abbot was stringing him along.

"I'm coming to that," Abbot said. "Cissie left the farm to Ernie for his lifetime and, in the event of his marrying and leaving children, to his offspring after his death." He stopped, took a shallow breath, and completed the explanation in a rush. "If he was to die before having children, the farm would come to the Alternative Therapy Centre."

"Why didn't you tell us that before?" Ramsay demanded. "You didn't say anything to the officer who came earlier in the week to take a statement."

"Shock, I suppose. Embarrassment. And at that time I only had Cissie's word as to what was in the will. She might have been leading me on. It would have been quite in character. But I had a phone call from her solicitor this morning."

"What do you mean Laverock Farm goes to the Alternative Therapy Centre?" Hunter asked belligerently. He saw the chance of a ruck. "You mean you sell it and split the profit between you? I don't know how many of you work in this place, but it'd be a tidy windfall. I'd call that a personal gain."

"No," Abbot said, interrupting forcefully. "It wasn't like that. The terms of Cissie's will were very exact. Occasionally we run weekend retreats like the one Val McDougal attended last autumn. It provides a chance for our patients to get away from the stress of everyday life which often lies at the root of their problems; charge, if you like, their spiritual batteries. . . . We have discussion groups, teach relaxation techniques, yoga, meditations. Look, as you said yourself, at the whole person."

"This is most instructive, but I don't understand what it has to do with Laverock Farm."

"In the past we've always gone to a place in Cumbria for the retreat. Juniper Hall. It's pleasant enough but expensive and inconvenient for people to get to. Cissie had a vision of Laverock Farm being turned into a centre where we could run retreats ourselves, weekend workshops, experiment with all kinds of different therapies in a residential setting. A place like that would attract visitors from all over the country."

"I bet the locals will love that," Hunter muttered.

"I'm sure they'll get used to it, Sergeant," Abbot said piously. "Besides, Cissie was hardly one for worrying about what her neighbours thought."

"Are you sure?" Ramsay asked. "Isn't that what this is really about? We know there was ill feeling between her and the Richardsons at Long Edge Farm. I suspect the will was her way of paying back her neighbours for what she saw as their spite. It was her final piece of mischief. Her revenge. Leaving them with what they'd consider a commune in their midst."

"Her motives hardly matter now, Inspector. You can be sure we'll put the place to good use."

"You seem to have given the venture a lot of thought," Ramsay said.

"I suppose I have. It was a dream, you know, that's all. An exciting dream. I never thought anything would come of it. Ernie Bowles was fifty-five. He could have lived for thirty years."

He could have lived for thirty years, Ramsay thought. But he didn't, did he?

13

After the interview with Abbot, Ramsay and Hunter separated. Hunter was sent to Long Edge Farm to talk to the Richardsons.

"See if you can find out if Richardson knew about Cissie Bowles's will," Ramsay said. "If he did, I think we've lost a motive for murder. He'd surely rather have a festival of New Age travellers once a year than have the hippies on his doorstep permanently. And see if any of the family knew Val McDougal. The wife, Sue, might have done. They'd be of a similar age. It's even possible that Peter, the lad, went to Otterbridge FE College before starting at agricultural college." At this point they were still looking for connections, hoping for luck.

Ramsay picked up Sally Wedderburn from the incident room and took her to interview Win Abbot. He had already established that she would be at home.

"Win?" Abbot had said dismissively. "Oh yes, she'll be there. Since the boys were born she's only worked part-time."

He must have warned her that the police were on their way, because when they rang the doorbell she let them in immediately, without asking what they wanted. Win was a tall, thin woman with wispy hair fixed in a pile on the back of her head with a tortoiseshell comb. The hairstyle and her clothes—a long skirt reaching almost to her ankles and a long shapeless cardigan—made her seem old-fashioned. Like a character from one of the adaptations of D. H. Lawrence that Prue made him watch, Ramsay thought. Somehow haunted and intense. Certainly she looked very tired. She came to the door carrying a toddler on her hip.

"Come in," she said, pushing a strand of hair away from her face. "I'm just giving them lunch. We're in the kitchen."

The house was one of a row of stone houses built into the side of the hill with a long steep garden behind it and a bay window at the front. The kitchen was an extension on the back. Another little boy sat at the table there. Win lifted the toddler from her hip into a high chair. She began to feed him slices of apple and whole-meal toast covered with an unappetising but obviously healthy spread.

"Sit down," she said. "I'm sorry about the mess."

She looked around the kitchen as if overwhelmed by the disorder, though Ramsay thought he had seen much worse. Often, for example, in Prue's home. There was a basket of laundry on the table, a pile of toys on the floor, some nappies soaking in a bucket by the sink. Nothing to explain Win Abbot's exhaustion.

"It must be a lot of work with two little ones," Sally Wedderburn was saying. "And your job at the Alternative Therapy Centre. Do you have any help?"

"No." The hand twitched nervously back to the escaping hair. "Not now. I had a girl in to look after the boys last summer, but now I try to manage on my own. I only go to the centre two evenings a week. Daniel has the boys then." She handed the toddler another finger of toast and watched while he squeezed it back out through toothless gums onto his plastic bib. "Can I get you something?" she asked. "Tea? Coffee?"

Ramsay shook his head.

"The main trouble is that they don't sleep very well," she went on. "I always seem to be tired."

So that was the explanation, Ramsay thought, for her drawn and grey appearance. Not guilt, the torment he'd imagined, but kids who wouldn't sleep. He should know by now not to jump to conclusions.

"Perhaps you could explain how the centre is organised," he said. "You and your husband are partners?"

"With my mother," she said. "She and Daniel work at the centre practically full-time. There are three treatment rooms. I use the third for my evenings. When I'm not there we let the room to other practitioners: Sam Lacey's an osteopath and Billy Brown's a chiropractor. They have two and a half days each."

"But they're not partners? They won't benefit under the terms of Cissie Bowles's will?"

"None of us will benefit personally," she said sharply. "And I'm sure we'll find a place for them at Laverock Farm."

"But you *will* benefit," he persisted gently. "Surely you'll have an increased income because of the new patients the centre at Laverock Farm will attract."

That seemed genuinely not to have occurred to her.

"I suppose it might," she said. "In the long term."

"And you'll split any profit three ways?"

"Oh no," she said. "I shouldn't think so. Magda put most money in when we started. It would be fair, I suppose, that she should take most out."

She leaned forward over the table. "But none of us has been motivated by money, you know. That's not what it's all about." She had the passion of a fanatic.

"What does motivate you?" he asked lightly.

"Healing," she said. "We want to show people that they can be well. That's why Laverock Farm's important. We can reach more people."

The boys had finished eating. She wiped their faces perfunctorily with a dishcloth and helped them down from the table, then opened the door to let them into the garden. Outside there were tricycles, a scooter. She shut the door on them gratefully.

"Peace," she said. "For ten minutes at least. Until they start fighting."

"You've heard from your husband that Mrs. McDougal's dead?" Ramsay asked.

She nodded.

"Tell me about her. Were you friends?"

"Friends?" The question seemed to bemuse her. She sat with her head on one side, considering it. Her eyes were grey and her skin was sandy and freckled, lined on her forehead with fine wrinkles. Ramsay guessed that she and Daniel were of a similar age, but she looked much older. "No," she said at last. "We weren't really friends, though I always felt we might be. I was putting it off, if you know what I mean, saving it for when I had more energy and time. Now I suppose it's too late."

"Val didn't make the effort to be friends with you?"

"No, but then she wouldn't have done. She was very shy."

"You never saw her professionally?"

"No. She had ten sessions of rebirthing with Magda. She came to the retreat at Juniper. I talked to her there, at meals you know, socially. But there was a lot going on that weekend. It was hard to concentrate on getting to know people."

"I would have thought that was what the weekend would be for."

"Usually, yes . . ."

"But something unusual happened that weekend?"

She looked up at him sharply, as if the question might be some sort of trick, then paused uncertainly and shook her head. She was lying, but he did not push it. There would be other people to ask.

"Do you ever attend your mother's Insight Group?"

"Occasionally," she flashed back bitterly. "When I can persuade Daniel to look after the children."

"Did Mrs. McDougal have any special friends there? Someone she confided in. A man perhaps?"

"She didn't have a boyfriend, if that's what you mean."

"What about Lily Jackman? Were she and Val friends?"

"What is this friendship business about?" Win demanded angrily. "I thought you were a policeman, not a psychologist."

"If she had any concerns for her safety, she may have confided in someone," Ramsay replied calmly. "That's why I need to know."

"I'm sorry," she said. "I hardly slept at all last night. That's why I'm so ratty. And the shock, I suppose. Val and Lily seemed to get on very well in the group. They seemed to understand each other right from the start. But I don't think they ever met away from the centre. Lily never mentioned it anyway."

"You've been very kind to Lily and Sean," he said.

"Not really."

"They come to your house for meals and baths. You found them somewhere to live."

"Well," she said, "I suppose I felt a bit responsible—for their staying in Mittingford when the rest of the convoy moved on."

"Why?"

"I'd talked to them a lot about the centre, how we organise it. I wanted them to see that they could have a lifestyle which didn't compromise their beliefs but was more purposeful than aimlessly travelling around in an old van."

She was like a missionary, Ramsay thought. He could see how Lily had been hooked.

"It was awkward," she said. "I think when the convoy moved on they expected that we'd put them up here. I wouldn't have minded. We've got the room and I'd have liked the company. But Daniel wasn't keen. He didn't want us getting too involved. . . ."

"So instead they moved into Mr. Bowles's caravan."

She nodded.

"Did you meet any other members of the convoy?" Ramsay asked.

"Yes. They used to come into the coffee shop in the Old Chapel. I saw them there occasionally."

"Do you remember a couple called Wes and Lorna? They might have been driving a blue Transit van. They had a baby, a little girl."

She shook her head.

"Sorry," she said. "Lily and Sean were the only people I really got to know."

"Could you tell me where you were on Saturday night?"

"The night Ernie Bowles was strangled?" There was a brief flash of humour.

He nodded. "It's a formality," he said. "We're asking everyone."

"I was here. I'm always here."

"And your husband?"

There was a perceptible pause before she answered: "Yes. He was here, too."

"Thank you," he said. "You've been very helpful." As they stood to go there was a yell from the garden, followed by the sound of a child sobbing.

"I'll have to go," she said, more in resignation than concern.

"That's all right. We'll see ourselves out."

"Poor cow," Sally Wedderburn said when they were out on the pavement.

"What do you mean?"

"Well, she seems so ground down by it all, doesn't she? Depressed."

Sally was right, he thought. There was more wrong with Win Abbot than a few nights' missed sleep. She might be tied to the children, but it wasn't as if she didn't get any break at all. There were her two evenings at the Old Chapel and they knew that she'd been in Otterbridge on Monday night with Daniel. Lily was obviously available to baby-sit and her mother lived in Mittingford. Surely she'd help if Win were desperate.

And she was desperate, he saw now. But why?

When they returned to the incident room Hunter was waiting for them, sitting on Ramsay's desk with a mug of coffee in his hand.

"Well?" Ramsay said. "How did you get on? How did Mr. Richardson take the news that there'd be a New Age centre at Laverock Farm?"

"He didn't set the dogs on me or get out the shotgun," Hunter said. "Though it was touch and go at first."

"Did he know already about the terms of Cissie Bowles's will?"

"He says not and I believe him." Hunter put his coffee mug onto the desk, leaving a ring in the wood. "At first he was pretty mad. He talked about getting an injunction. Something about a change of use from agriculture being against the planning regulations, but he didn't really seem to know what he was talking about. His wife soon calmed him down."

"How?"

"She said she thought the hippies would only be interested in the house, not the land. It was a way of getting a bargain."

"I had the impression that he has his eye on the farm," Ramsay said. "For the son."

"Aye well, it's the land the son's interested in, too, not a big draughty house. If he marries, Mummy and Daddy will build him a nice modern bungalow."

"So Peter Richardson's done very well out of Ernie's death, if the Abbots are willing to sell the land."

"Too bloody right," Hunter said, and slurped the last of the coffee.

"Did any of them know Val McDougal?"

"Never heard of her. So they claim."

14

It was Saturday, a week after Stephen Ramsay had walked with his lover in the hills and Ernie Bowles had dressed up to meet his date in the town. Lily had been invited to supper with Magda Pocock. Magda, the famous rebirther who, despite her wealth, lived very simply on the job in a flat built into the roof of the Old Chapel.

Lily was working and Magda had come into the shop, ostensibly to buy groceries but hoping to find Lily there. She was still wearing her smart conference clothes, looked very much the professional woman.

"Lily," she said. "My dear. What time will you finish work?" There was still the hint of the accent she had picked up from her mother.

Lily told her.

"Come and talk to me," she said. "Stay for supper. I'm worried about all these dreadful things that have been happening."

And she was worried, Lily could see that. She wasn't curious or excited like most of the customers who came into the shop to discuss the murders. Magda's anxiety troubled Lily more than all the other unsettling things that had been going on. It wasn't like her.

From the beginning Magda had taken Lily under her wing and Lily had become dependent on her.

"A mother substitute," Sean said derisively, usually when

he was jealous about the time Lily spent in Magda's company. And Lily supposed that was true. Certainly she would have preferred Magda as a mother than Bridget the politician. She almost said as much at one of the groups, but Magda had pushed the idea aside.

"You can't blame your parents for your unhappiness," she had said. "You've left them behind. You must take responsibility for your own life now."

But it seemed to Lily that it was harder to leave her parents behind than Magda supposed. Even last Sunday, at the Voice Dialogue workshop, when she'd been working with Val, a particular incident from her childhood had intruded. She'd had to live it again. She still remembered it quite vividly.

Her mother had been a workaholic, driven by political ambition and seldom there. Her father was an actor of sorts, but by the time Lily was a teenager hardly ever seemed to be in work. He drank like a fish and found his companionship in pubs and bars. Quite often he picked up friends there and brought them home to carry on drinking.

That was what had happened on the evening Lily remembered. She had got out of bed to go to the bathroom and almost fallen over a strange man who had collapsed at the top of the stairs. He had caught her around the waist and said in a thick Bristol accent:

"My, you're a beauty, a real bobby dazzler," and pulled her towards him to kiss her. She could still remember the smell of the whisky on his breath. She had screamed and screamed until he'd let her go and all the other men rushed out to see what was happening. Her father, shocked into sobriety by the noise, had been in turns defensive and apologetic. Why had she made so much fuss? he said. Then, pleading: there was no need, was there, to tell her mother.

Lily never discussed the incident with her mother, partly out of loyalty to her father and a kind of embarrassment, partly because she had so many late-night sittings that she was never there. But Bridget had found out somehow and Lily was never left alone in the house with her father after that. Strange girls were employed to "keep her company" or she was sent to friends' homes to sleep. She thought it was probably a relief all round when she packed her rucksack and left them to it.

"You're very quiet tonight," Magda said. She was setting the table, polishing heavy silver with a white napkin.

"I was thinking of Val," Lily said. "The last time we met."

"Ah yes," Magda said. "Poor Val."

"Did you talk to her on Sunday?"

"Only briefly."

After a week of sunshine it had begun to rain very heavily and there was thunder. Magda's flat had sloping roofs and windows you needed to open with a pole, and the water seemed to be all round them. It was only eight in the evening but already quite dark. The room was lit with scented candles. "To help me relax," Magda said. "What a week I've had."

It seemed to Lily that Magda had made too much of an effort. Usually she was so calm and unflustered. Tonight she fussed over everything; the food, the table, where Lily should sit. It made Lily uneasy.

Nothing important was said until they sat down to eat. Even then the conversation was careful, like one of those elaborate peasant dances where you go round and round in a circle. Magda started it off. She spooned food onto Lily's plate and said: "The police are coming to see me tomorrow. They wanted to talk to me today, but I said no."

"You could have seen them this evening," Lily said. "To get it over with. I wouldn't have minded."

But she would have minded really. She was glad to be here in Magda's warm and comfortable flat. She felt she couldn't have faced another evening of Sean mooching around the caravan. Especially in the rain. It made a terrible din, like stones rattling around in a tin bucket. It really got on her nerves.

"No," Magda said. "I need time. To decide what I'm going to tell them."

"What do you mean?" Lily said, startled. "What do you know about the murders?"

"Nothing. Of course. Nothing."

"Well then?"

"I wondered if I should tell them about Juniper. Val was there, after all."

Then Lily realised that was why she was here. Magda wanted to ask her advice. Magda, usually so confident and competent, who told them all what to do, had turned to her.

"I don't see that it's relevant," Lily said. "Faye died of natural causes, didn't she?"

Magda did not reply.

"Well? Didn't she?"

"I'm not sure," Magda said quietly.

"What do you mean?"

"I found her diary," Magda continued. "She was very unhappy. It could have been suicide."

"But not murder!"

"No," Magda said sharply. "Of course not. But now . . . Mr. Bowles could just have been a coincidence. But Val . . ."

"Have you talked to Win about this?"

Magda shook her head. "She's unhappy enough, don't you think?"

"Daniel?"

Magda's voice hardened. "No," she said. "I've discussed nothing with Daniel."

They sat, looking at each other. A flash of lightning close to the roof made Magda jump so she knocked over her glass.

"Well," she said. "Lily, my dear. What would you advise?"

Don't ask me, Lily thought. I can't even make decisions for myself. She forced herself to be rational, practical.

"Don't say anything," she said. "Not yet. Most murders are cleared up very quickly, aren't they? The police might already know who they're looking for. If you tell them your suspicions about Juniper, they'll have to reopen the case of Faye's death, won't they? And even if they decide that she died of natural causes, there'll be lots of bad publicity. Just at a time when you want people to accept the idea of an alternative therapy centre at Laverock Farm."

"That's another thing," Magda said. "I'm not sure we should take on Laverock Farm. It's not right to profit from murder."

"That's ridiculous!" Lily said. She had her own ideas about Laverock Farm and her place in it. Usually she would not have dared to speak to Magda like that, but today she seemed so vulnerable and uncertain. "Nobody would accuse you of murdering Ernie Bowles to get your hands on the farm. You're healers."

"I'm not sure what to think. Besides, I don't like the idea of accepting a gift from Mr. Bowles, even indirectly. He was such a *dirty* old man."

He was that all right, Lily thought, remembering the face pressed up against the windowpane, only partly hidden by grey net curtains. But I suppose that's no reason for being glad that he's dead.

"You wouldn't really turn down the chance of Laverock Farm, would you?" she said. "It's such a brilliant opportunity. Think what you could achieve."

"Tell me, dear," Magda said. "Why are *you* so interested?" And Lily realised that even now, when she was so stressed up, Magda was the most perceptive person she had ever met.

There was no point pretending. She shrugged. "I suppose I hoped there'd be a place for me there. You'd need someone living in to keep an eye on everything."

It needn't be much, she thought. A flat like this and I'd be as happy as a pig in muck.

Magda smiled suddenly. "Why not?" she said. "If we do decide to go ahead, why not? I see you as a sort of lady of the manor. You would be magnificent."

Lily thought she was being teased, but Magda seemed quite serious.

"But what about Sean?" Magda continued. "Do you see him having a place at the new Laverock Farm?"

The question made Lily suddenly feel very tired. Thoughts of Sean always made her feel like that. She had a picture of him in the caravan, restless, waiting for her to come home. He seemed to have stopped his wandering lately. She did not know which was worse—never knowing where he was or having him cooped up with her in the caravan.

"Well?" Magda said gently. "How are things between you and Sean these days?" There was something hypnotic about her voice. Lily felt the old compulsion to talk. Magda put so much into her listening and was so wise. Perhaps she would help her sort things out with Sean. That would be a relief. To come to some conclusion about where they stood. But she sat up straight in the bentwood chair and she could not catch Magda's eye.

"Fine," she said in a brittle voice. "Well, as fine as they've always been."

Then she sat back with a sigh and watched Magda carry out the dirty plates and return from the kitchen with a blue glazed bowl of purple grapes and a cheese board. Magda would know that things weren't really fine, but she wouldn't push it.

They sat for a moment in silence.

"What are they like, then?" Magda asked at last.

"Who?"

"The policemen in charge of the case."

"The inspector Ramsay's not bad really. For the fuzz." In her travelling days Lily had met plenty of the other sort of policeman. "Quite sensitive, I think. I don't know about the sergeant. He's a bit cocky, arrogant. . . ."

She looked up from her cheese.

"Have you decided? Will you tell them about Faye and Juniper?"

"I don't know. I suppose I'll sleep on it. Or not sleep probably. It's Win I'm worried about."

"Of course," Lily said, and hoped Win knew how lucky she was to have a mother who worried about her. She wanted to comfort Magda as she had been comforted in the past. She leaned forward across the table so her face was lit from underneath by the candle. "I'm sure it'll be all right," she said.

"Are you?" Magda's voice was bleak. "I expect you're right."

She stood up suddenly. In the distance there was a rumble of thunder. Rain was still washing over the windows.

"I'll give you a lift home," she said. "You can't cycle in this."

"Are you sure? I can stay if you like. I'm in no hurry."

"That's very kind, my dear, but I think now I have to be alone."

They hurried through the rain to the car, which was parked in the street. It spluttered before it started as if water had got into the engine. The windscreen wipers couldn't clear the screen. Magda drove with her head pushed forward over the steering wheel, peering into the gloom. When they pulled into the farmyard Magda switched off the engine so they could hear the rain bouncing off the roof. They kissed as they always did, lightly on each cheek.

"Take care," Lily said, and she sprinted away through the meadow to the caravan.

Sean was waiting for her. She threw herself into the caravan. She was drenched to the skin. He was holding a big white towel. He wrapped it around her and took off her wet clothes and dried her as if she were his baby. Then he sat her in the corner and made hot chocolate and told her he would look after her. It was like the old days, when they had first met up. Somehow he was his old self again.

"I'm sorry I'm late," she said. "Magda wanted to talk."

"Tell me about it later," he said.

He blew out the paraffin lamp and they made love to the sound of the rain.

15

The detectives based in Mittingford were starting to form a cohesive team. There were shared rituals, in-jokes, and a scapegoat called Newell who never washed his coffee mug or took his turn at making tea. Ramsay watched the team develop, sensed their frustration, wished he could give them a result.

Their world was this town and the surrounding farms. Ramsay knew the names by heart—Long Edge, Laverock, Denton, Holywell—could picture each of the farmers. They talked to retired farm labourers and the visitors staying in the Long Edge holiday cottages. Slowly they built up a picture of Ernie Bowles, the people he met, his weekly round of market and boozing. Then, when they took on the Val McDougal case, too, they concentrated on the Alternative Therapy Centre, made visits to the regular clients and the occasional visitors who dropped in for homoeopathic remedies and advice.

On a large old blackboard in the incident room these two groups—Bowles's acquaintances and the patrons of the Alternative Therapy Centre—were represented as two circles of names joined to the centre like spokes in a wheel. The circles only met through Lily Jackman and Cissie Bowles. There was no other significant connection. After a week that was the most important conclusion the team had come to. Because they were based in Mittingford, Val McDougal with

99

her home in Otterbridge seemed on the very edge of the Alternative Therapy circle, almost incidental. Ramsay was aware of that. They hadn't concentrated on Val enough. Next week he would send more officers to talk to her friends and colleagues and trace her movements in the days before her death. Then perhaps there would be a third circle and she would be in the middle.

But now it was Saturday night and they were all spending their overtime payments on beer in the small dusty bar the landlord had given them for their own use, to keep them away from the regular punters. Ramsay joined them for a couple of pints for the sake of team spirit, but he wasn't comfortable. It wasn't just police company that put him off, the blue jokes, the aggressive consumption of alcohol. He'd never enjoyed any sort of social gathering. Too many inhibitions, he supposed. Diana, who adored parties, had called him a boring old fart. Affectionately at first but then with irritation. He thought Prue was still to be disappointed by his lack of social skills. At ten o'clock he left the bar. He called good-bye but nobody noticed his leaving.

He found it impossible to sleep. In the hotel's restaurant the town's rugby club was holding its end-of-season dinner, and bawdy songs were being bellowed long after the party in the private bar had broken up. In the end he got up, and sat by the window and tried to plan his interview with the elusive Magda Pocock.

Hunter, on his way to bed, was attracted by the noise in the restaurant. He was a football man, had a season ticket to St. James's Park, and was rather suspicious of rugby, with all that mawling and rolling in the mud. But he was quite prepared to take advantage of the free beer that was swilling around, and it was almost three before he returned to his room.

The next morning at breakfast he was pale and unusually quiet. Ramsay hadn't often seen him with a hangover, and hoped it meant he'd keep his thoughts to himself when they interviewed the rebirther.

Despite his headache, Hunter ordered bacon and eggs. The

force were picking up the expenses of their stay and he intended getting his money's worth.

"Peter Richardson was here last night," he said. "At the rugby do. Shouting his mouth off. About Ernie Bowles and what he's going to do when the Laverock land's his."

"He seems to be taking a lot for granted," Ramsay said. "Even if the crowd from the Old Chapel decide to sell the land, surely there'll be an auction."

Hunter shrugged. "I had the impression that his old man had already done a deal with them."

"If that's true, Magda Pocock should know. She's the senior partner in the practice."

"That's the line we're going to take with her, then? She's the senior partner, so she's the most to gain from Ernie Bowles's death."

"No!" Ramsay said sharply. "I hope we can be more subtle than that. I'm just as interested in what she can tell us about Val McDougal. No one can explain what she was like. Quiet, shy, intimidated by her husband. Not a woman with any confidence or self-esteem, but there must have been more to her than that. If she was so inoffensive, why would anyone want to kill her?"

Hunter thought his boss was talking nonsense as usual. What did it matter what the woman was like? It was facts: forensic facts, blood samples, witnesses' descriptions that solved murders, not what the woman was like. The psychology of the victim, they called it, as if the poor cow had asked to be strangled. She hadn't and nor had Ernie Bowles, if it came to that.

It was Sunday, but the Old Chapel was open. It was their busiest day, and at ten o'clock, when Ramsay and Hunter walked along the wet pavements from the pub, there was already a coach pulled up outside it. A group of middle-aged Americans climbed out. They had the dazed look of people who are not quite sure where they are. Then enthusiasm took over again as they went in search of souvenirs, their midwestern voices drowning out the bells being rung in St. Cuthbert's Church across the street.

In the Alternative Therapy Centre Magda Pocock was waiting for them. Ramsay recognised her at once. She had been featured a few weeks before in a Sunday colour magazine. There was a Slavic look to her face. She had wide cheekbones, thick eyebrows, and a mane of grey hair. There was nothing of her daughter's sandy, faded look, nothing to suggest the two were related. Except the fanaticism, Ramsay thought. They had that in common. He could imagine Magda as a nineteenth-century Christian missionary converting whole continents through the joy of her certainty. Perhaps the image was so strong because of the word itself. Rebirthing made him think of being born again and fundamentalism.

"Sit down," she said. "Perhaps you'd like some coffee?"

"Thank you."

"We don't usually see patients on a Sunday," she said, "so we can sit here, in reception. More comfortable, I think, than my treatment room."

"But you run your Insight Group on a Sunday."

"Once a month, yes. I expect you'll want to ask me about that."

It must have been Rebecca's day off, too, because Magda went away to make the coffee herself. While they were waiting, Ramsay riffled through the leaflets on the coffee table until he found one on rebirthing.

Rebirthing is conscious connected breathing, it said. Which didn't tell him much.

"You should try it, Inspector," Magda said in a gently mocking voice. "It might change your life."

She handed him a cup of coffee.

"Did it change Val McDougal's life?" he asked.

"Yes," she said, serious now. "Really. I believe it did."

"In what way?"

She sat opposite to him.

"It gave her the power to take responsibility for herself. When she came to me she was deeply unhappy. Helpless, you might say, in her unhappiness. She came to see that she could take positive steps to bring about change."

"How did rebirthing help her to do that?" His voice was neutral.

"It's rather difficult to explain to someone who's never experienced it," she said. "Perhaps to you it sounds fanciful. . . . The breathing relaxes the body's natural energies. In Val's case it gave her a sense of control which she was able to take into her everyday life."

Did it? Ramsay thought. There was no indication that she'd found the courage to stand up to her husband. But perhaps she had. Perhaps she was planning to leave him. That would provide a motive for murder.

"Could you take us through one of your sessions with Mrs. McDougal?" Ramsay asked.

"You do realise that usually my work is confidential, Inspector."

Ramsay sensed that Hunter was about to be rude and anticipated him.

"Of course," he said. "But in the circumstances . . . What happened, for example, when she first came to see you? She was referred by your son-in-law?"

"By Daniel. Yes." Just in those words Ramsay sensed that she disliked Daniel Abbot.

"And that was last summer?"

"August," she said. "I looked it up when I heard you wanted to see me. But I'm not sure how relevant this is, Inspector. She came to my group, but she hasn't attended any rebirthing sessions since Christmas."

"All the same . . ." he said.

"Very well," Magda said. "If you think it will help. She was very nervous when she first came to me. Very tense. That is quite usual. I always spend time talking to my client before we start the breathing. I asked Val what she hoped to get out of the sessions. She was having panic attacks, she said. Very frightening panic attacks. She had gone to her GP, but he could only suggest tranquillizers. That, too, unfortunately, is quite usual. Most of all she wanted the panic attacks to stop. I suggested that the attacks were merely a symptom of her problems and that we should look more

103

deeply at what she might hope to achieve. We talked about her relationship with her husband and her children. It was clear that she felt uncomfortable in expressing her own needs. . . . There was a lot of frustration and resentment."

"How long would that part of the session have lasted?"

"Half an hour. Longer perhaps. Val was very reserved at that stage. Not used to talking about her feelings. I had to give her time."

"And then?"

"Then we'd begin the breathing. That's what rebirthing is, you see—a specific breathing technique."

"And that is?"

"To consciously breath correctly—to have no gap between inhaling and exhaling."

"That's it?" Hunter could contain himself no longer. "You charge fifty quid a session to teach them that?"

Magda laughed out loud. She was quite unoffended. "Not quite," she said. "During the breathing the client becomes aware of tensions. I can encourage the client to feel safe, to continue breathing while they are feeling whatever they are experiencing. This can integrate the feelings and resolve the tensions."

"What happened during Mrs. McDougal's sessions?" Ramsay asked.

Magda hesitated.

"In the first session she began to hyperventilate," she said at last. "That's not uncommon. Especially with clients who suffer from panic attacks. I helped her breathe through it. I showed her that she could control her own reactions. That gave her confidence."

"How long does the breathing last?"

"Usually between one and two hours."

"Don't they get bored?" Hunter demanded. "Just lying there for an hour and a half. Breathing?"

She laughed again. "Not at all, Sergeant. Really, a rebirthing session can be a most exciting experience. You should try it. I'd even give you a discount."

104

Money for old rope, Hunter thought. There should be a law against it.

"What happens then?" Ramsay asked. "After the breathing?"

"Sometimes we talk through the issues that have emerged during the session. In Val's case that was the relationship with her husband, her inability to assert herself."

"How many sessions did Val have?"

"Ten. That's usual. I like to arrange the length of the course before we start. If it's left open-ended, there's a danger of the client becoming dependent. That's counterproductive, of course."

"But you encouraged Mrs. McDougal to come to your Sunday afternoon group?"

"That's quite different, Inspector. Much less intense. Besides, Val and I became friends. We were, I suppose, mutually dependent. I'll miss her."

"What happened at the group on Sunday?"

Magda shrugged.

"For the last few sessions we've been looking at a technique called Voice Dialogue, which was developed by American therapists. I'd been working individually with group members, but on Sunday I put the group into pairs. One member would be the facilitator and the other the client. In Voice Dialogue the facilitator talks to different parts of the personality: the vulnerable child, the teacher, the critic. It's a way of developing a balanced and healthy ego."

More money for old rope, Hunter thought again.

"Who was Mrs. McDougal paired with?" Ramsay asked.

"Lily Jackman," Magda said.

"Who was the facilitator?"

"Both of them. They took it in turns."

"Did Mrs. McDougal seem especially distressed or upset?"

"She became emotional, but that was to be expected."

"But you don't know what emerged from the session?"

"No, Inspector. You'd have to ask Lily."

There was a brief silence.

"What were you doing on Saturday evening, Mrs. Pocock?"

"I was here," she said. "In my flat upstairs." She paused. "Val was here, too. I'd invited her for supper."

"Why?" Ramsay asked sharply. This, at least, was one gap filled. They knew now where Val had disappeared to on Saturday evening.

"Why, Inspector? Because we were friends. I wanted to spend some time with her."

"Did you meet her regularly?"

"No," Magda said. "This was the first occasion I'd invited her for a meal."

"How did she seem?"

"Relaxed," Magda said. "More relaxed than I'd ever known her."

"What time did she leave?"

"At about eleven."

"She wouldn't have had to drive past Laverock Farm to go home?"

"Not usually. But it was a pleasant evening. It's possible, I suppose, that she took that road."

And she might have seen something, Ramsay thought. The time would fit. Perhaps she passed a car she recognised.

"Where were you on Monday evening?" he asked.

"In my flat," she said. "On my own. Preparing my speech for the Nottingham conference."

There was a pause. Hunter was beginning to get restless. This talk was getting them nowhere.

"Did you know that Cissie Bowles had left Laverock Farm to you in the event of Ernie not marrying?" he demanded.

"Daniel had mentioned it."

"And were you aware that Mr. Bowles had taken steps to find a wife? He'd gone as far as consulting a dating agency."

"No," she said. "How could I know that? I had no social contact with the man."

"Rather a coincidence, don't you think?" Hunter sneered.

"That's insulting, Sergeant."

"Have you done a deal with Mr. Richardson at Long Edge Farm to sell him the land?"

"Of course not!" She seemed genuinely shocked. "It's not even been discussed."

"You might not have discussed it," Hunter said. "But someone has. Peter Richardson was full of it last night."

"No. There must be some mistake. Unless . . ."

"Unless?" Ramsay prompted gently.

"Unless Daniel has begun some preliminary negotiations," she said frostily. Again Ramsay sensed her antipathy for her son-in-law.

"But you would be glad of the use of the farmhouse," Ramsay said. "It would be more convenient than going to Juniper Hall for your weekend courses."

"Yes, yes." She was impatient and suddenly eager to be rid of them.

"If that's all," she said, "I'll see you downstairs."

16

Charles McDougal made no attempt to cook a family lunch that Sunday, though Richard, the older son, was home from university for the weekend. Instead he mumbled something about having work to do and disappeared to spend the day with Heather. Perhaps he had intended to cook one of his elaborate meals for her. Heather had become altogether kinder and more solicitous since Val's death, though whether this was because she was genuinely sympathetic, or because there was the possibility now that the relationship might become permanent and respectable, it was hard to tell.

The boys, Richard and James, were left to their own devices in the house where their mother had been killed. They had never been close and found now that they had little to say to each other. Richard, secretly, had thought for a long time that James was weird. All that New Age crap was a joke. Richard wanted to save the planet, too, but didn't believe it could be done with crystals in pyramids and astrological charts. He'd thought James had grown out of it. When he'd asked his mother, that's what she'd said. But his mother had been part of the problem and it seemed to Richard that they'd egged each other on, daring each other to accept greater follies, more bizarre ways of looking at the world. In the end he'd dismissed them both as potty and couldn't blame his father for looking for other women.

When Charles disappeared to Newcastle to be comforted by Heather, Richard suggested that the two of them should go into Otterbridge, spend the day together. There were a couple of pubs he knew where you could drink all afternoon. He thought after a couple of pints he might get through to James. He felt a sort of responsibility for him. He blamed that crazy girlfriend James had taken up with last summer. Before that he'd been almost normal. A bit shy, a bit intense, but not cracked. If he could get James to talk about *her*, Richard thought in a muddled, good-natured way, it might help him come to terms with his mother's death. He could see that Val's murder had affected James in a strange way. There seemed to be little grief, but an empty detachment. Richard, who had howled like a baby when he'd first heard, couldn't understand it.

"Come for a drink," he said. "The Shakespeare does food. And there's a good jukebox."

"Go by yourself," James said, quite abruptly. "You'll want to see your friends and they won't like me hanging around."

So Richard had gone, quite relieved in the end not to have to spend any more time with James. He'd never been one for navel gazing. It embarrassed him. He went into town, where he met some friends he'd played rugby with when he was at school. They'd heard about his mother and knew just what he needed. When he'd drunk so much that he was insensible, they took him home in a taxi, let themselves into the house with his key, and put him carefully to bed.

There was nobody in the house when Richard came home. James left almost immediately after his brother, only making sure that the street was clear before he went out. He walked through the suburban streets, with their smells of roasting beef and overcooked vegetables, into the town centre. Then he took the main road out of the town, which led eventually to the coast. He stopped only once, at a petrol filling station which had a shop attached and which sold cut flowers. He took three large bunches from the tin bucket and paid with a ten-pound note. The ten pounds he had stolen from his father's wallet early that morning. His father would have given him the money if he had asked for it, but stealing it was far more satisfying.

The cemetery was huge, bounded by a grey stone wall which stretched for almost a mile along the road. The entrance was marked by Victorian Gothic towers, and a flower seller stood there, a hard-faced, middle-aged woman with dyed blond hair tied up on the top of her head like the plume on a circus pony. James never bought his flowers from her, not only because he found her unsympathetic but because there was something shabby and unprepared in getting them at the last moment. There must be hundreds of regular visitors to the cemetery, but he had the sense that she recognised him and he felt her dislike as he walked past her with the flowers he had already purchased in his arms.

His mother would not be buried here. Charles had decided already that she would be cremated. The funeral had been arranged for the following week. By that time the police would be prepared to release the body. It would be a dignified affair, but there would be quite a show. The vice-chancellor of the university had agreed to read the address.

James always took the same path to the grave, though there were many that he could have chosen. He avoided the main track, which cut the cemetery in half and which was busy with people who seemed to have no real reverence for the place—families with children who dropped sweet papers and played kiss chase around the graves nearest to the track. Once, James had even seen a jogger there—a woman in black shiny cycle shorts and a sleeveless vest.

He took the path that followed the wall because he liked the smell of the ivy which grew there. That brought him to the grave he had come to visit. He had never met any other mourner there. That would have been unbearable. He needed to feel that he alone remembered her, though he knew that could not really be true and somewhere her parents would be grieving, too.

The grave was simple, the headstone obviously newer than most of the others. The flowers he had left on his last visit were dead and shrivelled. He didn't mind that. It meant that no one else had been there. He squatted cross-legged beside the grave, carefully took away the old flowers, and replaced them with the new ones. Then he began to talk to her.

He was sorry, he said, that it had taken so long to sort things out. But he hadn't forgotten her. He would pay them back in the end.

Faye Dawn Cooper—born 1974, died 1993—did not answer.

Lily was working. She saw Hunter loitering outside the health-food shop door, as inconspicuous, she said to herself, as a penguin in a desert. She was used to men staring at her, and turned away, but he came in and hovered at her shoulder as she tipped a sack of potatoes onto the shelf.

"Don't you usually go to the Abbots' for your dinner on a Sunday?" he said.

"Not today," she replied. "We haven't been invited. They want to be on their own."

"I suppose you do get a dinner break?" he said.

"Yes," she said shortly. "I'm off now."

"Come on, then. I was wanting a chat. I'll buy you a meal."

He took her arm and led her through to the coffee shop. Short of screaming, there was nothing she could do about it.

"I didn't think this was your sort of place," she said.

"Oh, I'm not fussy. I'll eat anything, me."

"Well?" she demanded. "What do you want?" Then she looked around to see if any of her friends were there. It wouldn't do her reputation any good to be seen socialising with a pig.

"To know what went on between you and Val McDougal last Sunday."

"What do you mean?"

"This Voice Dialogue business. What did she talk about?" Lily shrugged.

"The usual. That bastard husband of hers."

"The idea was that she spoke in different voices?"

"You know about that? I suppose Magda explained. I tried

to speak to the critic in her, the part of her that believed her husband when he put her down. It was amazing. It hardly sounded like Val at all."

"Did it do any good?"

"Well, at least it made her see what was going on. Later she talked about leaving Charles. She was starting to make real plans. She said she'd stay until James went away to college in September. She was always worried about James."

"Why?"

She paused. "He had a girlfriend. He was crazy about her. She was his first love, you know. She dumped him for someone else and then she died, really suddenly, in an accident. He couldn't handle it."

"Did she talk about that at the Sunday group?"

"Yeah," Lily said, "She did. She wished she could get James to come along."

"And what did you talk about?"

"My bloody father and mother and how they screwed me up." The answer was flip and automatic.

"Not Sean?"

"No," she said. "Why would I want to talk about him?"

"If you were frightened of him."

"Don't be daft." She gave a short, bitter laugh.

"Where was he on Saturday night?"

"Smoking dope with a couple of dropouts in a Ford Transit. Listening to old records. Remembering old times."

"You believe him?" Hunter was scathing.

"Yeah," she said. "Actually I do."

"We haven't traced the van yet."

"No?" she said. "Well, perhaps you haven't been trying very hard."

There was a brief angry silence.

"That's not true," he said.

"Well, I'm sorry, but it wouldn't be the first time a traveller was fitted up for something he didn't do."

"What will happen to the two of you when the Abbots and Mrs. Pocock take over Laverock Farm?" he asked conversationally.

112

She looked at him, suspecting a trap. "Sod it," she said. "You'll find out anyway. There'll be a place for us there. And work. And it'll be a bloody sight more comfortable than the caravan."

"So you're pleased Ernie Bowles is dead?"

She paused. "Okay," she said, "so I'm pleased that he's dead. That doesn't mean that I killed him."

They ate for a while. The food wasn't bad, Hunter thought. For vegetarian muck.

"How do you get on with them?" he asked. "The Abbots and Mrs. Pocock."

"Magda's great," she said enthusiastically. "Really special, you know. There are lots of people in the business of self-enlightenment and personal growth. Most of them are crap. Magda knows what she's doing."

"And the Abbots?"

"Win's okay. A bit heavy sometimes, a bit intense. And too wrapped up with her kids. But she's kind. She gives us meals. If it wasn't for Daniel, I think she'd have had us to stay—"

"You don't get on with Mr. Abbot?"

"I don't *not* get on with him. We're just not very close."

"What about Mrs. Pocock, Magda? Does she get on with him?"

Lily shrugged. "Not 'specially. But it's not an easy relationship, is it, being a mother-in-law?"

"I don't know," he said. "I've never been one."

She grinned despite herself.

"There must be more to it than that," he went on. "If she's such a special person, she wouldn't have taken against him for no reason."

"Oh," Lily said, "I think she had a reason."

"What reason? Was Daniel playing away?"

Lily nodded.

"And his wife never found out that he was seeing other women?"

"I think she knew. She just didn't want to admit it."

"Can you give me the names of some of these women?"

But Lily remembered her conversation with Magda the evening before and shook her head. Hunter didn't push it. He could make his own enquiries and he wanted Lily on his side.

"Do you know Peter Richardson?" he asked.

"I've seen him about," she answered cautiously.

"I was chatting to him last night," Hunter said. "He seemed to think that any offer he made on the Laverock land would be accepted. But Mrs. Pocock didn't know anything about it."

She looked awkward.

"That might be Sean," she said. "Jumping the gun a bit. I know he was chatting to Mr. Richardson when he came down to see to the animals."

"Nothing to do with him, though, is it?"

"We'd want to be involved," she said. "I told you, we've been promised a place if it goes ahead."

"What's the deal, then?" Hunter asked. "Richardson slips your laddie a few quid if he can persuade the Abbots to sell him the land without going to auction?"

"No," she said. "Sean wouldn't be involved in something like that."

But her voice was uncertain.

If Sean and Richardson were working together now, Hunter thought, perhaps they were working together before. Perhaps they were both behind the murder of Ernie Bowles. It was the closest he'd come to a motive for Sean and he felt quite cheerful.

"Have a pudding," he said "Some of that carrot cake."

She looked at her watch.

"No, I'd better go. I only get half an hour for lunch. Thanks anyway."

"No problem," he said.

He watched her walk back across the stone flags, her hips swaying, her thin jacket slung over one shoulder like a matador's cape.

17

W_{in} wished they had invited guests for lunch as usual. She and Daniel seldom communicated now unless they had an audience. This seemed not to trouble Daniel, but Win always felt tense and wretched when they were alone together in the house. She wondered how long she could carry on. Magda hadn't said anything directly, but Win could tell she thought the marriage was a mistake. It was all right for her, Win thought bitterly and irrationally. She'd lost her husband before it had had a chance to go wrong.

It had occurred to her recently that she should leave Daniel, but she knew she lacked the courage to be that decisive. She kept hoping things would get better. There were the two children to consider. Then there was the project at Laverock Farm. That would be a challenge, something they could work on together. She tried to convince herself that it would bring them close again.

When the telephone rang summoning Daniel away, it was a relief. One of his patients had gone into labour. She had fought for home delivery. She had found a sympathetic midwife and she wanted him there to help with pain relief. He went out cheerfully. He especially liked being present at births. It made him feel important and the patients were always very grateful. He said that Win shouldn't wait up for him. The contractions had only just started and he might be up all night.

In her paranoia she wondered if the patient in labour

was an excuse and really he had arranged to spend the night with another woman. The idea started as an idle fancy, but after an hour of worrying she became convinced by it. When the children were settled in the kitchen for their tea, she went to his desk and checked his diary. There was a woman he had supervised through pregnancy who had reached full term, so she supposed she would have to believe him.

As she was returning the diary to the desk, a photograph fell out. It had been slipped between the leaves at the back of the book. She had seen it before, might even have taken it. It was of the boys, playing in the garden last summer. They were splashing in a round, inflatable paddling pool and beside them, stretched out on a striped towel, was Faye Cooper. She was turned towards the children, shouting at them perhaps to take care. Win told herself that there was nothing suspicious about the photo. Daniel had kept it because it was a good one of the boys. All the same she took it back with her into the kitchen. There she cut it up into very tiny pieces and threw it into the bin.

Ramsay took the afternoon off. He needed time away from the case. He went first to his cottage in Heppleburn. It seemed as cold and unlived in as if he had been away for a month, and behind the door there was a pile of junk mail and free newspapers. From there he phoned Prue. He was tempted to turn up at her house to surprise her, but he thought she should be given the opportunity to make an excuse if she did not want to see him. He still lacked the confidence to take that for granted.

Prue said of course he must come and even to him she sounded delighted.

"Anna's off for the day with some chums," she said. "So we'll have the place to ourselves."

Anna was Prue's teenage daughter. She was nice enough, but she did tend to get in the way because she made Prue feel inhibited. As if, Prue told him, I was the teenager and she was my mother. And she definitely disapproved of Prue going out with a pig, even an enlightened pig like Ramsay.

She would be off to university in the autumn and then things would be easier.

Prue was waiting for him and her inhibitions had disappeared with her daughter. He found her giggly and flirtatious. She ran them both a bath so hot and deep that the old-fashioned bathroom, with its enormous enamelled tub and copper taps, was filled with steam. As usual her bedroom was a tip, with piles of clothes on the floor and an unmade bed, but there was a bottle of wine in a cooler and two glasses on the dressing table.

"Are you sure the phone's not going to ring?" she said suspiciously as she straightened the bottom sheet and wiped away a few biscuit crumbs.

"Certain. No one knows I'm here."

"What would your mother say?" She stretched across him to pour a glass of wine. "Sex and alcohol in the afternoon. And on a Sunday."

"Stop talking," he said.

They stayed there until it was dark and the orange streetlight came in through the half-closed curtains. He sat up and smiled at her.

"What, if it comes to that, will your daughter say?"

She pulled a pantomime face of horror.

"Shit," she said, "she'll be back in ten minutes."

Then there was a scramble of pulling on clothes and more giggling. When they heard Anna's key in the door, they were sitting at the kitchen table, sober and respectable adults, drinking coffee.

"I'm just going to start supper," Prue said. "Do you want some?"

"No thanks. I've already eaten," Anna ignored Ramsay and went off to her room. To work, she said. To express her disapproval, thought Prue.

"Your friend Maddy," Ramsay said. "Do you think she'll be in tonight?"

"Why?" She had her head stuck in the fridge, looking for inspiration for supper. "An omelette all right? And sautéed potatoes?"

"Fine," he said. "Is there enough for Maddy?"

"Why?" she asked again. "You've never bothered much with my friends before."

"You said she went on one of the weekend retreats organised by the Alternative Therapy Centre in Mittingford."

"That's right." Now he had her full attention.

"We think Val McDougal, the teacher who was murdered on Monday, was there, too."

"And you want me to invite her round here so you can ask her questions about it? Not very professional that, is it?" In her present mood he could not tell whether her indignation was genuine, so he decided to play safe.

"I'm sorry," he said. "Perhaps its a bad idea. I just thought it would save some time. And she might remember more if we talked informally."

"Would I get to see the great detective at work? You wouldn't send me upstairs with Anna?"

"Of course not."

"I'll phone her, then."

Maddy was younger than Prue, with waxed, spiked hair. She worked as a solicitor and Ramsay had come across her occasionally in court defending delinquent teenagers with a passion, dedication, and humour which made her unpopular with some of his colleagues. When she arrived she was out of breath, clutching a bottle of red wine and a handful of leaflets, eager to be involved. Ramsay was always surprised when other people thought his work exciting and glamorous.

"I'm not sure I can be much help," she said. "I haven't even seen the homoeopath lately."

"I thought you swore by her," Prue said.

"Yeah, well, she did help at first. But she always seemed so glum and I thought: if it doesn't even work for her, what am I going to get out of it? I didn't want to end up looking as miserable as Win Abbot." She grinned. "Besides, I've passed through my natural therapy phase. It's tap dancing and bungy jumping now."

"But you did go to Juniper Hall?"

"Yeah, last autumn." She pulled out a leaflet from the pile

she'd brought. "This is the publicity material. I thought you'd be interested."

Ramsay took it from her and read out loud: " 'An opportunity for real movement on a personal level and substantial healing on a planetary level. At Juniper Hall we expect fun, affirmation, sharing, creativity. We can work together to heal the global issues closest to your heart.' "

"Oh, Maddy," Prue exclaimed. "You weren't taken in by all that crap, were you?"

"Don't knock it," Maddy said seriously. "Not entirely. I've seen screwed-up, unhappy people change in a weekend, become more positive, somehow freed up, able to accept themselves."

"And how does this miracle take place? Just by talking?"

"Talking, sharing, meditation." Maddy opened the bottle of wine. "Magda Pocock was in charge. Have you ever met her?"

Ramsay nodded.

"She's the one person who makes all those claims seem possible."

"Was Val McDougal there?"

"Yes," Maddy said. "I just knew her as Val. When I saw her pictures in the paper earlier this week, I thought she was familiar. I couldn't place her then, but I definitely met her at Juniper."

"Did she tell you why she was there? Talk about her husband, her family?"

"She might have done," Maddy said. "But after all this time I can't really remember." She paused. "Something happened, you see, which cast a shadow over the whole weekend. Nothing else seemed so important after that."

"What was it?"

"There was a fatal accident. Juniper Hall is a big old house. It's got a swimming pool. A young girl went swimming by herself late at night and drowned."

"I don't suppose you remember the girl's name?"

"Yes," Maddy said. "It was Faye Cooper."

18

The anonymous letter arrived the next day. It was sent to the incident room at Mittingford police station and addressed to Ramsay personally. It was typed and literate, though brief.

"Sir, I suggest you find out what happened to Faye Cooper. She was the first." There was no signature, not even "friend" or "well-wisher."

"The first what?" said Hunter, who was reading the letter over Ramsay's shoulder.

The room was quiet. It had the untidy peace of a classroom when the children have gone out to play. Half Ramsay's team were trying to trace the people who'd been at Magda Pocock's Voice Dialogue workshop with Val McDougal. It wasn't easy. Magda's records were scanty. She usually made a note of group members' names but not their addresses. She had said it wasn't worth it—some only turned up once, then decided the group wasn't for them. The rest of the team were at the college in Otterbridge, talking to Val's colleagues, trying to find someone who remembered seeing the Abbots during the acupuncture lecture. Sunlight slanted over the desk and made Hunter wish he was outside, too.

"Well?" he said. "The first what?"

"The first death," Ramsay replied quietly. "I think that's what it must mean." He slipped the letter into a clear plastic folder. "Faye Cooper went on one of those weekend courses held by the Abbots for their patients and other like-minded groupies. It took place in a big house just over the border into Cumbria near Hadrian's Wall. They call it Juniper Hall. For most of the year the place runs adventure courses for stressed executives: mock battles in the woods, how to survive on the hills with a sheet of plastic and a scout knife. You know the sort of thing."

Hunter nodded. The force ran similar courses. He'd been half tempted to apply for one himself, but he knew he'd miss his beer.

"Once a year in early autumn the Abbots hire the place for the weekend and invite visiting lecturers. This is a brochure of the last one, when Faye died."

"Where did you get this, then?"

Ramsay paused for a moment. "A friend of Prue's was on the course." He waited for Hunter to make some comment about the arty-farty theatre crowd, but none came.

"One of the attractions of Juniper Hall is its swimming pool," the inspector went on. "It's not used much, except, I suppose, by macho executives who want to show how tough they are. It's outside. But the September of the Abbots' course was unusually warm, an Indian summer, and some of the more hardy souls did venture in. It provided a focal point in the evenings, an attractive place to sit. Faye Cooper was drowned in the pool. No one saw the accident happen. She'd been talking, apparently, about how good it would be to swim by moonlight. She must have come down when everyone else was in bed. Her body wasn't found until the next morning. The local police investigated but were satisfied in the end that it was an accidental death."

"You seem to know a lot, like." Hunter was suspicious. He thought Ramsay was following his own line of investigation again. They were supposed to be a team, a partnership. It made him look a fool if Ramsay refused to confide in him.

"No," Ramsay said, "not very much. I only found out about Faye Cooper last night. I got the Cumbria force to fax me the details this morning. It seemed a coincidence—

another death connected with the Alternative Therapy Centre." Not, he thought, that I have to justify my actions to you.

"What did you find out, then?"

Ramsay sat back in his chair, his eyes squinted shut against the bright sunshine. He did not need to look in his notes.

"Faye Cooper was just eighteen when she died. Left school at sixteen and left home at the same time. Set up in a bedsit in Otterbridge. She was a student at Otterbridge FE college, taking a secretarial course."

Before Hunter could interrupt he added quickly, "I've checked if she was ever taught by Val McDougal, but apparently not. She was quite a bright girl and never needed a remedial teacher."

"Why did she leave home?" Hunter asked. "It's canny young for a lass to be living on her own."

"I'm not sure," Ramsay said. "We'll have to check. I don't think the investigating officer was too impressed with her parents. He was certainly thorough—he talked to her college friends and checked her background, besides taking statements from everyone staying at Juniper Hall when she died. Reading between the lines, I'd say he suspected suicide, though no evidence of that was brought before the Coroners' Court. I'd like to talk to him, but it seems he's left the force."

"Why did he think she killed herself?" Hunter wasn't prepared to accept the judgement of some rural woodentop without question.

Ramsay shrugged. "He thought she was mixed up, lonely. There'd been a row with her parents. Her mam had remarried and she hadn't ever got on with her stepfather apparently. The college staff said she was a bit wild, especially when she first started there. She didn't join in the social life of the other students. Most of them said they only saw her in class. I suppose he just thought that suicide wouldn't have been out of character."

"Boyfriends?" Hunter asked. "Some teenage romance which went wrong?"

122

"I don't know," Ramsay said. "The report doesn't mention anything like that."

"How did she get mixed up with the bunch at the Old Chapel in the first place?" Hunter asked. "If she was living in Otterbridge and had no transport, she'd not come across them socially. It's not the sort of thing that would attract a young girl anyway. And how did she afford the weekend away?" He flipped through the brochure which still lay on Ramsay's desk and whistled. "Do you see what it costs? You'd need a second mortgage."

Ramsay did not answer. He was preoccupied. Hunter's question about boyfriends had triggered a memory. He was looking for the notes he had taken after his interview with James McDougal.

"Here we are!" he said at last, triumphantly. "When I talked to Val McDougal's son I asked how she'd got into alternative therapies. He said it was through him and he'd first become interested in New Age philosophy after travelling to festivals with his girlfriend. Whose name was Faye. That at least explains how she got to know the Abbots."

He tipped his chair forward, so his eyes were in shadow.

"That must be suspicious," he said. "Relevant anyway. The Alternative Therapy Centre is supposed to be all about healing, yet three people connected to it have died suddenly. Faye's death could be a coincidence, but it needs investigating. The writer of the anonymous letter certainly thinks so. Of course he might have his own reasons for that. It could be a distraction."

"Any way of tracing the writer from the letter?"

Ramsay shook his head. "Not unless you want to look at every typewriter in the county."

"Postmark?"

"Newcastle," Ramsay said. "The main post office in Eldon Square. Which at least shows a degree of intelligence. If it had been sent from Otterbridge or Mittingford, we'd have had somewhere to start."

"Means he must have transport if he lives in Mittingford. It's a good sixty miles into town."

"Not necessarily. There's a bus. One a day each way from here and one every hour from Otterbridge direct to the Haymarket."

"That's a lot of bother to go to," Hunter said. Ramsay always tended to opt for the over elaborate explanation. "Perhaps Faye Cooper had contacts in Newcastle and someone from there sent the letter. Where do her parents live?"

"Wallsend," Ramsay said. "Those houses by the river."

"It's a hell of a lot easier to get to Newcastle from Wallsend," Hunter said. "Perhaps the mother thought there was something odd about the lass's death—"

"And felt she owed it to the daughter to let us know. But didn't want to contact us directly for some reason. So she sent an anonymous letter. It's possible that her concern was triggered by the publicity surrounding the recent murders. The press has got hold of the alternative therapy angle." Ramsay was talking slowly, to himself. Hunter might not have been there.

"What do you want me to do about it?" Hunter demanded. He was already irritated at being ignored.

"Go and talk to the mother. If she admits sending the letter, she might have other information. Interview her, without the stepfather if you can. Find out what all the rows were about."

"Then what?"

"See the boy. James. Treat him gently, though. Don't forget he's just lost his mother."

"What do you take me for? An ignorant slob?"

Ramsay did not answer.

"I had the impression that the relationship between him and Faye was over before she died. Find out what happened. If he finished with her, we might be back to a reason for suicide. We need to know how involved she was with the crowd at the Old Chapel—"

"Yeah," Hunter said. "Okay . . ." No need to spell it out, he thought. I'm not some wet-behind-the-ears DC.

"And it will be useful to know how they met," Ramsay went on. He paused. "Don't disturb the lad at school. He's been through enough without having to explain you to his mates. Wait until four o'clock and see him at home. And if the father's there, for God's sake be polite. He's the type to stand on his dignity."

"Okay," Hunter said again. Generally it had all turned out much better than he could have hoped. A day away from the Mittingford sheepshaggers, the chance of a good lunch on expenses, and the possibility of actually moving the case forward. He could do with the recognition. He felt vaguely that he was always in Ramsay's shadow. If Ramsay had been a different sort of man, more of a character, more—he struggled with the idea—heroic, that wouldn't be so important. But to play second fiddle to such a dull dog did his image no good at all.

He was on his way out of the incident room when Ramsay called him back.

"Take Sally Wedderburn with you," he said. "She's on her break, but she'll be back in five minutes. She could do with the experience. And Faye Cooper's mam might find it easier to talk to a woman."

And at least Sal has a modicum of tact and discretion, he thought, but did not say.

"Yeah," Hunter said, trying not to show how pleased he was, trying to sound as if it were a chore he could do without. "Yeah. All right."

After Hunter had gone, Ramsay sat in the incident room and took out the file he was compiling on Faye Cooper. In a corner a DC was stabbing inexpertly at a typewriter. Otherwise the room was empty and still. Ramsay reread all the information and tried to form a picture of the girl. He wished he had a photograph. Beside the original police report into the accident at Juniper Hall and the coroner's statement, he had obtained records from her high school. What occurred to him most was that she had been abandoned by all the adults who had been responsible for her. It was clear that there had been no contact with her parents once she left home, and the staff at the college seemed to have been unconcerned about the way she lived. Perhaps they did not know. Or did not care. Val McDougal would have cared, he thought. She would have had the girl back to her home for meals, kept an eye on her. But once the romance between Faye and James was over, what would have happened to her then? He was becoming fascinated by her.

His teenage years had been stifling. Every move had been monitored by an overprotective mother and an extended family of aunts and cousins with nothing better to do than look out for his welfare. He tried to imagine what it must have been like to be left so completely alone. Exhilarating perhaps, but terrifying. He found himself groping towards an explanation for Faye's attraction to the people at the Old Chapel. She wouldn't be turned on by traditional religion. That would seem staid and irrelevant. But the philosophy of Daniel and Win, with their close family life, Magda's evangelical zeal, her charisma, would be more exciting. Belonging to that community of believers would give Faye a meaning to her life and the same sense of comfort as belonging to a church.

It occurred to him that Lily Jackman might have had the same sort of rootless past. More affluent, he thought, but similarly insecure, attracted to the group at the Old Chapel for the same reasons. He wondered what else the two girls might have had in common.

19

Faye Cooper's mother lived in a row of terraced houses which ran steeply towards the river Tyne. Her name after her marriage was Irving. Sally Wedderburn, who had done her homework and was as determined as Hunter to make her mark on the case, called her Joan.

"Just a few words, Joan," she said as they stood on the doorstep trying to persuade the woman to let them in. "We won't take up much of your time."

Hunter looked down to the Tyne, to a dredger moving slowly up the river. Two lads, sitting on the pavement with their feet in the gutter, stared back.

The woman was reluctant. The door was only open a crack and she was ready to close it again.

"No, thank you," she said, as though they were selling dusters and broom heads. Then: "My husband wouldn't like it."

"Come on, pet," coaxed Sally Wedderburn. "He need never know we've been here."

"Of course he'll have to know," the woman said sharply. She peered out, saw the lads on the pavement, and drew back her head. "The people round here have nothing better to do than mind other folk's business."

"Tell him we're the Jehovah's Witnesses," Sally said. "Come to convert you."

"I'll have no blasphemous talk in my house," Joan Irving

said, but by then somehow they were in, standing crushed together in a small hall. There was a smell of lavender furniture polish and bleach.

"Is the lounge through here?" Sally asked. She pushed open the first door she came to. "Nice little places, aren't they, these? Cosy."

The room they entered was small and square, dominated by the harmonium that stood against one wall. The colour scheme was brown and mustard. The smell of furniture polish had become overwhelming. It was impossible that anyone sat here and relaxed. The cushions propped against the brown leatherette settee were symmetrically arranged. There were no books or newspapers. The only ornaments were framed religious texts which hung on the walls and were propped up on the tile mantelpiece.

Hunter shivered. This wasn't what he'd expected at all. From Ramsay's description of the family he'd imagined someone feckless, a slut who'd got herself pregnant, then conned some poor bloke into marriage to get the rent paid and her brat cared for. Someone with loose morals who'd ditched the girl as soon as she could. Not this stern, pinch-faced woman who was only forty but looked older than his mam. He wasn't sure how to handle the situation, but he wasn't going to let Sally Wedderburn have all the running.

"Is your husband out at work?" he demanded.

She did not answer, but backed away from him, apparently panic-stricken, until she was pressed against the wall.

Christ, he thought. She's mad as a hatter.

"Well?" he said impatiently. She looked wildly about her. Still she did not speak.

Hunter swore under his breath.

"Haven't you got a call to make, Sarge?" Sally Wedderburn said.

"What?" He turned his anger towards her.

"A call. From the car." She motioned for him to leave the room. He stamped out, banging the front door behind him, then stood on the pavement smoking a cigarette. It came to something when you were ordered out of an interview by a

128

subordinate. Still, he told himself viciously, it was better to let a woman deal with the hysterics. It was all they were good for.

In the brown-and-mustard living room Joan Irving had begun to tremble.

"Can I get you something?" Sally asked.

The woman shook her head. "It's my nerves," she said. "I've always been bad with my nerves. There was no need for him to shout."

"No," Sally agreed. "Why don't we sit down and start again. I can explain properly why I'm here."

"I don't know," the woman said. "My husband's out at work. At Swan's. But he'll be back soon. They've been on short shifts since the receivers took over the yard." But she did as she was told and sat on a straight-backed, fireside chair, her knees locked together, her hands gripped in her lap.

"I'm here about Faye," Sally said gently.

"That's all over," Joan Irving snapped. "She's dead."

"Are you sure it's over?" Sally asked. "As far as you're concerned?"

"I don't know what you mean!" The panic was returning. She began to take gasping breaths. Sally moved closer to her and took her hand. She waited until the breathing returned to normal, then said:

"We had a letter about Faye this morning. We wondered if you'd written it."

There was a silence.

"No," Joan Irving said at last. "I don't understand."

"We're investigating two murders. A farmer at Mittingford and a teacher from Otterbridge. Perhaps you read about them."

Joan Irving nodded. Ron had pointed the items out to her in the *Chronicle*. A sign of the times, he had said.

Sally continued, "Then someone wrote to us and suggested that Faye's death could be linked. To these murders. Do you know why anyone would think that?"

The woman shook her head. She seemed genuinely bewildered.

There was a pause and Sally tried again. She could see the back of Hunter's head through the window. It was a sort of challenge.

"It must have been a shock hearing out of the blue that Faye was dead," she said tentatively.

"Of course it was a shock," Joan snapped back. "Wouldn't you be shocked? If it were your child?"

"I haven't got kids myself," Sally Wedderburn said. "Not yet. I'm working on it."

Outside the window Hunter began to pace up and down the pavement. Sod him, she thought. I'm not rushing this. "Did you go to the inquest?" she asked.

Joan shook her head. "Ron went. He thought my nerves wouldn't stand it."

"But you did accept the verdict? You did believe her death was an accident?"

"Nothing in this world is without purpose," Joan said piously. Then: "An accident, of course. What else could it have been?"

Sally didn't answer the question directly. "I'd like you to tell me all about Faye," she said, "if it wouldn't upset you too much."

"No. I want to. Ron doesn't like me talking about her. It's morbid, he says."

"Ron's your husband?"

She smiled. "He says she brought it on herself."

"In what way?"

"For getting mixed up with those people. The New Age hippies. We'd heard about all that in our church. No better than witchcraft, Ron says."

"And what do you think?" Sally asked quietly. "About Faye's death? Do you think she brought it on herself?"

"No," the woman said uncertainly. "No one deserves that, do they?"

She got suddenly to her feet. Sally thought for a moment that the panic had returned and she was running away, but she opened a drawer in a small sideboard and pulled out a photograph album. She held it out to Sally with an awkward gesture, as if she expected it to be rejected as unimportant. Sally took it carefully and opened it on her knee. Joan Irving sat beside her on the sofa and began to point out Faye as a baby, Faye on her first day at nursery school, Faye starring as Mary in a nativity play.

"She was very pretty," Sally said, and indeed the girl was attractive, fair-haired, blue-eyed.

"I look at it," Joan said, "when Ron's not here. It's all I've got of her."

"You never married her father?" Sally asked. "You brought her up on your own until you met Ron?"

"I'd made my bed," she said. "I had to lie on it." She paused, embarrassed but wanting to explain. "I was working in an estate agent's. He was my boss. It happened at the office party. My first time. Too much to drink. When I found out I was expecting I just left. I couldn't face seeing him again."

Bloody men, Sally Wedderburn thought. Hunter, on the pavement, was lighting another cigarette, cupping his hand around it to stop the wind putting it out.

"She looks very happy in all those photos," Sally said. "Was she a happy child?"

"Once she started school," Joan said. "She wasn't an easy baby. Always restless. The health visitor said she was bright and I should be pleased." For the first time she smiled and made an attempt at a joke. "I told her I'd have been pleased to get more sleep."

"You must have been very close," Sally said.

"I suppose we were. Then."

"How old was Faye when you met Mr. Irving?"

"She was twelve. She'd just started at the high school."

"Where did you meet him?"

"At the chapel. That was before we started to worship as a housegroup. He was kind. Took us out for treats. He said he liked kids."

I bet he did, Sally thought.

131

"I really married him for Faye, so she'd have a dad like the other children."

Then there was a silence. On the river a boat's hooter sounded.

"Twelve's a difficult age, isn't it?" Sally said. "They're just starting to grow up. Was Faye difficult?"

Joan Irving became tense again. Her spine straightened and her knees locked together.

"She never liked Ron," Joan said. "She made things difficult, right from the start."

"In what way?"

"Cheeking him. Not doing what she was told."

"Was he strict, then?"

Joan was defensive. "No," she said. "Not really. I suppose I'd let her have her own way too much. There just being the two of us. Ron said I'd spoilt her."

"Why did she leave home? Did Ron tell her to go?"

"No! He wouldn't have done that. He knows what's right."

But he made things so uncomfortable for Faye, Sally thought, that she was forced to leave.

Joan Irving was continuing. "He had rules," she said. "He wanted to know where she was and who she was with. There was nothing wrong with that. Faye was always wilful. She didn't see he wanted the best for her."

"So there were rows?"

Joan nodded. "About her staying out late and makeup, and the clothes she was wearing. Always rows."

"It must have been a relief when she decided to leave home."

Joan looked at her suspiciously. "Yes," she said. "I suppose it was."

"But you kept in touch with her? You went to see her? Helped her find somewhere to live?"

"I did at first. Ron works one weekend in four. On the Saturday he was working I'd go into Otterbridge to see her. To keep an eye. She was always wild."

"You went to her bedsit?"

Joan nodded.

"And was she all right? Managing?"

"It was tidy enough, but then she knew when I was coming. I don't know what it was like the rest of the time."

"Wasn't she lonely, on her own?"

"She said not, but then she would. Pride being one of her faults."

"Why did you stop going to see her, Mrs. Irving? Was it because Ron found out?"

She shook her head.

"Why then?"

"She got herself a boyfriend."

"And didn't she want you to meet him? Or didn't you approve? She was sixteen. Old enough to have a boyfriend."

"Not *that* boyfriend," Joan Irving said.

"Why?"

"He was bad for her. Took her off to pagan festivals. Introduced her to all that wickedness."

"Did you ever meet him?"

Joan shook her head. "He was called James," she said. "I remember that. Came from a nice home, too, according to Faye. He should have known better."

"She discussed the New Age ideas with you?"

"She talked about them, all right!" Even after all this time Joan was indignant. "She said it would help me. I ought to go along to some group. Meet this Mrs. Pocock. Then I wouldn't be so uptight. I told her, 'I'm not uptight, my girl. I just know right from wrong.'"

"So you stopped going to see her."

Joan nodded. "She would have thought I approved. Besides," she added honestly, "Ron would have killed me if he'd found out."

"And you never saw her again?"

Joan shook her head sadly. "I couldn't, you see, I had my principles. Faye would have understood that."

"Did she ever try to get in touch with you?"

"She sent me a postcard," Joan said. "The summer before she died."

"Where from?" Sally said. "Perhaps you kept the card?"

"No," Joan said. "Ron made me get rid of it. But I remember where it was from. Mittingford. There was a picture of the church. I thought she'd chosen it specially. She'd think I'd like that."

She sat back in her chair with her eyes closed.

"What was she doing in Mittingford?" Sally asked. "Did she say? Was she there on holiday?"

Joan shook her head. "She'd got a summer job there when she finished college in July. A sort of au pair. Minding a couple of bairns while their mother was at work. That's what she wrote on the card."

"Did she mention James?"

"No, I hoped she'd packed him in, left all that wickedness behind."

"Did she say exactly *where* she was staying?"

"No," Joan said. She looked at Sally Wedderburn, hoping for understanding. "If she had I might have gone there to see her."

Outside, Hunter had given up his wait on the pavement and was sitting in the car. He hit the horn impatiently.

20

Hunter was uncomfortably aware that he'd had too much to drink at lunchtime. He'd taken Sally to a little pub he knew near the river. He'd planned it before the farce at the Irving house, hoping to impress, but he'd needed a drink after that. Several drinks. There'd been a row. Now, sitting moodily in the car, waiting for James McDougal to come home from school, he thought he hadn't been interested in Sally Wedderburn. Not seriously. He saw vaguely that the desire to impress had become a habit, an object in its own right, and his thoughts returned to Lily Jackman, who wouldn't be taken in anyway by a smart pub lunch.

"Oh shit," Sally said. "He's been there all the time."

They had rung the doorbell, but when there was no answer had assumed that he was still out. Now they saw that he must have been in the garden, at the back. He came round to the front with a pair of shears and began to chop furiously at the privet which separated the house from the property next door.

Sally Wedderburn got out of the car.

"Do you want me to come?" Hunter said nastily. "Or do you think you can handle this better on your own, too?"

For a moment Sally was tempted to reply, but she shrugged and said nothing. The boy heard their footsteps on the gravel and turned to face them nervously, holding the shears in front of him like a weapon.

"It's all right," Sally said. "We're from the police." She held out her identification. The boy looked at it then relaxed.

"Sorry to be so jumpy," he said. "I know it's silly. . . ."

"Quite natural I'd have thought," Sally said. "I'm afraid we want to ask you some more questions. Is that okay?"

"I suppose so." He was unenthusiastic but not rude. He led them round the back of the house and in through the kitchen door.

"What a lovely garden!" Sally said.

"Yeah. Mum loved gardening. She did it all herself. It was starting to get untidy. Dad's not bothered. I wouldn't be normally, but Mum would have liked it sorted out." He flushed.

"You've been to school today?" Hunter asked. James was wearing black jeans and a T-shirt, but you couldn't tell. Sixth-formers were allowed to wear anything these days.

"I couldn't face it," the boy said. "They understand. . . ." He stared out into the garden then turned back to face Hunter. "How can I help you?"

"Did you know a girl called Faye Cooper?"

"Faye? Yes. She was my girlfriend. For a while."

"Until she died?"

"No. She packed me in before that. Found someone else." The words were bitter. He screwed up his face like a child trying not to cry. "I'm sorry," he said again. "I still get upset. I've never met anyone else like her. At least when she was alive there was some hope that we'd get back together. . . ."

He got up abruptly and pulled a can of Coke from the fridge. "You want one?"

They shook their heads.

"Do you know the name of the lad she went out with after you?" Hunter asked.

"It was no lad," James said angrily. "At least that was the impression she gave. Someone mature. More mature than me at least. She never told me his name. And then she took that summer job in Mittingford so I couldn't pester her. That's what she said. Just because I was younger than her, still at school, there was no need to treat me like a kid."

"You were jealous, then?" Hunter said.

"Of course I was jealous. I wanted her back." He ripped back the ring on the Coke can.

"Where did you first meet Faye?" Sally asked.

"In a pub in town. She'd just moved to Otterbridge and she didn't know anyone. We started chatting. We liked the same music, shared the same ideas."

"The New Age thing?"

"I suppose so, though I've never been sure what that means. It's only a label, isn't it, now? Used by the press. But she cared about more than making money and having a good time. I liked that. And her independence. She lived by herself, you know. Her parents had thrown her out. She had a bedsit over the bookie's in Bridge Street. She didn't have much money, but she made it really nice in the end. I helped her. Decorating, going to jumbles and car-boot sales to pick up stuff for her. I spent a lot of time in that place. . . ."

"The belief in alternative therapy was one of the things you shared?" Sally asked. She had to repeat the question. He was still dreaming of long lazy afternoons and Faye.

"Yeah. It was part of being open to new ways of looking at things. First we went to a talk by Magda. Faye was dead enthusiastic then and asked me to take her to the Sunday group in Mittingford. She never had any transport and Mum let me borrow her car."

"Then your mother got involved, too?"

"Yes. I explained to Inspector Ramsay about that. But Faye was always the most heavily into it. Mum and I were more detached, more critical. Faye swallowed it whole. I suppose she needed something definite to hold on to."

"Your mother was at Juniper Hall when Faye died?"

"Yes." He took a gulp from the Coke can. "What is all this about? Why are you so interested in Faye?"

"We received an anonymous letter this morning. It implied that Faye's death was connected to your mother's murder." Hunter paused. "I don't suppose you sent that letter?"

"Of course not. If I'd had anything to tell you, I'd have come right out with it."

There was a silence, then he asked: "Do you think Faye was murdered, too?"

"There's no evidence of that," Sally said carefully. "Did your mother tell you about the accident when she came back from Juniper Hall?"

"Of course. She was dreadfully upset. She'd liked Faye. Not just because she was my girlfriend."

"She never expressed any doubt that it *was* an accident?"

He shook his head. "She said no one knew how it happened. It was a mystery."

"When was the last time you heard from Faye?"

"At the beginning of the summer holidays when she went off to work in Mittingford." His voice became hard. "She was terribly kind. Told me there was someone else, that she was very fond of me, but that I was to leave her alone."

"Do you know where she was working in Mittingford?"

"Didn't you realise?" He was surprised by their ignorance, shocked by their incompetence. "She worked for Daniel and Win Abbot as a sort of nanny. She looked after the kids, did a bit of cleaning." He hesitated. "I don't think they were paying her very much, but when I asked her about that she told me to mind my own business. She said she'd have done it for nothing."

"It would help us to know if Faye was particularly lonely or unhappy just before she died. Do you know anything about that? Perhaps she talked to your mother at Juniper Hall? It sounds as if they were close."

He shook his head. "I don't know," he said. "Mum didn't say. . . ."

He seemed lost again in thoughts of his own. Through the open window they could hear a woodpecker drumming on one of the oaks at the bottom of the garden.

"Would Faye have been capable of suicide?" Sally asked carefully.

James considered.

"Yes," he said. "I think she would. She was wild, you know. You had the impression that in the end she had nothing to lose."

138

"Except the new boyfriend."

"Yes. Except him. If anything went wrong there, I think she'd have been pretty desperate."

He sat in a gloomy silence. Sally and Hunter looked at each other.

"Is there anyone else she might have confided in?"

"I don't think so. Magda perhaps. Or the Abbots."

"No special college friends?"

"No. She was always a loner."

He stood up. "Look," he said. "I don't think I can stand much more of this. I ought to get on with the garden."

"There's nothing else you can think of?" Hunter demanded. He was reluctant to let the boy go. He wanted a result from the interview and the bloated feeling caused by too much beer made him belligerent.

James paused. "If you want to know Faye's state of mind before she died, you should look in her diary. She might not have confided in the rest of us, but she bared her soul in that."

"She would have had it with her at Juniper Hall?"

He nodded. "She took it everywhere with her. And she certainly didn't leave it in the bedsit. Mum and I went and cleared all her stuff out of there."

He stood, quite still.

"I looked in her diary once. Just before she chucked me. Perhaps she meant me to see it. . . . We were in her bedsit and she went out to the bathroom. Usually she hid it away in a drawer somewhere, but it had been left out on the windowsill. I know I shouldn't have looked, but it was too much of a temptation. That's how I found out she was seeing another bloke." His face twisted into a miserable grin. "She called me 'sweet' in it. I suppose she meant that as a compliment."

"What did the diary tell you about her new boyfriend?"

"Not much." Then he recited, as if he had learned it by heart. " 'I wonder what it would be like to be a farmer's wife. I really like the idea.' I suppose then that the bloke she'd been seeing was working on a farm. And that she must have thought there was a future to the relationship. After all, she never talked about marrying me."

Hunter and Sally stared at each other. Surely Ernie Bowles couldn't have been Faye's secret lover. Not of a pretty young girl like that! James was quite unaware of the reaction he had caused. He picked up the shears from the kitchen floor and said firmly that he had nothing else to tell them.

Later he wondered if that was quite true.

When he finished in the garden he lay on his bed. It was still light and his father was not yet back from the university. He seemed to be spending less and less time at home. James tried to remember the last evening he had spent with his mother, the Sunday evening before she was killed. The details were remarkably vivid.

Charles had been sulking. He had spent all evening in his study and had hardly spoken to them. Val had gone off to Magda's group, and when she returned she was strangely subdued. When Charles was out of the way James had teased her about it. They were sitting in his bedroom. She was helping him pack for the geography field trip, piling clean clothes on the bed, but really just wanting the excuse to talk about what had happened. He'd switched down the music so they could chat.

"Was it good?" he had said, slightly mocking. After all, he felt that he had grown out of that. "New insights? Lots of personal growth?"

"I suppose so," she had said, but not so enthusiastic as she usually was.

He could picture her, still wearing the leggings and loose sweater she had put on for the Old Chapel group, squatting over his rucksack, looking up at him frowning.

"What went wrong?" he had asked. "Something blocking the energy? People too uptight to get anything out of it?"

"Quite the opposite," she had said. Then: "Don't you think there's a danger that we can know ourselves and other people *too* well. There's a need for privacy, even for self-delusion."

He had shrugged, not sure what she expected of him, not in the mood to be heavy.

"I don't think I'm going to go back there," she had said, and he had sensed that she shivered slightly, although the day was not cold. "It's served its purpose. It's time to move on."

Now, lying on his bed in the last of the sunshine, he wondered if she had told anyone else of her decision.

On the way back to Mittingford the atmosphere between Sally and Gordon Hunter was more cordial, or at least slightly less frosty. There was a shared sense of achievement. They had valuable information to take back to Ramsay. They had perhaps even discovered a connection between Val McDougal and Ernie Bowles. It was possible, they told each other, that Faye had seen in Ernie some sort of father figure, that he was the man in the diary.

But when they returned to the Mittingford incident room, Ramsay could not accept it. The Faye he had come to know through reading the police reports was passionate, enthusiastic. She would have nothing to do with the grubby, overweight farmer from Laverock Farm, no matter how much she needed a father. He settled the matter by phoning Win Abbot. She would not talk to him for long. In the background he heard a baby screaming and she seemed preoccupied. But she knew that Faye had had a boyfriend. He sensed rather that she disapproved.

"Was he a local man?" Ramsay asked.

"Oh yes," she said. "She went out with Peter Richardson. His father farms Long Edge."

"The farm next to Laverock?"

"Yes," Win said. "That's right. I'm not quite sure what she saw in him."

21

S*ean* Slater was setting about making himself indispensable. Whatever happened to Laverock Farm he wanted to be involved. After years of drifting he thought he had found a project he could believe in. At least that's what he told Lily. At the back of his mind there were other ideas which he would have found hard to confess to her. Marriage, children. He saw Laverock Farm as a way of finally tying her down.

Already they had moved from the caravan into the house. Somehow he had persuaded Bowles's solicitors that it would be safer. The security was dreadful and they could keep an eye on the place. The Abbots had not been able to refuse.

"It's only camping," Sean had said to Lily. "But at least there's room to swing a cat." And it stakes our claim, he thought.

If Lily realised what he was up to, she made no effort to escape. She even seemed to encourage him in his plans. The day the anonymous letter arrived at the incident room, Magda Pocock and the Abbots came out to the farm, to survey, as Daniel grandly put it, their new estate. It was evening and the low sun made the place more attractive, warming the grey stone, hiding the rubbish with long shadows. Sean and Lily were in on the meeting and Sean was full of ideas.

"I think Stan Richardson up the valley would buy most of the land," Sean said, hardly giving them time to get out of their car. "I talked to him about it. In general, you know. No commitments. That would give you the working capital to convert the house. I thought we might turn some of the outhouses into staff accommodation. That would leave the house for guest rooms and lecture halls. There's plenty of space."

"You had no right to talk to Richardson," Magda said sharply. "The house has nothing to do with you."

Lily was surprised by Magda's anger—it wasn't like her—but Sean was unabashed. "The police took the livestock up to Long Edge," he said. "I had to speak to Richardson about that. Then he dropped some pretty massive hints that he'd be interested in the land. The sooner the better, surely, from your point of view. Once you've got the money you can start on the house."

"We mustn't get carried away," Daniel warned, but he seemed to be getting carried away himself. He could imagine the place humming with people and ideas. They would attract the best teachers from all over the world. There'd be other spin-offs—books, for example. He'd always wanted to write. And perhaps a training facility for other practitioners. The new EC directives would make further qualifications essential. And money. He had to admit to himself that he imagined the prospect of making money. "Still, I think Sean's got a point, don't you? It would be great to make a start."

Magda said nothing, though Lily could sense her disapproval.

"I thought an organic garden," Sean suggested enthusiastically. He was leading them across the farmyard. "To provide food for the centre. It shouldn't take long to get Soil Association approval. It's run wild since we've been here and I shouldn't imagine any pesticides were used even in Cissie Bowles's day. Look, it's a wonderful place."

He pushed open a rotten wooden door in a high stone wall and they were in an enclosed garden. Once there had been glass houses built against the wall and paths and fruit trees. Now it was an overgrown wilderness. The panes of glass had shattered and rotting vegetation lay everywhere.

143

"It's sheltered from the north wind by the house," Sean said. "You could grow anything in here."

"It would take a lot of work to get it straight," Daniel said, but he saw it with Sean's eyes, pictured neat rows of organic vegetables, the trees and fruit bushes pruned back. "We could have a herb garden. Medicinal and culinary herbs. There'd be nothing else like it in the country. . . ."

"I wondered if you'd like me to make a start on it," Sean said diffidently. "Just clear out the rubbish. Dig it over perhaps. So when you take the place over we'll be ready to start."

"I'm not sure—" Daniel hesitated.

"I don't think that would be wise," Magda interrupted briskly. "Not before all the formalities have been completed. That's the time to take stock of the situation and to decide which way we want the project to go."

"I can't see that it would do any harm for Sean to make a start," Daniel said. Win stood beside him, silent and tense.

"And do you propose paying him?" Magda demanded. "Or will we expect him to work out of the kindness of his heart? Excuse me for being blunt, Sean, but what's in it for you?"

Sean smiled easily. "I just want to get involved," he said. "We both do. Really. We so much admire what you've done at the Old Chapel. You and Daniel and Win. We want to help."

There was a silence, then Win blurted out:

"I had a phone call just before I came out, from that policeman, Ramsay."

Daniel looked at her sharply. "You didn't say. Why didn't you tell me before?"

She shrugged awkwardly.

"What did he want?"

"To ask about Faye?"

"Faye? What has she to do with anything?"

"I always knew," Magda said, "that poor child would come back to haunt us."

"Nonsense." Daniel was dismissive. "Why should she? She has nothing to do with this business."

"I'm not sure." Win spoke slowly. "The police think that she has."

"Why?" Daniel demanded. "What made you think that?"

"I don't know." Win looked wretched. "Ramsay said they'd received 'certain information.' And he seemed so serious, so formal."

"He's always like that," Daniel said. "It's a pose. You shouldn't allow yourself to be intimidated. What did he ask?"

"He wanted to know about boyfriends," Win said. "Did Faye have a boyfriend?"

"And of course you told him that she did?"

Win nodded. "I said when she was living with us, she was seeing Peter Richardson, that she seemed very keen on him though she never really discussed him. I said I couldn't see it lasting because they had so little in common. . . ." Her voice trailed off.

"That's all right, then. They can go up to Long Edge and bother young Richardson. I never liked him." Daniel had recovered his poise.

"That wasn't all," Win said. She paused and swallowed hard. "He asked about a diary. Did we find Faye's diary among the rest of her belongings at Juniper Hall?"

"What did you tell him?"

They had to wait again for her to reply. The sun had fallen below the horizon. The air was very still. There was the distant buzz of a tractor and wood pigeons called from the trees behind the house.

"I said that I knew Faye kept a diary, but we didn't find it. She must have left it at home in Otterbridge."

"Quite right," he said. "You did very well." He gave a strange little laugh. He was staring directly at Magda, challenging her to contradict him. "It's the truth after all. We didn't find it. And it won't come to light after all this time. Faye will be able to rest in peace."

Magda turned abruptly and walked away, through the arch into the farmyard. Daniel gave another of his little laughs. "Mother-in-laws," he said.

Win watched the woman go anxiously. She seemed about

145

to follow her, but Daniel caught hold of her hand and pulled her towards him.

"You know," he said, "I'm not sure Magda's really committed to the Laverock Farm project. I'm not convinced that she'd fit into a therapeutic community. It's not her style. She's too much of an individualist." He put his arm around Win's shoulders. "We'll have to talk about it seriously," he said. "Decide where she'd be happiest."

Lily expected some protest from Win, but she stood miserably cradled in Daniel's arm and said nothing. They walked slowly back towards the car.

"What about the garden, then?" Sean asked. "Do you want me to make a start on it?"

"Oh, I think so," Daniel said expansively. "I definitely think so."

Lily and Sean stood in the farmyard and watched the car drive off.

"What was that all about?" Lily asked. "The police can't really think Faye's death had anything to do with these murders."

"Who knows?" Sean said. He seemed pleased with himself. "You should ask your friend Gordon Hunter."

"He's not my friend," she said automatically.

"He thinks *I* killed Ernie Bowles." But today not even that troubled Sean.

The Abbots' car disappeared round a corner in the lane.

"It seems very quiet without the animals," Lily said. "The hens and that smelly dog of Cissie's that Ernie kept chained up all day." She looked towards the house. "I can still see him there in the kitchen, looking out at me from behind the net curtains. I can't believe that Faye's come back to haunt me, but I can believe in the ghost of Ernie Bowles, dirty old man." She clapped her hand to her mouth. Sean led her inside.

"Ernie Bowles," Ramsay said, "is a problem."

It was seven o'clock and they were in the small private bar that the pub's landlord had said they could use. "You'll get no peace if you sit in the public," he'd said. "Folks'll be asking questions all night, sticking their oars in."

Ramsay thought he just wanted them out of the way. Murder had novelty value, but after a while having cops within earshot cramped the punters' style. It was bad for business. The room was dusty and smelled damp. At one table sat the team who had been tracing the participants in Magda Pocock's workshop. A bunch of weirdos, the team agreed, but harmless enough. One significant detail had been confirmed. For most of the exercises Val McDougal had worked with Lily Jackman. No one could remember if Val had been especially anxious or upset, but they told the detectives that Lily would know. Lily had been with Val all afternoon, real buddies.

At another table made of dimpled copper, sticky with drink rings, sat Ramsay, Hunter, and Sally Wedderburn.

"What do you mean?" Hunter demanded. "Ernie Bowles is the problem."

"I don't see where he fits in. Everyone else knew each other. Faye, Lily, Val, the gang from the Old Chapel. They all had similar ideas and met socially. Ernie Bowles wasn't any part of that. They despised him. So far as we know, the only connection he had with that group was through his mother."

"And the fact that the rest of them inherited his farm," Hunter said. "Even the two hippies will have benefited from that. The Abbots are hardly likely to turf them out of the caravan, and Ernie might have done if he suddenly turned nasty. I still think Slater was involved. That blue Transit never turned up."

"Are we certain that the old lady *did* die of natural causes?" Sally asked suddenly. "I suppose Abbot didn't stick an acupuncture pin in one of her vital organs? She'd been ill for ages and she was getting on. The doctor might not have looked too closely for a cause of death. I should think an attack like that might be hard to trace anyway."

Ramsay smiled. "Perhaps, but I've checked with the doctor who signed the death certificate. Pneumonia killed her in the end. Nothing more exciting than that."

"What about Richardson?" Hunter asked. "He's a sort of connection. If his dad buys the Laverock land and he was going out with Faye."

"Yes," Ramsay said. "I thought I'd go to see young Richardson this evening."

"Want me to come with you?"

"No. I don't think so. I thought an informal approach."

"Suit yourself," Hunter said. He stood up in a huff to fetch another round of drinks.

"What's the matter with him?"

"He had his nose put out of joint," Sally said, "because Faye Cooper's mother would only talk to me."

"We knew that was likely," Ramsay said. "We knew she'd probably be more comfortable with a woman."

He looked across at the group of officers at the other table and frowned. They were becoming rowdy. They'd already had too much to drink. He knew they were frustrated. They thought the case was going nowhere. He did not really want the drink Hunter had bought for him, but he took it anyway, finished if off quickly. Hunter was in a mood to take offence.

"I'll go, then," he said. "See what Peter Richardson has got to say for himself."

Outside, a group of teenagers stood, looking bored, at the bus shelter. They stared as he walked past and he thought that everyone in Mittingford knew who he was. It was inconceivable in a place like this that someone did not know who had strangled Ernie Bowles. The town was already in shadow, and the air was suddenly cold. He walked quickly past the Old Chapel towards the police station.

In the incident room staff were still on duty, manning the phone, being available to talk to members of the public who came in off the street with scraps of information, most of it irrelevant. "I remember the last time I saw Ernie Bowles at market he seemed very peculiar. Odd, you know. I thought you'd be interested. He bought me a pint and he's never done that before in his life. He wanted to talk about his mother. . . ."

It was all written down and processed. Anything of interest was copied and left on Ramsay's desk. When he saw the paper that had accumulated there in his absence, he felt overwhelmed by it. He left a message saying where he was going and drove into the hills.

22

W_{hen} Ramsay arrived at Long Edge Farm the lights were on but none of the curtains had been drawn. There was enough light from a thin moon to see the family cars pulled up in front of the house: Sue Richardson's red Fiesta, a Land Rover, and a big Volvo Estate. Either local hill farmers were crying wolf about the Common Market sheep subsidies or the holiday cottage business was booming. Ramsay walked round to the kitchen door and knocked there.

The Richardsons had obviously just finished a meal. Sue was piling plates into a dishwasher, with astonishing deftness and speed. Stan was slumped in his wicker chair watching a small television which stood on the breakfast bar. The smell of the meal—something spicy and Oriental which Ramsay guessed Stan would have turned his nose up at—lingered in the room and made Ramsay realise that he had not eaten.

"Oh, it's you," Stan said. "What are you after now?"

"A few questions," Ramsay said easily. "Is Peter in?"

Sue turned from rinsing pots in the sink. "He's in the bath. Just getting ready to go out."

"You won't mind if I wait, then?"

Stan gave a bad-tempered scowl, but Sue jumped in before he could speak: "Of course not. Sit down. Would you like a drink? Tea? Coffee?"

"Coffee, please." It had been a long day. He could do with a shot of caffeine to keep him going.

"Turn off the television, Stan," she said chidingly, as if he were a child. He grumbled under his breath but did as he was told. Ramsay thought that despite his rudeness he always did. He was probably instructed to keep away from the paying guests. Unless he could be polite.

"I understand that you're interested in the Laverock Farm land," Ramsay said.

"Oh, aye. Who told you that?"

"It seems to be general gossip in the town."

"Well, you're best not believing anything you hear."

"It's not true, then?"

"Depends on the price," he admitted reluctantly. "And what sort of deal I can get."

"Even with a load of 'hippies' living in the house?"

He snorted.

"I've told Stan I don't think that will be a problem," Sue interrupted again. "I've seen the sort of operation they run at the Old Chapel. I like to shop there, actually. Some of my guests prefer organic produce. It's very professional. I don't think we'd have anything to worry about if the Abbots took over. It might even work to our advantage. Some of our visitors might be attracted by the facilities they'd provide. Anything would be better than Ernie Bowles, with his smelly old dog, swearing at anyone who went near him."

So Cissie's plan had backfired, Ramsay thought. She had hoped to upset the neighbours. Instead they saw the Alternative Therapy Centre as a tourist attraction.

"What do you want with the lad, then?" Stan demanded.

"Some information," Ramsay said. "It'll not take long."

"I'd best go and fetch him for you. He'd spend all night in the bloody bathroom, given the chance. Then I'll be in the other room watching television if you want me."

He stomped out of the kitchen. Sue watched him go with an indulgent smile. Through the open door they heard him yell up the stairs to Peter: "That police inspector wants to see you. Get your arse down here!"

Sue slammed shut the dishwasher door and pretended not

150

to hear. She poured coffee for Ramsay and set it before him with a slice of fruitcake.

Peter swaggered in ten minutes later. He was wearing the trendy Geordie's uniform for a night on the town: expensive and immaculately fitting jeans, a short-sleeved open-necked shirt, and a lot of gold. This was standard dress in Newcastle even when there was snow on the ground and ten degrees of frost.

Sue Richardson looked at her watch. "If you don't mind, Inspector, I'll leave you to it. Another family is moving into one of our cottages tomorrow. There's a cot to put up and I want to check that everything's ready for them."

She flashed him a professional smile and disappeared.

Peter stood with his back to the Aga. "Inspector," he said, sneering. "What a surprise! How can I help you?"

"I want to ask about Faye Cooper," Ramsay said. "She was a friend of yours?"

It wasn't what he had been expecting and the mask of arrogance slipped. He played with the gold chain on his wrist.

"Yes," he said uncertainly. "I knew her for a while."

"I wouldn't have thought she was your sort," Ramsay said.

Peter did not answer.

"But she was your girlfriend?"

"I suppose so."

"Where did you meet her?" He had been anxious about that from the start. They would hardly have had many friends in common.

"In the Old Chapel." He seemed almost ashamed of admitting that he had ever been there. It didn't fit in with his image. "In the coffee place. Mum asked me to get some stuff from the health-food shop and I stopped for a drink. She'd been visiting the Abbots. We got talking. She said she was a student in Otterbridge. I'd just finished at the agricultural college. There was something about her . . . I asked her out. On the spur of the moment, you know."

"And she agreed?"

"Yes, she agreed. I was surprised. I suppose I was just trying it on." He paused. "We arranged to meet in a pub in

151

Otterbridge because she didn't have any transport. I almost didn't go. She wasn't my type really. Too serious. Too intense. But, like I said, there was something about her."

"Did she tell you she already had a boyfriend?"

"Yeah. I thought that was a good sign. I didn't want to get into anything too heavy."

"How long did you go out with her?"

"It wasn't like that. I mean, it wasn't as if we were engaged or anything. She still had her boyfriend, James, and I was seeing other women.... We talked mostly. Went for walks. I didn't really think of her as my girlfriend."

The relationship with Faye had obviously confused him. Girlfriends you took out to clubs and pubs. If they let you, you screwed them. If they didn't, you dumped them. His friendship with Faye had been different, less clear-cut. He hadn't known how to handle it.

"But Faye did consider herself your girlfriend, didn't she? She told James about you. And last summer she got a job in Mittingford so she could be close to you."

"I told her not to do that," he said. "I knew it would be a mistake."

"Cramp your style, you mean?"

"If you like!" The macho lout had returned. "I wasn't ready to be tied down. Not to a lass like her."

"Is that what she wanted? To be tied down?"

"Oh," he said, "I never knew what she wanted."

"Did your parents know that you were seeing Faye?"

"They knew I was seeing someone called Faye. They never met her."

"Wouldn't they have approved?"

"It wasn't that." It was because she wasn't leggy and ornamental, Ramsay thought. She was pretty enough, but she would have worn the wrong clothes, given the wrong impression altogether. He would have been embarrassed to be seen out with her. "None of my friends knew," Peter said. "They wouldn't have understood."

"Did Faye understand?" Ramsay asked. "Didn't she mind being kept a secret?"

"I don't think she realised," Peter muttered. "She really liked me, you see." Then, trying to be flippant, a man of the world: "Women are such romantics, aren't they?"

"You went out with her all that summer?"

He nodded. "Not often, though. The Abbots were real slave drivers. She didn't have much time to herself."

"Did she ever meet Ernie Bowles?" The question suddenly occurred to him.

"No. Not when she was with me. Why?"

Ramsay did not answer. "Did you ever consider putting an end to the relationship?" he said. "If she was such an embarrassment . . ."

"Of course I considered it. But I liked her. She listened. And I wasn't sure how she'd handle it. She didn't have anyone else. I suppose I didn't have the guts. Besides, I knew she'd go back to college at the end of the summer. I thought it would die a natural death."

"Instead," Ramsay said, "she died a natural death."

Peter flushed. "I'm sorry. I didn't mean to make a joke. Not about that."

Suddenly he became almost likable.

"Tell me about her," Ramsay said. "You must have known her better than anyone."

Peter shrugged. He wasn't used to putting feelings and impressions into words.

"Everything was black or white with Faye. She either loved you or hated you. She hated her stepfather. 'I had to get away from that house,' she said, 'or I'd have killed him.' The crowd at the Old Chapel were her heroes. She quoted them all the time: Daniel said that or Magda said this. It really got on your nerves. . . ." He paused. He had more to say, but he wasn't sure how to put it. "She didn't play safe," he said. "There was no pretence. If she liked you, she said so. If she wanted something, she asked for it. There was no . . . protective layer between her and the world."

He blushed again. "This must sound dead stupid. Do you know what I mean?"

153

Ramsay nodded. "I think so. It would have meant that she'd be easily hurt."

"That's why I found it so hard to tell her that I didn't want to see her again."

"Did you tell her that?"

"In the end."

"What happened?"

"Like I said, I expected we'd stop seeing each other so often when she went back to Otterbridge. She'd become too demanding. I wouldn't have minded meeting her occasionally. . . ." On your own terms, Ramsay thought. To have your ego massaged. To be flattered by her admiration. "But that wasn't enough for her. She seemed to be obsessed. She even phoned me here, begging me to go out to Otterbridge to meet her."

"I expect she was lonely," Ramsay said. "It must have been hard to go back to her bedsit after having had company all summer."

"I suppose it was." He was so self-centred that the idea had never occurred to him before. "Anyway, I thought I should make a clean break of it. Tell her straight that I didn't want to see her again."

"When did you do that?"

"I'm not sure exactly. Not long after she left here to go back to college."

"How did she take it?"

"She seemed all right," he said. "Quite controlled. She didn't burst into hysterics or anything, which is what I expected. It was a bit hard to tell because I told her on the phone. I couldn't face a mega-scene in public. At least she stopped bothering me."

So you could forget all about her, Ramsay thought. You could go back to your mates in the rugby club and making money. And a much more suitable girlfriend.

"Then I heard she was dead," Peter went on bleakly.

"Who told you?"

"Mrs. Abbot phoned me. She'd never liked me, but she thought I should know."

154

"She didn't blame you in any way?"

"What do you mean?"

"She didn't suggest that Faye killed herself because of the way you'd treated her?" He realised that was cruel, but he felt vaguely that Peter deserved it.

The boy was defensive and all the bluster returned. "Of course not. I'd finished with her a couple of weeks before that. She'd had time to get over it, hadn't she? Besides, I thought it was an accident." He thrust his head towards Ramsay. "You can't go around making that sort of allegation. What's this got to do with you anyway?"

"I don't know," Ramsay said as he let himself out of the house. "I really don't know."

When he returned to the hotel most of his team were still in the bar. He hurried past the door to the stairs so no one should see him. From his room he phoned Prue. She seemed pleased to hear from him, and when he replaced the receiver he was comforted, more optimistic.

23

Early the next morning the Abbots sat over muesli and apple juice. Win was still in her nightdress, a long, shroudlike garment. She looked faded; her skin had the dusty, dried-out texture of dead leaves. Daniel felt a shudder of irritation, even of disgust. He had never found her sexually attractive. Now her lethargy repulsed him. But not enough, he realised, for him to consider leaving her and risking all that they had achieved together.

The telephone rang. It was Ramsay, requesting an interview.

"I'm seeing a patient at nine," Daniel said.

"I must see you this morning." Ramsay was polite but emphatic.

"I could be free by eleven-thirty," Daniel said. He replaced the receiver slowly.

"He'll want to talk about Faye," Win said. She looked at him anxiously.

"Of course . . ." He paused. "I wonder who's stirring up trouble after all this time."

He spooned yoghurt onto his muesli and said, as if he were changing the subject completely: "Do you think Lily would have the boys this afternoon?"

"I expect so. I think it's her afternoon off. Now they're staying in the house I could phone and ask." Win faced him uncertainly across the breakfast table. He realised she was frightened of him and felt an exhilarating rush of energy.

"I was wondering if you'd go to see the lad, James. To express our sympathy. Someone from the centre should do it and I'm busy."

"I don't know," she said quickly. "Surely he won't want to see us."

"Why?"

"Well, first Faye. Then Val. I should have thought we were the last people—"

"Nonsense," he interrupted. "I think it would be a welcome gesture." Then, persuasively: "Val was very close to him, wasn't she? If she confided in anyone, it would have been in him. Find out if she talked to him before she died. You're good with kids."

"All right," she said. "If you think it's a good idea." He smiled because he had known all along that he could make her agree.

In the Alternative Therapy Centre his patient was already waiting for him. Daniel introduced himself and began mentally, almost automatically, the process of diagnosis: rigid posture, he thought, firm grip, cold hand. All that could be relevant.

"Just give me a couple of minutes," he said, and let himself into his treatment room. He put on a clean white coat. Other acupuncturists might practise in jeans and a sweatshirt, but he had never been comfortable with such informality. He looked at his equipment with satisfaction. He loved this work, cared more about it than anything else in his life. There was the plastic case of sterile, disposable needles; the akabani, the sticks which warmed the skin to test for an imbalance between the left and right side of the body; and the moxa, the herb which was burned on the acupuncture points to warm the energy. The tools of his job, he thought. Then, suddenly: healing gave you power. That's why he got such a buzz out of it.

He rang through to Rebecca to send the patient in.

The man complained of migraine.

"I've been to the doctor," he said, "but he just tells me it's stress-related. Of course I'm under stress. All the time. I'm running my own business in a recession. Who wouldn't be?"

"Today I'll do a TD," Daniel said. "A traditional diagnosis. If I can help, we'll start the treatment in the next session."

He already had the man down as a wood causative factor. He could even hear the shout in his voice. Woods could be rigid, overindependent, needing to control. Cissie Bowles had been a wood causative factor, though she had mellowed with treatment and become almost human by the end.

"I'll take a personal history," he began. "I'd like to concentrate on the first five years of your life. Perhaps you could tell me something about that time."

The businessman claimed not to remember anything, looked at Daniel as if he were wasting time.

"That's not unusual," Daniel said, but probing gently he discovered that the father had been a merchant seaman, away a lot. The patient had spent much of his early childhood with his grandmother.

"Now," he said, "what about your present family?"

There was a wife apparently, who had a successful career in her own right, two teenage children. All the time Daniel was looking for the secondary gain. What did this man get out of being ill? Attention, it seemed. The wife made a fuss of him when he had a migraine attack and at other times dismissed him as a failure. In Daniel's experience there usually was a secondary gain. In Cissie Bowles's case her arthritis had allowed her to ease up on the farm and boss poor Ernie about.

Poor Ernie! Daniel gave a little grin. The businessman looked at him suspiciously.

"I'll ask you to undress now," Daniel said, trying to concentrate, "so I can do a physical examination."

While he was waiting for his patient to strip, he went out to reception. Rebecca was opening the mail. She heard him coming, looked up nervously.

"Yes, Mr. Abbot. Is there anything I can do?"

"I'm sure there is, Rebecca. I'm sure there is. But not just now."

He walked round behind her so he could look over her shoulder at the letters on the desk. His hand rested on her waist. As he walked away he tapped her on the buttocks.

"Very good," he said. "What a fast little learner you are!"

Back in the treatment room he completed his diagnosis. He took the pulses, six on each wrist. He waved the burning akabani over the man's fingernails and waited to see how long it took for the skin to feel warm. He took his blood pressure.

"Now," he said, "we have to decide what to do next. I think we'll clear any polluted energy that may be in your system," Daniel continued, explaining the test for aggressive energy in the best way he knew how. "It's always safest to do that first. It involves thirteen needles in your back, but you'll feel no real discomfort."

The patient was impressed. Daniel felt the old satisfaction in knowing that he could help. He realised that he really was very good at this.

After making a new appointment with Rebecca, the businessman hovered in reception. Although he had been so unforthcoming at the beginning, now he was reluctant to leave. Eventually Daniel walked down the steps with him, and through the Old Chapel to the street. The man was still talking about his wife.

In the health-food shop Lily Jackman was at work. The place was empty and she stood listlessly behind the counter while the two other assistants carried on a conversation over her head. Daniel nodded at her and paused for a moment. He wondered whether Win had phoned her at Laverock Farm to ask about the baby-sitting. Perhaps he should check. In the end he decided to leave it. It wouldn't be a good idea to make an issue of it.

When he got back to the centre Magda was in. The door of her treatment room was open and she was on the phone. But by the time Ramsay and Hunter arrived at eleven-thirty, she had a client with her and she refused to be disturbed. That suited Daniel very well. He thought he could handle the police better by himself. The successful session with his patient had given him confidence.

"I'm sorry, Inspector, I'm afraid I'll have to do," he said, standing up to greet them. He was still wearing his white coat. The room smelled slightly herbal. Hunter sniffed the air disapprovingly. "Besides," Daniel went on, "we've all given statements already. I don't think we can add to what we've told you."

"I think you can," Ramsay said. "I'm interested in a girl called Faye Cooper."

"What possible interest could you have in Faye?"

"We've been given information which links her death with the recent murders."

"I don't know who could have put that idea into your heads. It's ridiculous."

"Are you quite sure?" Hunter leaned forward. He played the part of the heavy too convincingly, Ramsay thought. And Daniel Abbot was too clever to be taken in by it.

"Of course," Daniel said. "You must have looked at the records, seen the inquest verdict. Faye's death was accidental."

"I understand that you employed Faye for several weeks last summer," Ramsay said. "As a nanny."

"It wasn't such a formal arrangement as that," Daniel said. "Not really. She was at a loose end during her college holidays. We invited her to stay with us and in return she did some baby-sitting."

"I see." Ramsay sounded sceptical. "Did the arrangement work?"

"Yes. The children seemed to take to her and we found her a very pleasant girl. Very accommodating."

"Was she working on the weekend when she went with you to the retreat at Juniper Hall?"

"What do you mean?"

"I presume that by then she'd returned to college for the autumn term. She was living in her bedsit in Otterbridge again. Did you invite her to accompany you to look after the

160

children so you were free to participate in the weekend's activities?"

"You make it sound very calculating, Inspector. It wasn't like that. We thought she'd benefit from the retreat. And she was very keen to go. She did look after the children on occasions during the weekend. Win and I were both very busy. But we waived her registration fee."

That was big of you, Ramsay thought.

"Perhaps you could tell me exactly what happened that weekend," he said.

"I'm sorry, Inspector, it's not that I'm not keen to help, but I don't see how that's relevant to your present enquiries."

"I've explained that certain allegations have been made," Ramsay said quietly. "They may be malicious, but you do see that I have to follow them through."

"I suppose these were anonymous allegations!" Daniel said petulantly.

"I'm sorry, sir, you can't expect me to discuss that."

"Why don't you just tell us what happened," Hunter said threateningly, "on that weekend that the lassie died."

Daniel seemed about to protest but looked at Hunter and thought better of it.

"We picked Faye up in Otterbridge on Friday lunchtime," he said. "She didn't have classes in the afternoon, or if she did she was prepared to skip them. She seemed in an emotional mood, rather withdrawn. I kept expecting her to burst into tears. We discovered in the course of the trip to Cumbria that a boy she'd been seeing, Peter Richardson, had finished with her. I don't think it was ever a particularly close relationship, but she seemed to be taking it rather badly. I hoped that the weekend would be good for her, do something to rebuild her self-confidence. Certainly by the time we arrived at Juniper Hall she seemed more cheerful. . . .

"It was a beautiful weekend, very hot and sunny. Everyone talked about it, said how unusual the weather was for that time of year. We kept expecting it to break, for there to be a thunderstorm. It had that sort of feel. But it stayed fine."

He paused. He would have found it easier to deal with

161

specific questions. But Ramsay and Hunter just waited for him to continue.

"Juniper's a beautiful house," he said. "Elizabethan, I think. All chimneys and pointed gables. More the sort of place you'd expect to find in the Cotswolds. You could tell that Faye had never seen anything like it before. There wasn't much arranged for the Friday. Some of the people had a long way to travel and didn't arrive until late. We had a meal. There was a session where we all started to get to know each other."

"Val McDougal was there?"

"Yes. She arrived in time for dinner."

"And Lily Jackman?"

Daniel paused. "Yes. She got a lift with Val."

"How did Miss Jackman afford it, then?" Hunter thrust his face towards Daniel's. "I've seen the brochure. It doesn't come cheap."

"You'd have to ask Lily that. I presume she thought it was worth it."

"Did Faye have her own room?" Ramsay asked.

Daniel nodded.

"She died late on Saturday night or early Sunday morning. Did anything unusual happen on Saturday?"

"No. It had all gone very smoothly. There was a great sense of sharing and openness. Everyone seemed very close."

"Did Faye go to all the sessions that had been arranged?"

"I don't think so. You'd have to ask Win. She'd be more likely to remember. Faye definitely took the kids out for a walk in the morning while I was running a group, but in the afternoon I think they went for a nap so she could join in."

"And what session was that?"

"It was Magda's Voice Dialogue."

"The same thing she was doing with her group on the Sunday before Val died?"

Daniel nodded. "It's a technique of consciousness-raising," he said. "A way of achieving self-acceptance. You know."

"Not really," Ramsay said brightly. "But I'll take your word for it. Were they working in pairs?"

"Yes. That's how Magda works it."

"Who was working with Faye?"

He paused again.

"Come on, Mr. Abbott. You must have some idea."

"I think it was Magda herself. There was an uneven number, so she joined in."

"And that session lasted all afternoon?"

Daniel nodded.

"How did Faye seem? Was she still upset?"

"I didn't notice," Daniel said dismissively. "Magda would know."

"What happened then?"

"There was a period of free time before dinner. For people to reflect quietly in their rooms or explore the garden."

"Or go for a swim?" Hunter demanded.

"Yes. Some of them went for a swim."

"But not Faye? She didn't swim until later, did she?"

"No," Daniel said awkwardly. "That's right."

"Tell us about that," Ramsay said confidentially. "Tell us exactly what happened."

"I don't know," Daniel cried. "I wasn't there. No one was."

"Take me through the evening, then."

"We had dinner. Helped clear up. That's part of the deal at Juniper. Everyone mucks in. After the meal there was a talk by a visiting speaker. He went on rather. It was gone ten by the time he'd finished. We had coffee, then most people drifted back to their rooms."

"Wasn't that unusual?" Ramsay asked.

"What do you mean?"

"Well, I get sent on conferences, too. Not so uplifting, of course, and I expect the food's better, but the setup's similar. I always mean to get to bed early, but I never seem to manage it. There's too much going on. People you've not seen for years. I always find myself up until the early hours chatting."

"It's hardly the same, Inspector. Our sort of programme is

163

very intensive. Emotionally draining. People need time to come to terms with what they've learnt about themselves."

"They don't all go off to the pub, then?"

"We don't need alcohol, Sergeant. That's not encouraged."

"And yet," Ramsay said, "after a long day of looking after the children and this intensive group therapy, Faye decided to go swimming. By herself. I wonder why she should do that."

"I don't know, Inspector. All I know is that she was found drowned the next morning."

"Who found her body?"

"My wife did," Daniel said. "She'd gone out for a walk before I was awake. Of course she was terribly distressed. She came to find me, and once we realised Faye was dead, we called the police."

"Yes," Ramsay said. "I see."

There was a silence. Daniel looked at his watch. "My next patient will be coming soon, Inspector. If there's nothing else . . ."

"Faye's diary," Ramsay said.

"What about it?"

"It wasn't among her belongings at Juniper Hall. Not when the police arrived."

"She must have left it at home, then."

"In your house? Did you ever find it?"

"No," Daniel said. "Not in our house. In her bedsit. I don't know what happened to her stuff there."

"Did Faye ever meet Ernie Bowles?" Ramsay asked. The questions came quickly. He knew that his time was running out.

"Of course not. Why would she?" He found it hard to contain his impatience. The telephone rang. "That's my next patient, Inspector. I'll have to ask you to go now."

"All right, Mr. Abbot. Perhaps we could see if Mrs. Pocock can help us."

But there was no sign of Magda and she'd left a message with the receptionist to say that she'd be out for the rest of the day.

24

When they got back to the incident room, they noticed a change of mood. They had left the team submerged in an air of morose quiet, which had little to do with hangovers, the result of the night before. Nothing was happening and nothing, the team felt, was likely to happen. The case had reached a stalemate. But now there was conversation, a lift of spirits. It was clear that they had been waiting impatiently for Ramsay's return.

"Well?" he said. "What's been going on?"

"We've traced those hippies, sir. The gang Slater claims to have spent the night with when Ernie Bowles was killed. A postie said he saw their blue Transit up a track just west of Berwick. A man, a woman, and a kid. It must be them. We reckon they must have been hiding out up there. They might even have been in on the murder."

They looked at him expectantly. They all wanted to go to check it out. They were like children, he thought, waiting to be chosen for the school football team. He wouldn't have been surprised to see hands in the air, to hear cries of "Pick me, sir. I'm the best."

"I'll do it myself," he said, not out of diplomacy but because he felt like a trip out. He could do with a fresh perspective on the case. "You come with me, Sal. You can play with the bairn while I talk to the adults."

He saw her turn away and realised he'd offended her.

Stereotyped again, she was thinking. Why couldn't Hunter mind kids as well as her? He could hardly explain that he'd only said it to save Hunter's pride. Really he wanted her along because she was so sharp. She could sniff out a liar better than anyone he knew.

She spent most of the trip in silence to express her disapproval. She was driving and Ramsay followed the route on an Ordnance Survey map. They came to a scattered village with a school, a pub, a shop built into the garage of a stone cottage. A sandy track led on to a piece of overgrown woodland and the Transit had pulled off that. If they had not known it was there, they would have missed it, though when they walked in through the trees, there were traces of a fire, and a makeshift line with washing hanging on it. A few weeks earlier the ground would have been covered by bluebells. Now most were dying, though the colour remained in patches, out of the sun.

A little girl with black curls squatted in the leaf mould and rolled out Play-Doh on a tin tray. Sally crouched beside her.

"What are you making?" she asked.

"Cakes." The girl was not curious about them. She did not look up.

"They look lovely. Can I have one?"

"Of course not!" The child was contemptuous. "They're not cooked. You can't cook Play-Doh."

"What do you want?" The question came with a slight stutter. They turned to see a tall man in his late twenties who had followed them on foot into the wood. He had a thin face and long straggly hair and reminded Sally of images of Jesus she had seen in stained glass windows. He carried a rucksack on his back. It must have been heavy, because he swung it with relief onto the ground. Cans of beans and soup, loose vegetables rolled out.

"What do you want?" the man said again, not aggressively but with resignation.

"I'm Inspector Ramsay. Northumbria police."

"Inspector? They've never bothered with an inspector be-

166

fore. Hey, Lorna! We've got an inspector come to visit." His voice was Welsh, nervous, rather bitter.

A woman climbed out of the back of the Transit. She wore a crushed velvet skirt, over scuffed suede desert boots, and a long sweater with holes at the elbows. Her hair was tied back with a scarf flecked with silver thread. Ramsay thought she looked more of a gypsy than Romanies he had met.

"You can't make us move," she said. "This is common land. We checked."

"Common-land law is very complicated," Ramsay said. "But we're not here to move you on."

"What then? We've done nothing." She was the stronger of the two. She stood with her legs apart, her hands on her hips, facing them out.

"Some questions," Ramsay said. "That's all."

"We don't claim dole." She nodded towards the groceries in the rucksack. "We paid for all that ourselves. I make jewellery. Silver and enamel. I can show you. . . . And Wes gets work whenever he can."

"Though there's not much call for a classics graduate in rural Northumberland," Wes said. The stutter was more pronounced.

"You're a classics graduate?" Sally looked at Ramsay to apologise for butting in, but she was intrigued.

He nodded.

"Then why . . . ?"

"Do I live like this?" He finished the question for her, mocking.

She nodded.

"Because I'm happier." He paused. "I had a sort of breakdown. Stress disagrees with me. You wouldn't think there was a lot of stress teaching Virgil to ten-year-olds in a crummy prep school, would you? But it was too much for me."

"So you dropped out?" Sally said.

"Or dropped in. Depending on your perspective. Concentrated at least on the important things."

"It can't have been easy, with a baby."

"I don't think babies are ever easy, wherever you are. We'd like to find somewhere to settle now. Briony's getting older, you see. She should be at play group soon. We could afford to pay rent, but no one wants us. Travellers don't make ideal tenants apparently. Once we could have had a council house, but they've been sold off. Except flats on city estates, and that would make me mad again. So we're here. Camping out on common land. Doing no harm to anyone. Hoping that eventually people will get to know us and trust us enough to rent us a place. Even a plot of land to put a caravan."

The phrases came in sharp bursts. Then he seemed to run out of steam and gave a lopsided grin to show he realised the hope was misguided.

"How long have you been here?" Ramsay asked.

"All winter. About six months." Sally caught Ramsay's eye. So Hunter was right, they both thought. Slater was lying all the time.

"You can confirm, then, that you weren't on a road near Mittingford the week before last."

"Why?" It was Lorna again. Suspicious.

"Haven't you realised that we've been looking for you?" Ramsay demanded. "Don't you ever read the newspapers?"

Wes shook his head.

"Listen to the radio?"

"Yes," Wes said. "But only Radio Three."

"There was a murder. A farmer in Mittingford was killed. We think you may have been witnesses. But if you can prove you weren't anywhere near the place . . ."

"We might have been there," Wes said. "On the Saturday night. We'd been to a show in Durham. Lorna sells her jewellery wherever she can—agricultural shows, craft fairs. We'd driven down early on Saturday morning. We had a good day and we were late packing up. By the time we got to Mittingford, we were both shattered, so we decided to pull into the gypsy transit site and spent the night there. What are we supposed to have seen anyway?"

"Did you meet anyone that night?"

168

"Yes," Wes said slowly. "A guy called Sean Slater. Why?"

"What time did you meet him?"

They found it impossible to say. Perhaps it was just getting dark. He appeared there at the van, out of the blue. They hadn't seen him for ages. They could have done with an early night, really, but Sean seemed keen to talk. They listened to some music, drank some wine. The inspector would understand. By that time it was so late that they suggested Sean should crash out with them. There wasn't much space, but they'd managed to fit another sleeping bag on the floor.

"What time did Mr. Slater go?" Ramsay asked.

They considered. "Probably at about seven," Lorna said at last. "We were back here by nine. The bells were ringing and all the old biddies were on their way into church as we drove through the village."

"Mr. Slater is an old friend of yours? You know him well?"

"Oh yes," Wes said. "Sean and I go back years."

"And how did he seem that night?"

"Fine. Perhaps a bit jealous, you know. He was playing with Briony before she went to sleep. I had the impression that he would have liked a kid of his own. He was living with a woman he really seemed to care for, but she didn't want to be tied down."

"He didn't take you to the caravan where he was living?"

"No. We dropped him at the end of the track in the morning, and he said he'd walk from there to the farm."

"Did he seem upset or anxious?"

"Of course not. We'd had a good night catching up on each other's news, talking. . . . What is all this about?"

"I think," Ramsay said, "you've just cleared your friend of murder."

They returned to Mittingford more slowly. Ramsay was driving and he was always more cautious.

"Well?" he said. "Were they telling the truth?"

"Definitely," she said. "They had no idea what we were doing there at first. The story wasn't prepared."

"So Slater's in the clear," Ramsay said. "At least for the Ernie Bowles murder."

"Sir, can I ask you something?"

"What?" He was surprised and did not know what to expect.

She grinned.

"Let me be the one to tell Gordon Hunter he's been wrong about Slater all this time."

25

W_{in} handed the boys over to Lily at two-thirty. Lily had her bike with her. The basket was full of fruit and veg which were too old or misshapen to sell. She wore dungarees and red canvas baseball boots.

"I thought I might take them out," Lily said. "To the park. They always like the park. What do you think?"

"Great," Win said. But Lily thought that nothing about Win seemed great. She looked harassed, tired, worn down. If that was what marriage and kids could do to you, Lily thought, Sean could bloody well think again. He hadn't spoken any more about marriage, but she could tell what was in his mind. He'd begun going gooey over kids lately, too, even the Abbot brats, and he'd told her more times than she could remember about the little girl who lived in the blue Transit van. How she'd been really sweet and no trouble really. Her parents were still on the road, weren't they? They hadn't sold out.

That morning Lily had left him working in the garden at Laverock Farm and the picture of him bent over his spade had made him seem domesticated and suburban. He wasn't any different from his father, she thought. Next thing he'd be wanting a semi on a new housing estate, weekly trips to a garden centre, and a shed to hide in when she was at the moody time of the month. She knew she should be grateful, but she couldn't settle for that, not even for him.

When the phone call had come from Win, Lily had asked him if he minded her going.

"It's not as if it's that important," she said. "Win's only playing Lady Bountiful. She thinks she should offer our condolences to James McDougal. As if he'd want to see her. I expect Daniel put her up to it. He probably wants to know what Val said to James about Juniper Hall. They were very close. I suppose it could be useful to find out just what she told him."

Sean rested on his spade. "You go," he said. "We could do with the money. I want to get on with this anyway."

Lily watched Win drive away, then got the boys into their coats and strapped them into the double buggy. The road down to the park was steep. She imagined letting go of the pushchair handles and watching it bump down the hill and into the burn at the bottom, swept away perhaps by the high spring water. What's wrong with me? she thought. I don't hate kids. I just don't want Sean's.

When Hunter saw her from the window of the police station, the boys were out of the buggy. One was on the slide and the other was squatting down and playing with the wood bark which was supposed to make a softer landing, and which all the neighbourhood cats loved to use as a lavatory. Lily was rolling a cigarette, very thin. He watched her pinch out the ends and cup her hand to light it. She was staring out across the town to the hills, taking no notice of the children.

"I can't stand this waiting," he said. There had been no news from Ramsay about the blue Transit. "I'm going out for a breath of fresh air."

They let him go without comment. Gordon Hunter could be a moody bastard and you were best not to cross him.

When he got to the park she had not moved. She took a last drag of the cigarette and pinched it out.

"It's all right," she said. "It's only tobacco."

"I thought you were a health freak. I didn't think you'd touch that."

"Oh!" she said airily. "I've got all the vices." She sat on

172

one of the swings with her legs stretched out in front of her. "What are you doing here?"

"They let me out occasionally."

She leaned back so her arms were straight and she was looking at the sky.

"I'll give you a push if you like," he said.

"Better not. There's probably some byelaw. About adults on the swings. We couldn't have you mixed up in criminal activity." She pulled herself upright again.

I wouldn't mind, he thought. With you. He nodded towards the boys. "They've got you playing at nanny now, have they? I hope they're paying you."

"What do you mean?"

"Didn't they have that kid Faye Cooper skivvying for them last summer?" While he was there, he thought, he might as well find out what she knew.

She took a tobacco tin from her dungaree pocket and began to roll another cigarette.

"You're making me nervous," she said. "I don't usually smoke this much. I'd heard you'd found out about Faye. The Abbots won't like that. How *did* you find out?"

He took a gamble. "We had an anonymous letter," he said. "You wouldn't have had anything to do with that?"

She shook her head. "What did the letter say?"

"It linked Faye's death with the recent murders."

She laughed, which disconcerted him. It was the last response he would have expected.

"Faye wasn't murdered," she said.

"Why? How do you know? Did you see anything that night at Juniper Hall?"

She shook her head, but he thought that she did have things to say. She just didn't trust him.

"Faye wasn't murdered," she said. "No one there would have had the guts."

"How did you get mixed up in all that stuff?" he asked suddenly.

"A nice girl like me?"

"Don't be like that," he said. "I'm trying to understand."

173

And he wanted the moment to last. He liked the sound of her voice. The sense of intimacy, sitting side by side on the swings with only the kids to overhear. But half the squad was watching, he thought suddenly, glancing up at the old police station, imagining his colleagues crowded round the window, the obscene remarks, the gestures. Sod them, he thought. Let them think what they liked.

"Well?" he asked.

"They seemed to have all the answers," she said. "To be so certain. If you're mixed up yourself, that gives you something to hold on to."

"Who, exactly, are we talking about?"

"All of them, I suppose," she said. Then: "No. It's Magda really. She's the one who holds it all together. She was the one who attracted me in." She leaned forward. "Look," she said, "I'd screwed up everything. At home, at school. I suppose she gave me some confidence again. In the beginning I was like Faye. I thought they were all heroes."

"And now?"

She shrugged. "Just because I don't believe in heroes anymore doesn't mean I don't admire them, think they do good work."

"Did Faye lose faith, too?"

She did not answer.

"Well?" he demanded.

She shrugged. "We all have to grow up sometime."

"What does that mean?"

"Nothing," she said. "Nothing." Again he had the impression that she wanted to confide in him.

"I'm still grateful to them," she said suddenly. "For what they taught me."

"What was that?" he asked warily. He felt as he did when people come to the door talking about the Good News.

"Openness. Understanding." She pushed back on the swing. "I still remember the first group I went to. Magda was running it. We were working in pairs. I still remember my partner. He was a dentist. That seemed strange. I always thought dentists would be really straight."

"Like policemen," he said.

"Yeah. Like policemen. I found myself telling him things I'd never told anyone before in my life. About my father and my shitty mother and blokes I'd known. And suddenly I found myself bursting into tears."

It didn't sound a barrel load of fun, Hunter thought.

"You get close to people very quickly," she said. "I suppose it makes you vulnerable. . . . And you learn you've got to move on."

Hunter wanted to say something intelligent, but the words wouldn't come. At least with the Jesus freaks you could just slam the door.

They realised then that one of the boys had fallen and was crying. Lily went reluctantly to pick him up and dust the shavings from him.

"I'll have to go back," she said. "Get them some tea."

"Where's their mam?"

"She's gone into Otterbridge to see James McDougal."

"What would she do that for?" His voice was suddenly sharp.

"Nothing suspicious." She was laughing at him. "A gesture of sympathy, that's all. I'm not expecting her to be long."

She bundled the boys roughly into the buggy and fastened the straps.

"Do you want a hand up the hill with that?" Hunter said, imagining the gibes of his mates when he returned to the incident room if she agreed. "Never had you down as a family man, Gordon," they'd say. Sniggering.

"No," she said easily. "I can manage."

He walked with her to the edge of the park. There, their ways would separate.

"We're not just cranks, you know," she said.

"No," he said, unconvinced.

"Look," she said, "talk to Rebecca in the Alternative Therapy Centre. That might give you some idea what happened to Faye."

She walked on quickly, and though he called after her asking what she meant, she did not turn back.

Gloom had settled once more on the incident room. Ramsay was back and had reported in a clipped detached voice on the interview with Wes and Lorna. Hunter came in just in time and glowered silently for the rest of the day. The frustration was more than any of them could bear. They'd all had Sean Slater down as the murderer—the midnight wanderings, that crappy alibi, a feeling that he was really *weird*. Weirder than that crowd at the Old Chapel. Whatever you might think of *them*, at least they made a decent living. And Hunter was feeling ratty.

The phone went. A uniformed WPC took the call. She grinned at her friends and shouted to Hunter.

"I think you should take this one, Sarge."

"Why? What is it?"

"A witness. It might be important."

"Put it through, then," he said grudgingly.

He listened for a few minutes, grunted, then replaced the receiver.

"Very funny, Constable," he said.

"Who was it, Sarge?" They sensed a wind-up and they needed cheering up.

"A lunatic," he said. "Some poor bugger who's spent too long up here in the hills. He says he's just seen the ghost of Ernie Bowles in Mittingford High Street."

They all laughed and Hunter stomped out.

26

Hunter drove from the incident room to the Abbots' house. When Lily opened the door he was surprised but pleased to find her still there.

"Oh, it's you again," she said. The confiding mood had gone and she was prickly, bad-tempered. "What do you want now?"

"A few words," he said.

"I've nothing more to say to you. . . ." But she stood aside to let him in. "I've been giving the kids their tea. I expected Win back by now."

In the kitchen there was food on the floor and a smell of charred toast. A piece of mashed banana stuck to his shoe.

"I want to talk to Rebecca," he said, "like you said. But I need her address. Unless you want me to bother her at work."

He knew it was an excuse. Really he wanted to talk to her.

"No," she said quickly. "Don't do that. She lives with her parents in one of those modern bungalows up on the hill. I'm not sure of the number. It's got a blue gate. You'll find it easily enough."

"What's her surname?"

"Booth." She paused. "Look, perhaps I shouldn't have said anything. You mustn't blame me if this is all a waste of time."

They stood awkwardly. The children were suddenly quiet.

"It would be a lot simpler if *you* told me what's going on," he said.

She shook her head.

"I'd best go and talk to Rebecca, then," he said sharply. "She will be home by now?"

They looked at the hall clock. It was five-fifteen.

"I think she finishes at five, so she'll be back in the next few minutes."

When she saw him to the door he hesitated, but inside one of the children was crying and she slammed the door shut without a word.

In the car he swore out loud and wondered how he could have come to make such a bloody fool of himself. He'd go and see the girl anyway, he thought. See if he could salvage something from the afternoon. But a call came onto the radio summoning him back and he did not get to see Rebecca Booth that night.

James McDougal left school early again. At lunchtime he wandered down the drive with a gang of sixth-formers who were going to the chip shop, and just didn't bother going back. That afternoon was double English, which he usually enjoyed, but he knew he wouldn't be able to concentrate on *The Waste Land*. He had other things to think of.

He walked home along quiet suburban streets dappled with sunshine, lost in thought. In the house he drank a can of Coke and played some music, but he could not settle. On impulse he picked up the telephone and dialled the number he had found in the local paper. A voice on the other end of the line said, "Mittingford incident room." He hesitated for a moment, then replaced the receiver. He could have asked to speak to Ramsay, but what would he say? That his mother had become disillusioned with alternative medicine? So what?

A little later he left the house and began the walk to the cemetery to visit Faye, only because he could think of nothing else to do. He stopped, as usual, to buy flowers at the garage. He walked with his head bent and he did not look round. There was a big redbrick primary school on the main road which he had never really noticed before, because he'd always come at weekends, when it was quiet. Now it was home time and the pavement was crowded with parents. There were cars parked all the way back to the garage and on as far as the cemetery wall. A lollipop lady was shepherding children across the road. The girls wore red-and-white gingham dresses newly bought for the summer. They chased past James to find their mothers. Still he did not look behind him.

There was no sign of the flower seller at the cemetery gate. Her trestle table was still set up as normal, but it was empty except for an upturned bucket. James missed the confrontation with her and imagined her at home. She would live in a council house with a rottweiler in the garden and a brutish lover who drove a truck and had tattoos. He smiled briefly at the cartoon picture. What would his mother have thought of his prejudice? Then he walked in between the massive wrought-iron gates.

He had never known the cemetery so quiet. There was birdsong, but it seemed to come from the surrounding gardens. There were no joggers, no dog walkers, no other mourners. It was the hottest day of the year so far, and after the walk he felt drained of energy. He came to a bench which had been donated by an alderman of Otterbridge Town Council in 1961. He sat there and began to doze. A peacock butterfly settled on the wooden plank beside him. It was the last thing James saw.

James's body was found on the grass next to Faye's grave at five o'clock. The old man who had almost stumbled over it was quite sure of the time when Ramsay questioned him later. Five o'clock exactly. He was a retired railwayman and knew the importance of precision. He said he came to the cemetery every afternoon for a constitutional before his tea. Not to visit one of the graves. His parents were buried in Newcastle and his wife was still alive, thank God. They'd celebrated their golden wedding in February. No, he liked the cemetery because it was a quiet and pleasant place to walk.

179

Better than the main road with all those diesel fumes at any rate, and he wasn't one to be bothered by the thought of dead bodies. He'd been a stretcher bearer in the war.

"Did you touch the body?" Ramsay asked gently. They were standing by the cemetery gate. The whole area had been cordoned off. It was evening by now, and the place was in shadow.

"Aye. It was still warm. But then it was in the sun."

"Did you see anyone else in the cemetery? When you were out for your walk?"

The man thought.

"My eyesight's not what it was," he said. "Not long distance."

"But you think there might have been someone there?"

"I heard something," the man said. "Footsteps running. But not in the cemetery. Along the pavement on the other side of the wall. Just before I found the lad." He looked at Ramsay sadly. "I'm sorry," he said. "That's not much help. It could have been a kid, anyone."

"Did it sound like a child?" Ramsay asked.

"What do you mean?"

"A child would be lighter. Have smaller paces."

The old man considered again.

"So it would," he agreed. "No. You're right. It was an adult. In a hurry. Someone fit and not very heavy."

"It could have been a woman, then?"

"Aye, I suppose it could."

"Which way were they running? Back towards the town?" This time he was certain immediately.

"No, the other direction. North towards the dual carriageway."

"And the footsteps just faded away?"

"No," he said carefully. "There was a car. The footsteps stopped and there was the sound of an engine starting."

"Thanks," Ramsay said. "I'm sorry to have kept you hanging around for so long."

"I don't mind." He was a little, round-faced man, irrepressibly cheerful. "Beats mowing the lawn, which is what the wife would have had me doing. You did send someone round to explain where I was?"

"Of course."

"That's all right, then. She'll have had my tea ready for hours and I'm more scared of her than of any bloody corpse."

Hunter ducked under the red-and-white tape to join Ramsay. He'd been quiet since he'd arrived. Usually murder brought out the worst in him, made him loud and facetious. Ramsay wondered if the squad's teasing had got through to him.

"The lad wasn't killed where he was discovered," Hunter said. "They found his scuff marks in the grass where he was dragged to the Cooper girl's grave. Not very far, but you wonder why anyone should bother. It was risky enough anyway attacking him in broad daylight."

"Was he strangled?" Ramsay asked.

Hunter nodded. "With a thin nylon rope. Like his mother." He paused. "Win Abbot was coming to see him this afternoon."

"How do you know?"

Hunter paused again, embarrassed. "Lily Jackman told me. She was minding the Abbot bairns in the park. She gave me some information, not much, but a lead. She suggested we should talk to that young receptionist at the centre. I went to the Abbot house later, hoping for more details, on the off chance Jackman would still be there. She was pretty fed up because she'd been expecting Mrs. Abbot back sooner."

"At least that puts Lily Jackman in the clear," Ramsay said. "You must have been there around five?"

Hunter nodded. "Left at quarter past." He had made the point he had intended. Lily could have played no part in James McDougal's murder.

"She was baby-sitting when Val was killed, too," Ramsay said to himself. "I suppose that's a coincidence. . . ." He looked up. "What was Mrs. Abbot going to see the lad about?"

181

"Jackman said it was a gesture. Mrs. Abbot went to offer their sympathy."

"And a homoeopathic remedy to put it all right again, I suppose," Ramsay muttered under his breath.

"What was that, sir?"

"Nothing. This lot are starting to get on my nerves." He looked at his watch. It was gone seven, but still the day seemed unusually hot and airless.

"Track them all down," he said. "The Abbots, Magda Pocock. I've no idea where she's been all day. And someone had better see what Sean Slater's been up to. We know he's clear of the Bowles murder and he's unlikely to be involved here because he's got no transport, but we can't rule him out. The sooner it's done, the better."

Hunter nodded gloomily and walked away.

But later, when the information was put together, it seemed that none of them had a satisfactory alibi. Except Lily, of course, who'd been seen by Hunter.

Mrs. Abbot was jumpy and tense. She admitted, in a voice so low that he could hardly hear, that she had gone into Otterbridge intending to see James McDougal.

"What happened?" Hunter demanded.

"When I got to the house no one was in. I waited for quite a long time, thinking he might be on his way back from school, held up, you know, but at five o'clock I gave up and drove home."

"You sat outside the house for more than an hour?" Hunter was sceptical.

"I suppose I did," she said. "Actually I quite enjoyed it. The peace, you know. There's not a lot of that here."

Daniel Abbot said he had spent the afternoon in a private home for the elderly in Otterbridge. It was run by an enlightened matron who believed that complementary medicine had a place in work with old people. It was a regular commitment. He went once a month.

He was very happy to give Hunter the name of the nursing home, but was vague about the time he had left. Late afternoon, he said. He couldn't be more specific. He hadn't noticed the time. He'd finished treating his patients at about three, but he liked to stay on to chat to the residents. The old dears didn't see many new faces; some had no visitors at all. When pushed by Hunter, he said he thought it was at least five when he left. The residents had been given tea. He was sure of that.

But when his story was checked with the matron of the nursing home, she said that none of her staff had noticed Daniel after three-thirty. He could have been there, of course. It was a big building and he visited so often that he was almost part of the furniture, but no one could honestly remember seeing him.

Magda Pocock appeared to have disappeared into thin air. She was not in her flat and her car was missing. She had not been seen since early afternoon.

Ramsay decided to see Sean Slater himself. Hunter volunteered to visit Laverock Farm, but Ramsay told him to take a break. It had been quite a day.

He found himself unusually moved by the death of the boy. He rarely knew the victims of the crimes he investigated. He could remember James alive, imagine the conversation they had had in his bedroom, and that made a difference.

Lily was sitting on the kitchen step of the farm, her hands cupped around a mug of tea. She greeted him with amusement. "I haven't been able to get away from your lot today. What have I done now?"

"There's been another murder," he said.

She looked at him sharply. "Who?" There were no hysterics. She did not pretend to be shocked.

"James. James McDougal."

"No," she said quietly. "Not James." She stood up and clutched her arms around her body as if she were cold.

"Where's Sean?" he asked.

"He's in the garden," she said. "He's been there all day. I'll show you."

Sean had taken off his shirt and his shoulders were pink

183

from the sun. Lily led Ramsay through the gate in the wall, so at first he only saw her.

"I was going to call it a day," he said. "I'll be in now." There was a square of brown earth and a pile of weed and bramble. "Not much to show for a day's work, is it? I'll tell you one thing, I'm bloody unfit."

Then he saw Ramsay and put his hand above his eyes because he was looking directly into the setting sun. "Inspector. How can I help you?"

"James McDougal's been murdered," Lily said.

He thrust his spade in the earth and walked over to her. He put his arms around her and stroked her hair while she cried on his shoulder.

27

In the morning Ramsay gathered his team together in the incident room. They looked washed out and lethargic. James's death was like a personal insult. They knew that they'd been outwitted. They had no answers. The sun was shining again. There were no blinds at the windows and they squinted awkwardly against the light, waiting for the inspector to speak, not expecting too much.

Ramsay knew he should provide positive leadership. He had seen it done. A charismatic officer could pull together a team in minutes, make them believe in themselves again, send them away with renewed enthusiasm. But that had never been his style. He wasn't up to it.

He looked out at them. They sprawled across desks or in chairs tilted back against the wall. Hunter was perched on a windowsill with his feet on a filing cabinet and stared out towards the children's playground. In the last few days there had been none of the sarcasm, the deliberate attempts to undermine Ramsay's authority, which usually marked their relationship. Ramsay supposed he should be grateful, but Hunter's disengagement from the enquiry was beginning to worry him. It was another problem which would have to be sorted out by the end of the day.

He stood to speak. Sally Wedderburn flashed him a smile, not of encouragement but of pity.

He began by giving them the details of James's death in a flat, matter-of-fact voice.

"The boy was strangled between four-thirty and five. At four o'clock he was seen by a school crossing patrol in the road leading to the cemetery. Neither his father or his school friends knew that he was planning to visit the cemetery that day, so we must assume that neither did his murderer. The implications of that are obvious. . . ."

He paused and looked into blank, gum-chewing faces. The room was wreathed in cigarette smoke and dust. There was no response, so he continued.

"James must have been followed from his house. Either on foot or by car. The kids were just coming out of Otterbridge Primary School. Parents were waiting for them. That means there were lots of witnesses. It gives us something to work on. Sally, I want you outside the school at home time today. Talk to the mums. Take a photo of James. Was there a car travelling particularly slowly? A pedestrian nobody recognised?"

She nodded.

"James was strangled several metres from where he was found. He'd been sitting on a bench. The ground was dusty and the footprints of his trainers were quite distinctive. Then he was dragged to Faye Cooper's grave and left to lie there. Any ideas why?"

There was a silence. A hand was raised at the back of the room. It was Newell, an ex–public schoolboy and graduate entrant whom no one could quite take to. He had an army haircut and a Home Counties accent. The general opinion was that he was a pompous prat. It didn't help that he came from the south and knew nothing about football. Ramsay felt some sympathy for Newell but knew that to intervene would only make matters worse.

"To make a point, sir."

"What sort of a point?"

"Well, sir, if the murders are motivated by revenge—for Faye's death—there would be more satisfaction in making a

186

show of it. There's always an element of ritual in revenge, isn't there?"

He might be an arrogant young sod, Ramsay thought, but he was brighter than most of them.

"That's certainly possible," he said. "Any other explanations for moving the body?"

"Someone's trying to piss us about." It was Hunter, contemptuous. "Like that anonymous letter. All the evidence is that the girl's death was accidental. It's an attempt to distract us and waste our time."

"Why would anyone do that?"

"To lead us up the bloody garden path."

"I think it might have been to divert us from the real motive," Ramsay said. "But we can't ignore Faye. Even if the letter and the moving of James's body is some sort of elaborate game, it's significant. The murderer must have known her, known that there was some uncertainty about her drowning, so we'd waste time investigating it."

"Are you saying that the murderer was at Juniper Hall?" Hunter said abruptly.

"Either that or he was close to someone who *was* there. It narrows the field, doesn't it?" He paused, turned back to Hunter. "Didn't you say you had more information on Faye Cooper?"

"It's not much," Hunter said reluctantly. "A hint, that's all. Lily Jackman suggested that I talk to young Rebecca, the lass who does the clerical work in the Alternative Therapy Centre. I thought I'd catch her at dinnertime. Apparently she usually goes home. . . ."

Ramsay nodded his agreement.

"We need the Abbots' alibis checked again. Properly checked. Talk to the McDougals' neighbours. Was Mrs. Abbot's car really there as long as she claims? And what about another strange car? If James was followed to the cemetery, the murderer must have been hanging around somewhere. It was a fine day. People will have been in their gardens. It's an area full of retired people and housewives. There will have been folks about."

187

He sensed that the mood in the room was changing slightly. It wasn't quite optimistic. But they started to realise there might be a way forward.

"I'll talk to Magda Pocock," Ramsay said. He knew Magda was important. He saw her as a big spider who had attracted them all into her web. Trapped them and controlled them.

"Above all we need publicity," he said. "The murderer didn't get to Laverock Farm and the McDougal house on a magic carpet. Someone must have seen him, seen his vehicle. We'll prepare a request for information and try and get it on the television tonight."

They began to file out of the room. Not enthusiastically. But at least with a sense of purpose.

Rebecca Booth clip-clopped up the hill in a pair of platform sandals which she'd bought with last week's wages. Hunter, sitting in a car outside her parents' house, watched her. When he was young he'd made stilts from cans and pieces of string, and he thought she looked as if she were balancing on those. Otherwise she was smartly dressed in a sleeveless black pinafore dress and a white blouse. It could have been a school uniform. She looked that young.

The house was a small detached bungalow with big plate-glass windows and wood cladding on the gable, which had been built in the sixties. There was a steep terraced garden with little stone walls separating immaculate lawns. She let herself into the bungalow, opening the door with a key. Hunter hoped that meant both her parents were out. If he knew anything about young girls, she'd say nothing in front of them.

He rang the bell. She opened it nervously, just a crack. She'd been well brought up. Told not to talk to strangers.

"Oh," she said, relieved. "It's you. You're the policeman."

She opened the door wide to let him in and he saw that she was barefoot and there were plasters on her heels.

"Are your mum and dad in?" he asked.

"No. Dad's working. He's the postmaster." She was proud.

"Mum's a community nurse. She usually works evenings, but she's gone into Newcastle shopping. For my sister's wedding." She blushed. "You don't want to hear all this. . . ."

"Do you always come home for your dinner?" he asked. It wasn't far. A ten-minute walk up the hill, but this was her first job, you'd think she'd want a bit of independence.

"Yes," she said. "Mum gets a bit lonely on her own all day. . . ." It sounded lame, like an excuse.

"Is that the only reason?" he asked.

He'd followed her into the kitchen. Her mother had left her a tray. A plate of sandwiches covered with clingfilm, a packet of crisps, a slice of homemade cake.

She blushed again and did not answer. "Do you mind if I get on with this? I don't have long. . . ." She made him a mug of instant coffee, offered him a sandwich, hoped perhaps that he'd forgotten the question.

"Well?" he said, quite gently. "Is that the only reason?"

She shook her head and he saw that there were tears in her eyes. "I don't like it at the centre when there are no patients," she said. "It's nice to get away."

"Why don't you like it? They all seem very pleasant."

"Mrs. Pocock's all right," she said. "She's kind. But she's not always there."

"What's happened?" he asked.

"It's Mr. Abbot," she said, in a rush. "At first I thought he was just being friendly, making me feel welcome. You know."

"But it wasn't just that?"

She shook her head. "It's the way he looks at me," she said. "And he always tries to be on his own with me." She turned away. "He touches me. Wandering hands, you know."

The phrase was strangely prim and he was moved. "Couldn't you tell anyone?" Hunter said. "That's sexual harassment." Listen to me, he thought. I never believed anyone'd catch me saying that. "Couldn't you tell Mrs. Pocock?"

"I was frightened I'd lose my job," she said. "I was so pleased to get it." She hesitated. She was desperate to explain. "My sister's training to be a nurse," she said. "She was always brighter than me. Took A Levels. I was never much good at school. Mum and Dad wanted me to stay on into the sixth form. I did the first year, but I couldn't face exams. I've never stood up for myself much, but I stuck out for getting a job. In the end they said if I found one I could leave. When I got taken on at the Old Chapel at Easter, I was over the moon. I was determined to make a go of it."

"What about your parents?" Hunter said. "Couldn't you explain to them?"

"It would have been like admitting I was wrong," she said. "It's not that they'd be horrid about it. They're dead nice. But that's part of the problem. I'd feel that I was letting them down."

"Of course," Hunter said.

"I don't know what to do," she said, her eyes brimming with tears.

"You did talk to someone about this, didn't you?"

She nodded.

"Lily," she said. "The girl who works in the health-food shop. I met her in the café and she asked me how I was getting on, if I was enjoying it. She seemed almost to have guessed that there was a problem, so it was easier to tell her."

"And what did Lily say?"

"That I should tell someone. She asked if I wanted her to tell Mrs. Pocock. I made her promise not to. What would Mrs. Pocock think? Mrs. Abbot's her daughter." She hesitated. "She might think I'd been leading him on."

"What else did Lily say?"

"That I mustn't take it personally. It had happened before. He just fancied young girls."

"When did it happen before?" Hunter asked.

"They had a girl working for them in the house. Her name was Faye. Lily said you could tell Mr. Abbot was letching after her all the time she was working there, though Faye never noticed. She was too innocent, Lily said. Too naive. He didn't try anything on then because she had a boyfriend.

Peter Richardson. He went to school with my sister. Do you know him?"

Hunter nodded.

"Lily said Mr. Abbot was frightened of Peter. He knew he'd not stand him mucking about with Faye. He's known for his temper. He had a scrap with Ernie Bowles once. But then she stopped going out with him and Lily said Mr. Abbot was all over her."

"Lily saw that?"

Rebecca nodded. "They went away together. All of them. On some sort of course. Apparently it happened then." She shivered again slightly. "They're planning another course," she said. "Mr. Abbot wants me to go. . . ."

"Of course you won't go," Hunter said. "And you must speak to someone. If it's happened before, there's proof that you're not making it up."

"No," she cried, and he realised at last just why she was so frightened. "Don't you see, there's no proof! Faye's dead. They said it was an accident, but I can't help wondering. . . . Perhaps she threatened to tell someone. . . . I'm worried that the same thing will happen to me."

Ramsay had spent the morning trying to pin down Magda Pocock. She was at work and she spoke to him eventually on the telephone, but she seemed reluctant to see him.

"I have patients all morning," she said. "Actually, you've interrupted me now."

"I'll come at lunchtime, then," he said.

"No. There's someone I have to meet for lunch."

There was a brief silence, and she seemed to reach a conclusion. "I'll come to you," she said. "In the incident room. Fourish? Would that be convenient?"

And he had to leave it at that.

28

"*The* way I see it," Hunter told Ramsay, "that gives us a motive."

They were sitting in the back room of the pub. It was three o'clock and even the public bar was quiet. They were on their own. If they wanted a drink, they had to call through to the landlord, who shuffled in with poor grace to serve them.

"Daniel Abbot tried it on with Faye at Juniper Hall. Perhaps it wasn't a serious assault, but nasty, unwanted. She trusted him, and if he'd called her into his room, she'd have gone without question. Or if he'd suggested a walk by the pool or a midnight swim. She strikes me as having more fight in her than Rebecca, who's a smashing lass but a timid little thing. I can see Faye throwing a wobbler, threatening to tell his wife or Mrs. Pocock. Even the press. They'd be onto the story like a ton of bricks. Wasn't there all that fuss a while back about a doctor who took advantage of his female patients when they were under hypnosis? They'd have a field day with an acupuncturist and nubile young girls. She wasn't a strong swimmer. We know that from the report, don't we? She panicked if she got out of her depth. So he just pushed her in the deep end and waited for her to die. There would be no way of proving it was anything but an accidental death."

He set his glass on the table triumphantly.

"It's certainly plausible," Ramsay said slowly. "But I don't quite see how that provides a motive for the recent murders. It might explain the attack on Val McDougal. She was at Juniper Hall. She knew Faye well and might have guessed what was going on. But Ernie and James weren't even there. And why after all this time?"

"I was wondering," Hunter said tentatively, "about blackmail." He was enjoying this talk. It was like the old days, just the two of them working together. He had his complaints about Ramsay's methods, but that didn't mean he wanted Sal Wedderburn and Rob Newell brownnosing in and taking his place.

Ramsay said nothing. He waited for Hunter to explain.

"Ernie Bowles seems to me a classic blackmailer," he said. "Always prying. You can imagine him listening at keyholes, reading other people's mail. Lily Jackman said he was always hanging round the caravan at one time. She certainly knew that Abbot fancied Faye—she told Rebecca as much. He could have overheard her discussing it with Slater, even speculating about murder. We know the farm was going down the tube. He was even considering holding a New Age festival to make some money. Perhaps he thought it would be easier to blackmail Daniel Abbot instead."

"It certainly fits in with his character." Ramsay's voice was bland. Hunter was slightly disappointed that he wasn't more enthusiastic. "What about Val McDougal and James? I'd hardly put them down as blackmailers."

"Of course not," Hunter said crossly, "but she was there, wasn't she? She might have stumbled across them, worked out what was going on. After Abbot killed Bowles, perhaps he wanted to make certain that no one could try it on again."

"Perhaps," Ramsay said. "And James?"

"As I see it," Hunter said, "by this time Abbot's in a state of complete panic. He's not thinking properly. . . ."

Ramsay pictured his last interview with the sleek and charming Abbot and thought that he'd hardly seemed panic-stricken. He said nothing.

"He hears that we've received an anonymous letter linking

Faye's death with the murders. Who could have sent it? If Val was the only person who saw him with Faye at Juniper Hall, it must have been James. Everyone knew how close they were. Val would have told James everything. To be absolutely certain that his secret was safe, he'd have to kill James."

He drained the last Vaux Bitter from his glass. "Well?" he demanded. "What do you think?"

"I think it's the best theory we've got so far," Ramsay said.

Well, Hunter thought, talk about damning with faint praise.

"What do you think we should next?" Ramsay asked.

"Pull in Daniel Abbot and see what he's got to say for himself."

"I'm not sure," Ramsay said slowly, "that would be wise at this stage. It's all speculation just now. We've no proof. We need something to fix Daniel at the murder scene. His car. A witness. He's a clever bastard. Smooth. We'd never get him to confess. And even if we did, these days that wouldn't be a lot of use in court without corroboration."

"What then?"

"Mrs. Abbot has given him an alibi for the night of the attack on Val McDougal. They were supposed to be at a lecture together in Otterbridge College. If we could persuade her to admit that he slipped away for a while, it would be a start—"

"Do you want me to see her?" Hunter was on his feet, ready to go.

Ramsay hesitated, tried to be tactful.

"Do you think we should leave it to Sal? She took the original statement and Mrs. Abbot's nervy. We don't want her hysterical."

"Job for a woman, then, you think?" He sank back into his chair.

Ramsay nodded. "I would like you to talk to Lily Jackman again. Though she obviously feels a certain loyalty to the Abbots. She's kept quiet all this time, after all. But the fact that she sent you off to Rebecca Booth must mean that she's not happy with Abbot's behaviour. You might be able to persuade her to talk to you."

Hunter never walked anywhere unless he couldn't help it. Walking was for the woodentops and he'd left that behind long ago. But now, when he came out of the pub, he decided to walk to the Old Chapel, where he presumed Lily Jackman would be working.

He tried to drag all his prejudices to the top of his mind. He thought of the New Age travellers who'd stoned the police keeping them from Stonehenge. They were all the same, he thought. They smoked dope, lived like animals, crapping where the fancy took them. Hunter, who had been known to drive forty miles out of his way to find a public convenience rather than piss behind a tree, shuddered at the thought.

He walked through the restaurant to the health-food shop. The heavy smell of spices and yeast and garlic turned his stomach. He told himself he couldn't live with that all day. The restaurant was empty. The staff recognised him and nodded, not in an unfriendly way, but ironically, as if they could never allow their relationships with the police to be straightforward. At the door he paused and looked for Lily. He felt suddenly nervous. He thought she must be some sort of witch. No one else had ever affected him like this. Still flustered, he went into the shop.

The anaemic boy with the shaved head was on duty. He, too, recognised Hunter, but he did not let on.

"Yes?" he said carelessly.

"I'm looking for Miss Jackman," Hunter said.

"She's not here," the boy said. He had on a long, bleached apron tied at the back and reminded Hunter of a mortuary assistant.

"Where is she?"

"How would I sodding know? It's her day off."

So Hunter walked back to the police station, picked up one of the pool cars, and drove to Laverock Farm. He parked in the yard beside Ernie Bowles's old Land Rover. He opened the car door and swivelled in his seat to pull on the Wellingtons he'd had the sense to bring with him.

Lily was hanging washing on a line in the farmhouse back garden. He stood for a moment, looking at her, before she realised he was there.

"Making yourself at home," he said sarcastically.

"We've had permission to stay in the house," she said quickly.

"Where's lover boy?"

"I thought they taught you manners these days," she snapped.

"Sorry." He walked towards her. "Sorry . . ."

"Sean's gone up to Long Edge Farm to talk to Stan Richardson."

"What for?"

"I don't know. Something to do with the farm, I suppose. He was talking about getting some hens again."

She picked up the plastic laundry basket and walked into the house. He followed her. The kitchen was even more untidy than when Ernie Bowles had lived there. A mound of dirty plates was piled in the draining board and a box of washing powder stood on the windowsill. There was a smell of stale joss sticks. A candle stood in a bottle in the middle of the table and wax had dripped onto the surface.

"Why do you live like this?" he demanded before he could help himself.

"And how do *you* live?" she spat back. "In a nice tidy semi, on a nice tidy estate, with a nice tidy wifey to cook your meals?"

He grinned. "With my mam in a council house."

"So you're a mummy's boy," she said. But her anger had dispersed. He felt she was teasing him.

"No," he said. "It's just convenient."

She made instant coffee in grubby mugs. There was no milk or sugar.

"I did as you suggested," he said. "I went to see Rebecca Booth."

"Did you?" She seemed awkward. "A nice kid, isn't she?"

"Too nice to be messed around by Daniel Abbot."

196

"She told you, then? I wasn't sure she would." She stood up, rinsed her mug under the tap.

"Why didn't you tell me about him and Faye Cooper before?" Hunter demanded.

"I didn't think it was relevant," she said. "I still don't. Not to the murders. But Rebecca shouldn't have to put up with that every day. No one should."

"Has Daniel tried it on with you?" he asked suddenly.

She gave a laugh. "Of course not. I'm too old. And I've got a boyfriend. Daniel always makes sure his victims are unattached. He might look tough, but he's a coward."

"What happened that weekend at Juniper Hall?" Hunter asked.

"I'm not sure. He was pretty discreet. But on the Saturday evening I found Faye in tears in the ladies'. She blamed herself. She was scared Win would find out."

"What did you say?"

"That he was just a dirty middle-aged man and she should stand up to him. She wouldn't have done, though. She'd just been dumped by Peter Richardson and she'd lost all her confidence. She was in no state to stand up to anybody."

"Are you sure?"

"What do you mean?"

"Are you sure she didn't threaten to tell his wife, or Mrs. Pocock, or the press? Are you sure he didn't drown her to keep her quiet?"

"Of course he didn't drown her!" Lily's voice was emphatic. "I don't like him any more than you do, but he wouldn't have done that. He's a healer."

There was a moment of silence. In the hall Cissie Bowles's clock began to chime.

"Did Ernie Bowles know about Mr. Abbot's habit of harassing young girls?" Hunter asked.

"I shouldn't think so. How could he?"

"You said he was a snoop."

"He was that, all right. Made it his business to know everyone's business. But I can't see how he could have found out about that."

"You didn't tell him?"

"Of course not."

"Did he have any reason to go to the Alternative Therapy Centre?"

"When Cissie could still get about he used to take her in the Land Rover for her acupuncture treatment. He used to sit in the waiting room while she saw Mr. Abbot. I suppose he could have overheard something, but Faye wouldn't have been around then."

"And when Cissie was bedridden?"

"She was taking some homoeopathic remedies prescribed by Win. Ernie collected the tablets from the centre. I offered to get them for him, but he seemed to like going himself."

She returned to the table and sat down again, opposite to him. He thought she seemed unusually restless. He could tell that her concentration was wandering.

"We think Ernie could have been a blackmailer," he said, hoping to hold her attention. "Did he ever try to blackmail you?"

She laughed. "What would be the point? I've no reputation to lose anyway."

"But he would be capable of it?"

"Oh," Lily said, "he'd be capable of anything. We all are, aren't we? In the right circumstances. Put under enough stress."

"What do you mean?"

She paused. He had the impression that she was weighing him up, deciding how far she could trust him, wondering even if she should ask him for help. She seemed about to speak when the door opened and Sean Slater walked in.

"This is very cosy," he said. He stood in the doorway with the sun behind him, breathing heavily as if he'd been running. Something had annoyed him. He was spoiling for a fight, but Hunter had just enough sense not to be provoked. He knew Lily Jackman wouldn't be impressed by fisticuffs anyway.

"I'm just asking Miss Jackman a few questions," Hunter said.

"I thought you'd be leaving us alone now," Slater said. "You found my friends in the blue Transit, didn't you? You know we couldn't have killed James McDougal. So why do you keep tormenting us?"

"I'm not tormenting you," Hunter explained reasonably. And you'd soon know about it if I was, he thought. "I'm asking for information."

"Or is there another reason for your interest?" Sean said nastily. "Another reason for you sniffing around here all the time?"

Hunter pretended not to understand. He stood up and walked out of the house. Slater leaned against the frame of the door and watched until his car was out of sight.

29

W_{in} Abbot had been crying. She pretended at first not to be in. Sally Wedderburn rang the doorbell over and over again, but there was no reply. She could have given up and gone back to the station. Why should she always be the one to deal with nervy women anyway? But she was too persistent for that. An alley at the end of the terrace led into a footpath which ran along the back of all the gardens. Beyond that there was open hillside: bracken and sheep-grazed grass. Most of the gardens had a gate onto the footpath. The Abbots had stiff bolts, presumably to prevent the children from escaping. Sally gave up trying to shift them and climbed over. She pulled a thread on the pair of Benetton trousers she'd bought in the sales, but was rewarded by a glimpse of Win's terror-stricken face at the kitchen window.

"Mrs. Abbot!" she called, knocking on the kitchen door. "Please let me in."

Win must have made an effort to pull herself together, because when she opened the door she was red-eyed but calm.

"I'm sorry," she said. "I had the radio on. I didn't hear the bell."

"Could I come in for a while?"

"I don't know. It's not very convenient."

"There are just a few points to clear up about the acupuncture lecture," Sally said.

Don't confront her about her husband, Ramsay had told

Sally. We don't want to scare him off. That can come later. Don't ask her anything about Juniper Hall. Nothing tricky. Get her confidence and stick to the lecture in the college. See if you can break the alibi.

"You'd better come in, then," Win said, as if she wasn't really bothered after all.

The lunch things were still on the table. There were cartons of hummus and olives, half a quiche, a tub of salad. Most was untouched. It seemed Win hadn't had much of an appetite. It looked as if everything had been bought specially. Not the sort of snack a woman would rustle up for her and the kids. Win saw Sally looking at the table.

"Magda was here for lunch," she said. "My mother, you know. She brought the food. The restaurant at the Old Chapel do a carryout service, if you're hungry just help yourself. . . ."

Sally shook her head. She wondered what the meal had been about. Some sort of peace offering perhaps.

"Where are the boys?" she asked.

"Upstairs having a nap. I couldn't face their noise today."

She had a feverish burst of activity, cleaning plates, snapping lids onto plastic cartons, then stopped, quite suddenly, before the job was finished. Sally thought she was close to the breaking point. It was just as well, she thought, that they hadn't sent Hunter. He'd push her right over the edge.

"Are you married?" Win Abbot demanded.

Sally shook her head. "Thinking about it." She smiled. "Would you recommend it?"

"Yes," Win said very quickly. "Of course." She leaned forward across the table towards Sally. "I couldn't regret marrying Daniel. He's a great man, you know. He has a gift." Her eyes shone with fanaticism. "You can't expect gifted people to behave in ways we understand."

She knows her husband likes chasing young girls, Sally thought. And she's going to do nothing about it. Selfish bitch.

"I was very ill as a child," Win went on. "It took someone

201

like Daniel to make we well again. Now he's helping other people. It's worth making sacrifices to support him in that."

Sally did not know how to respond. "Hallelujah" might have been appropriate. Like in a Pentecostal church when someone's given witness.

"About the lecture . . ." she said.

"Yes?" Win said brightly.

"Perhaps you could take me through the evening again."

"Lily was baby-sitting. We drove to Otterbridge College. Daniel wanted to arrive early. He was making the introductory speech. He was with me all the time."

And even if he wasn't, Sally thought, you wouldn't let on.

Magda was late arriving and Ramsay was debating about whether he should go to fetch her when the man on the desk said she was there. "I'll be a quarter of an hour," he said. "Put her in an interview room." He wasn't usually into power games, but with Magda, he thought, he needed all the advantage he could get.

But when he saw her he thought he had misjudged the situation. She was subdued, uncertain. They had given her a mug of tea. His mug, he noticed immediately. One that Prue had given him. It was covered with painted pigs. Her idea of a joke. The interview room was taller than it was wide, and could once have been a cell. The bare stone walls had been covered with thick cream gloss paint. The window was very small, close to the ceiling, protected by wire mesh. Although it was a sunny afternoon, the room was gloomy and lit by an electric lightbulb hanging from a dangerous-looking flex. Magda, however, seemed not to notice her surroundings.

When he went in she stood up and held out her hand.

"Mrs. Pocock," he said, "we've been trying to talk to you. . . ."

"About the boy. I know."

"Where were you yesterday?" His voice was pleasant, only slightly curious.

"I went to Juniper Hall," she said. "I needed somewhere to think. It seemed fitting. There were no guests staying and the staff were very kind. They allowed me to walk in the gardens. It was quite late when I got back, and then Win phoned me and told me about James. I think I had decided to give you this anyway, but I couldn't keep quiet after that."

From her bag she took a notebook. It was A4 with hard covers, the sort which might be used in an office as a ledger.

"Faye Cooper's diary," he said.

"Yes. Faye's diary." She paused. "Don't expect too much, Inspector. I don't think it will solve your case for you. This hasn't been a conspiracy to protect a murderer. I really don't see that it can have anything to do with the attacks on Mr. Bowles or the McDougals. That's what I've been telling myself, you see. That's why I didn't come forward before. Then I thought you were an intelligent man. You would use the information wisely. And that any information, even of a negative kind, would be of use to you. Was my judgement correct?"

He nodded.

"Was Faye Cooper murdered?" he asked.

"No," she said. "Not . . . technically. Morally perhaps there was a responsibility, but nothing, I think, which would interest you. Nothing legal."

"She committed suicide?" he said.

"You guessed?" She was surprised, rather impressed.

"I thought it was a possibility."

"She committed suicide," Magda said. "It's quite certain. She makes her intention very clear in the diary. She wanted the record set straight."

"But it wasn't, was it? Not publicly at least. Because you stole the diary. Why did you do that?"

She shrugged heavily and he was reminded again that her mother had been a foreigner. "For a number of reasons," she said. "None of them were very well thought out."

"To protect Daniel?"

"Him? No. To protect my daughter perhaps. She must have guessed at his proclivities, but she would not admit it even to herself. Perhaps it was my fault. I brought her up to believe that those who can heal are special. She's still infatuated with him, at least the idea of him. I went to see her at lunchtime to show her the diary, to explain what I had to do. She wouldn't even read it. She had persuaded herself that he was just showing these young girls kindness. Perhaps when the story is out in the open, she will not find it possible to maintain the self-deception. I hope that is the case. I would like her to leave him. We could make a life for the children. . . ."

She paused and looked up at him.

"And then," she said, "I was protecting myself. I had a part in the girl's death, too."

"Tell me what happened," Ramsay said. "I'll read the diary, of course, but I'd like to hear it from your point of view."

She sat back in her chair and shut her eyes.

"It was such a hot weekend, Inspector, and such a beautiful place. The leaves had started to change colour, but otherwise you'd think it was high summer. The . . . tone of these weekends is usually set very quickly, depending on the people who are there, how they respond to each other. On that occasion it was affected, too, by the weather. Everything seemed feverish, sultry, highly charged. You understand what I mean?"

"I think so."

"You will see from the diary that on the Friday night Daniel invited Faye Cooper to go with him for a walk. She went without question. She was a lovely girl, no parents to speak of, no boyfriend. If anything Daniel was for her a father figure. I'm not sure precisely what happened on that walk, the diary is not specific. An unwanted advance at least. A forced kiss. Perhaps something more serious . . ." She hesitated again, sat more upright.

"You can see how that would have affected her, Inspector. She had invested all her hope for the future in the practitioners at the centre. We were her friends and her family. She was unbalanced anyway. You can understand why she took the option of suicide. She looked forward to a life of loneliness—"

"But she didn't kill herself that night?"

"No. It was the following night. The Saturday."

"You say that you feel responsible in part for her death. Why was that?"

"On the Saturday afternoon I was leading a session. Voice Dialogue. It's a form of therapy I've trained in. Faye Cooper was there, taking part. The others were all in pairs, so I worked with her myself."

"She told you what had happened?"

"Using one of her voices. Her victim voice. Yes."

"You were acting as facilitator. What did you say?"

"Nothing during the session, I just asked Faye's victim voice questions so that she could more easily understand that part of herself. Afterwards, though—I don't know why, I think it was own sense of frustration for her—I suggested that she had a responsibility to take charge of her life. Blaming others for her situation would do her no good."

"You blamed her for what had happened?"

"No!" she said. "Of course not. I wanted to give her the strength to prevent it from happening again. But I can see that she might have taken it that way." She paused. "Yes, if you look in the diary, you will see that she blames herself. She writes: 'Magda thinks it was all my fault.' "

"How did she seem after the session?"

"Quiet. Listless. That's not unusual. It can be draining."

"She had a meal with you?"

"Yes. I never saw her again. She wasn't at the talk after supper. She went upstairs. I presumed that she'd gone to help Win with the children, though later Win said that she hadn't seen her. She must have been in her room, writing her diary. Then, when the house was quiet, she went to the pool and drowned herself."

She sat upright, very still.

"Did Daniel know you'd taken the diary from Faye's room?"

"Yes. But he never read it. He did not know what it contained."

"Why did you keep it all this time?"

"It would be wrong, I thought, to destroy it." She pushed the diary towards him and across the table in a gesture of relinquishing all rights to it.

"You see, Inspector, it's not so very exciting after all. Not so very important. There is no motive for murder here. Only the story of a sad young girl whose ideals had been shattered and who could not face going on without them. Perhaps now you can leave Faye in peace. Her death has no relevance to your enquiries."

She stood up to leave. At the door she stopped and turned back.

"Will you be talking to Daniel about these matters, Inspector?"

"Oh yes," Ramsay said. "We'll have to do that."

"Good," she said. "Good. I hope you scare him."

She gave a quick smile at his surprised face and left.

When she had gone he remained in the interview room to read Faye's diary. There'd be no peace in the incident room. Sally Wedderburn and Hunter would be back vying for his attention.

It was all as Magda had said. There was no doubt that Faye had committed suicide. There had been no trick with forgeries, no elaborate lie. The same handwriting had been used throughout, the same confused and unhappy voice described her disillusionment with Daniel Abbot as noted her rejection by Peter Richardson.

And yet, Ramsay thought, in one way Magda was wrong. Faye's death *was* relevant to his enquiries. He was beginning to understand the connections. He saw the case as the symmetrical patterns of a kaleidoscope, a series of mirror images like the warm-up exercises Magda Pocock got her students to perform. He was groping towards a solution.

30

They left a skeleton team in the incident room to man the phones. The rest decamped to the pub, where they persuaded the landlord to move a television into the private bar. There they gathered around to watch Ramsay appear live on the local news. The press conference was taking place in the entrance hall of the old police station. It was packed with journalists from all the local papers and some of the nationals, besides TV and radio. Usually Ramsay avoided that sort of publicity, but today he had volunteered.

Sniggering, the team in the pub watched him begin his spiel. He said he needed specific information. The McDougals lived in Ferndale Avenue in Otterbridge. Did anyone see an unfamiliar car parked in that street between eight-thirty and ten P.M. on Monday, May the tenth? He was interested, too, in Ferndale Avenue on a more recent date, the previous afternoon. Perhaps the same vehicle had been seen? Did anyone notice the driver of these cars, or see anyone behaving at all unusually in the vicinity of number 32?

The detectives in the pub waited for him to ask for information about vehicles seen near Laverock Farm, but Ernie Bowles was not mentioned at all.

Ramsay continued: "We're planning a reconstruction of James's walk from the high school to his home, and then on to the cemetery tomorrow. Officers will be in position all along the route to jog memories and ask questions. I'm sure you'll be cooperative. In the meantime, will any member of the public who feels they can help call the Mittingford incident room."

There was a shouted question from a crumpled, middle-aged man at the back of the room.

"I can take it, Inspector, that you're looking for one culprit for all three murders?"

"I'm not prepared to rule anything out at this stage."

A young reporter from Radio Newcastle, with hair cropped so short that she looked like a baby seal, raised her hand, thrust a microphone towards him.

"Yes?" Ramsay said.

"I understand that you've been investigating another death connected with Mittingford Alternative Therapy Centre," she said in a clear voice. "Can you confirm that?"

Ramsay was obviously thrown for a moment.

"We have been following many lines of enquiry," he said, noncommittally. "So far none of the leads have been particularly encouraging."

"Is it true that the person in question was a young girl called Faye Cooper, who drowned last year at a hotel in Cumbria? The inquest verdict was accidental death, but you believe there may have been foul play."

The room was hushed, waiting for his reply.

"I'm sorry," he said, "I'm not prepared to answer that question."

"Why didn't he just deny it?" Hunter shouted to the assembled gathering in the pub. "I said all along someone was trying to piss us about. We know now that the poor kid killed herself." He fancied *himself* on the television. His mam would love it. She'd get all the neighbours in to watch.

In the police station the cameras were switched off and the reporters began to gather up their equipment. Ramsay approached the young woman from Radio Newcastle who was checking her tape.

"Where did you get that information about Faye Cooper?" he asked. "From her mother?"

"No," the reporter said. "At least I don't think so." She looked up sharply, smelling a story. "Why? Is it important?"

"It could be."

"There was a phone call to the newsroom this morning. Anonymous. No proof, of course, but I thought I'd just give it a whirl, see what response I got."

"Was the caller male or female?"

"I don't know," she said. "I didn't take it myself. I can probably find out for you if you like. Give you a ring here later this evening."

"Please," he said. Then: "There's no truth in the story, you know. It's not worth following up."

"Why didn't you say that on air?"

Ramsay did not reply. He was not quite sure himself.

When the team trooped back to the incident room, the phones were already starting to ring. Ramsay stood by his desk, accepting the cheers and the backhanded compliments.

"You didn't do bad, sir, even if you're not the prettiest thing that's been on the telly this week."

"At least you didn't fall off the platform like that DCI at the press call in Newcastle."

"Well, Gordon?" he asked as Hunter came in. "What did you think?"

"I was wondering why you didn't scotch the story that Faye Cooper was murdered." It was Hunter in his most truculent mood, graceless and offensive.

"I think," Ramsay said, "I wanted to keep the murderer guessing."

Hunter was not going to give his boss the satisfaction of asking what that meant. He mooched on towards his desk. The inspector called him back.

"Can I have a word? I've got a job for you." Something you'll enjoy, he thought. Something that's right down your street.

"What is it?" Hunter asked.

"Let's get out of here, shall we? I could do with some fresh air. I've been stuck in this place all day."

"If you say so," Hunter said rudely. "You're the boss."

Ramsay led him down the path to the children's playground by the river. They sat on the bench. There were two teenagers, a boy and a girl, standing on the swings, talking shyly, but when they saw the policemen they disappeared.

"Perhaps they recognised you from the telly, sir," Hunter said snidely. "You must be famous."

Ramsay said nothing, though of course all the town knew who they were by now. They didn't need the television for that.

"What do you want me to do, like?"

"Talk to Daniel Abbot," Ramsay said. "It seems clear now that the girl committed suicide and the diary's too vague for us to charge him with sexual assault. But let him know that we're onto him. Make it clear that if anything of that sort happens again, we'll be down on him like a ton of bricks."

Hunter was staring across the river and did not answer immediately. Ramsay was surprised by the lack of enthusiasm. Usually Hunter jumped at the chance to intimidate.

"Scare him away from Rebecca Booth, you mean," the sergeant said at last.

"Aye," Ramsay said. "If you can."

"Oh, I can manage that, all right." But there was no real pleasure in the thought.

They sat in silence.

"Are you all right?" Ramsay asked tentatively.

"What d'ya mean?" Hunter demanded aggressively.

Ramsay shrugged. "You don't seem yourself. I wondered if something was bothering you."

Hunter frowned, did not answer directly.

"Do you mind if I ask you something, sir?"

"Go on."

"Do you think there's anything in this alternative medicine crap?"

Ramsay was amused but knew better than to show it.

"I'm not sure. I suppose I try to keep an open mind."

"I was wondering, y'kna, if I was missing out on something. Personal growth. Isn't that what they call it? Finding out about yourself." He looked at Ramsay earnestly.

"You seem to have survived without it," Ramsay said.

"But I just can't see it working!" Hunter went on. "Needles in the hand to cure headaches. Energy forces in the body. And that rebirthing—lying on your back for an hour, just breathing. That's all bullshit, isn't it?"

"It's not illegal," Ramsay said, "which is all that concerns us at present."

But he could see that more than that concerned Hunter. Oh my God, Ramsay thought. He's fallen for the girl.

Lily Jackman was thinking about Hunter, too. When she and Sean had first moved into the Laverock farmhouse, they had stayed in the kitchen. They put their sleeping bags on the floor each night to sleep and they washed in the sink. After all, they had come into the kitchen when Ernie was alive. They were more comfortable there. The rest of the house had seemed out-of-bounds.

Later, however, they took the place over. They even slept upstairs, in the room that had once been Cissie Bowles's. It still smelled faintly of the moxa herb used in acupuncture and there were pots of homoeopathic remedies on the huge Victorian dressing table. And in the evenings they went into Cissie Bowles's lounge, with the grandfather clock and scratched leather chairs, and watched the television. They were sitting there, eating beans on toast from a tray, when the police press conference came on.

"Isn't that the policeman?" Sean said. "Not the one that's been sniffing round you all week. His boss."

He switched the sound up, motioned to her to be quiet until it had finished. When it was over he seemed pleased with himself.

"Sean," she said, "I've been thinking. . . ."

Something in her voice made him turn round sharply. "What?" he demanded.

"I wanted to ask you. . . ." she said, then her voice trailed away. "Oh, it's nothing. Probably it's nothing."

211

At Long Edge Farm the Richardsons were watching the local television news while they were finishing their evening meal. Mrs. Richardson had made a venison stew, braised in brown ale. She still had plans to open a restaurant at the farm for visitors and she'd been practising. She thought the food should have a local flavour.

"What do you think?" she said to Stan.

"It's all right," he said grudgingly. "At least there's meat in it."

Because she had taken to cooking vegetarian meals, in preparation for when the Abbots took over Laverock Farm. They might pick up quite a few customers from there, she thought. She felt very optimistic about it.

"Look," she said, "there's Inspector Ramsay on the television." She giggled. "Doesn't he look dishy!" She still used words like that. "Dishy" and "smashing" and "jolly good show." It was as if she were stuck as a schoolgirl in the early sixties. Nothing could shake her enthusiasm, not even her husband's indifference. She turned to her son, who had been eating, steadily and silently. "You never did tell me what he wanted the other day, Peter."

"You've never been here to ask," he said.

"I *have* been busy," she said complacently, knowing that it was only her effort which was keeping the farm together.

Stan Richardson pushed his plate away from him. His attention was still on the television. He watched the young reporter ask her questions about Faye Cooper, saw Ramsay's awkwardness, the noncommittal reply.

"Didn't you know a lass called Faye a while back?" he asked his son.

"So what?" Peter said defiantly.

"Nothing. I just wondered if it was the same girl, that's all."

"Why should I care? I moved on from that ages ago."

He slammed his plate on the draining board.

"Can I borrow your car tonight?" he asked his mother.

"Of course, pet," she said, absentmindedly finishing the last of her meal.

"It's about time you got a car of your own!" Stan shouted after him as he left the room. "I pay you enough. It's about time you stood on your own two feet!"

Magda Pocock did not possess a television, so she did not see Ramsay's appeal for information. The inspector saw her, silhouetted against the lighted, sloping window of her flat when he went back to the pub to phone Prue. He would be working for most of the night and he needed a break. From Hunter, as much as anything, who was still self-absorbed and short-tempered. Even a successful interview with Daniel Abbot had failed to cheer him up, though he described it with a gloomy satisfaction.

"I had him snivelling like a bairn," Hunter said. "He blamed it all on the lass, of course. Said she overreacted to a simple gesture of friendship. But we'll have no trouble from him again."

Magda moved her head, her hands, her feet in slow, fluid movements. Ramsay stood in the street and watched her. She could not see him because it was almost dark. Besides, her concentration was complete. Tai chi, he thought. Weren't Chinese parks full of elderly men at dawn, performing the same sort of actions? What could they hope to get out of it?

There must be something positive. Even the cynical Hunter was wondering if he was missing out.

Ramsay walked on up the street, and when he turned back to look at the Old Chapel, Magda was sitting perfectly still, in some form of meditation. Perhaps he should give it a go, he thought. Because he had the feeling that he now had all the information he needed to draw the enquiry to a conclusion, and if he was sufficiently focused and concentrated, he could come to an answer.

Prue answered the phone immediately, so he thought she'd probably had an early night. Often she worked in bed. He could imagine her there, surrounded by books and scripts, a bottle of wine on the bedside table, a packet of chocolate biscuits.

"Saw you on the telly tonight," she said. "Very impressive."

"Did you think so?" He was rather flattered.

"Very. You got over what you wanted from the public and gave them no information at all."

"Oh."

"When am I going to get you back, then?" she said. "I don't much like being a single woman again."

"Soon," he said. "Very soon. I think it'll all be over tomorrow."

When he went back to the incident room, Magda was still sitting by the uncurtained window, her legs crossed, her eyes shut.

31

A_s expected, there were plenty of calls from cranks and exhibitionists. People with a grudge wanting revenge. People with an axe to grind. The link made by the press of the murders to the Old Chapel gave the venom a particular flavour. Supporters of the Natural Therapy Centre claimed the police investigation had been an establishment plot to discredit complementary medicine. Religious bigots made accusations about New Age ideology: satanic ritual and paganism.

But there were genuine callers, hesitant and embarrassed, who stumbled over their explanations: "I don't suppose it's important but . . ."

When Ramsay returned to the incident room, the phones were still ringing. There had been a quiet period after eight o'clock, but the appeal for information had been broadcast again at nine-thirty and there was renewed activity.

Rob Newell was sitting at the desk nearest the door. He looked quite incongruous, dressed in a Young Conservative's idea of casual clothes—twill trousers, a shirt in boy-scout khaki, and a tweedy tie.

"Well?" Ramsay asked. "Any pattern emerging?"

"Several people have phoned about a car parked in Ferndale Avenue that Monday evening," Newell said. "It was parked outside the McDougals' house for a couple of hours, though no one seems to have seen the driver."

"Description of the vehicle?"

"Small red hatchback. Nova or Fiesta. We'll send people out with photos tomorrow and try to narrow it down."

"What about the day James McDougal died? Was the same car seen then?"

Newell shook his head.

"We've had a disappointing response on that," he said, "though a neighbour confirms that Mrs. Abbot was there. Saw her from an upstairs window. Apparently there were residents at home, but none of them had any reason to go out into the street. It was early afternoon. Kids were still at school. The people who did venture out only got as far as their back gardens to sit in the sun."

Ramsay allowed his impatience to show. He raised his voice so the whole room could hear. He wanted them to know how important it was. "Are you telling me that Ferndale Avenue was empty all afternoon?" he demanded. "Because I don't believe you. What about tradesmen? What about bin men? Window cleaners? Find out what time the post box in Ferndale Avenue is emptied and talk to the postman. Find out if any charity envelopes or advertising junk was delivered in the area that afternoon. Do any of the elderly residents have home helps? You get the idea. Use a bit of nous and imagination."

The impatience was real. He knew what he was looking for. He knew who had committed the murders and how it was done. He only had to prove it.

Newell was impressed by the list of instructions, almost happy. He was always more comfortable obeying orders than working under his own initiative.

"Right," he said. "I'll start checking at once."

"Sir!" Sal Wedderburn called from the other side of the room, her hand over the telephone receiver. "Another witness has called about the red car parked in Ferndale Avenue on Monday tenth. He's convinced it was a Fiesta. M reg. Do you want to talk to him?"

The caller was a computer freak with his own consultancy business. He's just landed a contract with a chain of travel agents and, he told Ramsay, he was feeling pretty good that night driving home. That's why he remembered the date so well. The next morning there'd been police all over the place, though no one had asked him any questions. He'd left before the house-to-house enquiries started. He was never there really. He worked all the hours God sent.

"Why did you notice the red car?" Ramsay asked.

"Because I'd never seen it before. That time it's mostly neighbours' vehicles on the street."

"What makes you so sure it was a Fiesta."

"I was thinking of getting one for the wife. She's always nagging about a car of her own. It's her fortieth birthday next month. I checked it out, thought it was a smart little motor."

By the time he had replaced the receiver, Ramsay remembered where he had recently seen a new Fiesta. He called to Hunter.

"Come on," he said. "We're going visiting."

"Where are we going, then?" Hunter asked when they were outside. He looked at his watch. It was only ten o'clock, but the town was deserted. Like a bloody morgue, he thought. He'd treat himself to a Friday night in town when this was all over, in one of the pubs where the barmaids went topless. That was probably all he needed to sort himself out: a few beers and a bit of smut.

"Long Edge Farm," Ramsay said. "Mrs. Richardson drives a car that matches the one in Ferndale Avenue."

"You don't have her down as the murderer?" Hunter said. "I can't see it myself. Not that I've met the woman, like. And wasn't it a bit daft to park right outside the victim's house for all those hours? You'd think she'd have moved it up the street a couple of hundred yards. Unless it wasn't premeditated, of course. But she was hardly just there for a chat—"

Ramsay cut through the rambling. "The lad, Peter, drives his mother's car," he said. "And he *is* a bit daft. But let's see what he has to say for himself."

There was no Fiesta standing outside the farmhouse. A full

moon had come up over the hills and they could see quite clearly. The living-room curtains were drawn and there was the sound of the television, rather loud, a burst of canned laughter. Ramsay led Hunter round to the back door.

Through the uncurtained kitchen window they saw Mrs. Richardson. She was dressed in a fluffy pink dressing gown and her hair was wrapped up in a towel. She was sitting at the table, obviously working on the farm's accounts. There was a calculator on the table beside her and she pressed at the buttons quickly and efficiently. She was wearing pink-rimmed spectacles. Ramsay watched her through the window when Hunter knocked at the door. She remained seated and still concentrating on the figures in front of her and called: "Come in!" She sounded a little surprised to be disturbed so late at night, but not anxious. Perhaps she was used to the guests from the cottages turning up at all hours, but Ramsay thought there was more to her calm response than that. Owning land gave people confidence. It wouldn't have occurred to her to be frightened.

He pushed open the door and walked in ahead of Hunter.

"Inspector," she said, and frowned. "What is it? It's not Peter, is it? There's not been an accident?" Still she remained quite composed.

"No," he said. "Nothing like that."

"Can't it wait until the morning, Inspector? It's been a very long day."

"I'm afraid not."

"You'd better sit down, then." She set the papers with their rows of figures aside and suddenly became more of her old self. "Would you like a drink? Tea? Coffee? Or could I tempt you to a whisky?"

He shook his head.

"Did you know Val McDougal?" he asked.

"The teacher who was killed in Otterbridge? No, I don't think so."

"She was about your age," Ramsay persisted. "Perhaps you met her before you married. Her maiden name was Brown. Or perhaps you came across her at Otterbridge College, where she worked. They run courses for people setting up in the holiday business. I've checked."

"I haven't been on any courses, Inspector," she said, good-naturedly. "I never found the time. I've had to pick it all up as I went along."

"Can you explain what your car was doing outside Mrs. McDougal's house, then, on the day she died?" It was Hunter, blunt and impersonal. She looked at him in surprise. People she invited into her kitchen didn't usually speak to her like that.

"Of course not," she said. "Because it wasn't."

"Where is your car tonight?" Ramsay asked politely.

"Peter asked to borrow it."

There was a pause while the implication of the words sunk in.

"Did he borrow it on the night of Monday May tenth?"

"I'm not sure," she said uncertainly. "That's more than a week ago, isn't it? I'd have to check my diary. See what I was doing that night."

"Perhaps you would do that for us, Mrs. Richardson."

"Yes," she said. "Of course."

She was fumbling in her handbag for the diary when they heard a car come too fast down the drive, the squeal of brakes, the crunch of gravel.

"I'd not let that lad drive any car of mine," Hunter muttered.

"There's Peter," she said gratefully. "You'll be able to ask him yourself."

The door opened and Peter stood, blinking and a little unsteady, just inside the room. Ramsay thought it unlikely that he would pass a breath test, but that was hardly his concern now.

"Peter," he said, "I'd like to talk to you."

"Well, I don't want to talk to you!" The boy was full of beer and mock bravado. "I'm off to my bed." He swayed slightly forward. "Unless you're planning on arresting me." His mother gave a nervous little giggle.

"I'll do that, too, if I think it's necessary," Ramsay said calmly. "Sit down."

Peter sat.

"Did you know James McDougal?" Ramsay asked. "He was Faye's boyfriend, before you."

"No." Peter was dismissive. "She told me about him. He was only a kid, wasn't he?"

"And Mrs. McDougal? She taught at Otterbridge College." He shook his head, yawned in a parody of disinterest.

"Do you often borrow your mother's car?"

"Yeah," he said. "She doesn't mind."

"Did you borrow it on the evening of May tenth?"

"I don't know. I might have done. Why?"

Ramsay slammed his hand flat on the table. "Because that's the evening when Mrs. McDougal was killed and a car like your mother's was parked in the road outside her house."

"It's a common car, that. Thousands of them about. It could have been anyone's."

"But I don't think it was anyone's. I think it was yours. Where were you on that Monday night?"

"I don't know." The aggression had gone, but he was sullen and determined not to cooperate.

"He was with us, Inspector." Mrs. Richardson had retrieved her diary and was peering at it through her spectacles. "Don't you remember, pet? It was the FWAG do at the agricultural college."

"What's a FWAG when it's at home?" Hunter asked.

"The Farming and Wildlife Action Group," Sue Richardson said. "Stan's not very keen on it, but I thought we ought to belong. It looks good on the publicity we put out for the holiday cottages. And you can get some useful information on subsidies, how to create a pond or maintain woodland. You know the sort of thing." Her tone was determinedly cheerful.

"And there was a FWAG meeting on the tenth?" Ramsay asked sceptically. He couldn't imagine Peter Richardson going along to a talk on the rise and fall of the corn bunting.

"Not a meeting," she said. She gave another of her little giggles. "You'd not get Stan along to a meeting. No, it was the annual dinner. The college put on quite a good spread, didn't they, pet? And there was a bar. It was just a good opportunity to meet old friends."

"Were the three of you there all evening?"

"Of course," she said. "It went on longer than I expected. It was gone midnight when we got home."

"Which car did you go in?"

"Not the Fiesta," she said quickly. "The Volvo."

"You left the Fiesta parked outside the farmhouse?"

"Of course."

"Was the car locked?" Ramsay asked.

She laughed. "I don't expect so. We're rather naughty about security out here, Inspector."

"Did you notice if the car had been tampered with? If there was extra mileage on the clock?"

"No," she said. "I'm sorry."

"You wouldn't have left the keys in the ignition?"

"Of course not, Inspector. I'm not a fool."

"Did you keep a spare set in the house?"

"Yes," she said. "On the hook over there." A row of mugs hung on hooks from the dresser.

"And I don't suppose you always bother locking your back door?" Ramsay said.

"No, Inspector, I'm afraid I don't."

"So someone could have stolen your car, and replaced it without your noticing?"

"What a ridiculous idea, Inspector! Why would anyone want to do that?"

They sat for a moment in the car, looking out over the moon-lit valley. Hunter shivered. All that space made him uneasy.

"What was that about?" he demanded.

Ramsay spoke slowly. "The problem was always how he covered the distance," he said. "How he got all the way to Otterbridge without transport. At least now we've got a possible explanation."

"Who are you talking about, man?" Hunger said impatiently.

"Slater," Ramsay said. "I think it was Slater."

"So it *was* that bastard all the time." Hunter was ecstatic. "Mind you, he couldn't have nicked Mrs. Richardson's car on the afternoon James was killed. It was broad daylight and there'd have been folks in and out of the house all the time. It'd be too risky, that."

"He didn't need to steal a car, then," Ramsay said.

"What do you mean?"

"Think, man! Can't you work it out?"

Hunter thought and only looked nonplussed.

"You took a phone call, didn't you, on the afternoon of James's death, from a drunken farmer who said he'd seen Ernie Bowles's ghost in Mittingford. What exactly do you think he'd seen?"

"A bloody hallucination."

"No," Ramsay said. "Not a hallucination. Ernie Bowles's Land Rover. If he'd seen it from a distance, he'd have recognised the vehicle—there aren't that many farmers let their cars get in that sort of state—but not the driver."

"And by then Slater had moved into the house at Laverock Farm and he'd found the Land Rover keys!"

"Quite."

"What about motive, though, sir? I can see why he would have wanted Bowles out of the way, but not the McDougals. And what about his alibi?"

"I've got an idea about that," Ramsay said.

32

They went to Laverock Farm that night. Hunter, knowing Ramsay's reputation for caution, for sticking to the rules, insisted on it, pushing the argument to the point of insubordination.

"We've got to take Slater in tonight," he said stubbornly, although in fact Ramsay had voiced no disagreement. "Charge him with the car theft, if nothing else. Anything to get him out of that house, prevent another death." Then, his voice almost hysterical: "Come on, man, you must see that Lily Jackman's in danger! We can't take the risk of leaving it until the morning."

"No," Ramsay said quietly. "I don't think we can."

It was almost midnight when they got to Laverock Farm and there were no lights on. Washing still hung from the line in the orchard and a white sheet billowed in a sudden breeze like a sail in the moonlight. They parked in the farmyard and waited.

There was a sudden noise in an upstairs room. Slater pushed open the sash window and the sound of the creaking wood running up the cords was shocking in the still air.

"Who is it?" he shouted. "What do you want?"

A lack of control in his voice made Ramsay cautious. He opened the car window and shouted back: "It's me. Ramsay. Why don't you come down? We can talk."

"Are you on your own?"

223

"No, Sergeant Hunter's with me."

"That's the bastard that's been hassling Lily. Keep him out of this."

"All right," Ramsay said easily. "I'll come in on my own."

"No," Slater said. "Just stand in the yard where I can see you. You can talk from there."

"It would be more comfortable inside."

"Maybe it would. But you'll do as I say." He swung round violently and they saw he was carrying a shotgun. He waved it wildly out of the window and repeated, "You'll do as I say."

"Where's Lily?" Ramsay asked.

"She's here with me. Where she belongs."

"Is she alive, Sean?"

"Of course she's alive. Do you think I'd hurt Lily?"

"Why don't you bring her to the window? So I can see her."

"No!" Slater said. "Just sod off!"

In the silence that followed, Ramsay heard Hunter on the radio, calling for backup, specialist officers. He knew that the nearest firearm officers were in Otterbridge and it would be hours before they'd get out here. He thought it would all be over by then.

"Where did you get the gun, Sean?" he asked, for something to say, just to keep him talking. It hardly mattered now and shotguns were two-a-penny in the countryside.

"It was Ernie Bowles's," Sean shouted back. "I found it in the glory hole under the stairs. Your blokes must have missed it when they searched. I knew he had one and it must be somewhere."

There would be plenty of questions asked about that, Ramsay thought. Recriminations. Passing the blame.

"I know why you did it, Sean," he shouted. "I know why you killed the McDougals."

There was a brief pause.

"You know nothing!" Sean yelled back angrily. He pointed the shotgun into the air and fired it. The noise was like an explosion and made Ramsay turn away. It was followed by the sound of wing beats as a barn owl was frightened from its roost in the tractor shed. The big white bird glided across the farmyard and settled on a tree behind the house. Everything was quiet and still again.

"Well, why don't you tell me, then?" Ramsay asked. "Why don't you tell me how it happened?"

He moved closer to the house, away from the car, hoping to establish a more intimate contact. He stood under Slater's window and spoke in a lower, conversational voice. He'd gone once to a seminar on hostage situations, but he could remember nothing now of what he'd been taught. He didn't even know if this *was* a hostage situation. From where he was standing he could not see inside the room.

"Well, Sean? Why don't we hear your side of the story?"

"You wouldn't understand!" Sean screamed. "You wouldn't bloody understand!"

"I might," Ramsay said. "If you explained. Just put the gun down and tell me." He might have been speaking to a child throwing a temper tantrum.

"They didn't think I was good enough for her." Sean turned his head so the light caught his face. Ramsay saw that he was crying. His voice became broken by sobs. "Just because I wasn't taken in by them, by their talk. Because I wouldn't go to their bloody groups. Inner knowledge and inner healing. What does that mean anyway? I didn't need all that. I always knew what I felt. I bloody showed them."

"But that wasn't why you killed them, Sean, was it?" Ramsay's voice was quiet, considered, interested.

"I did it for her!" The words came out as a bellow and reverberated around the valley, sending the monkey-faced owl into the air once more.

Hunter watched Ramsay move away from the car. When he was sure the inspector held the boy's full attention, he opened the passenger door slowly. Then waited. There was no response from Slater. The car was parked sideways-on to the house and the passenger door was out of his line of view.

Hunter rolled out of the car and into the shadow of the tractor shed. He lay still, breathing heavily. In the distance he heard the conversation between Ramsay and Slater continuing. There was a smell of grain and old sacking. The floor was covered with dried hen droppings.

He crawled on his stomach away from the car, keeping to the shadow, thinking that this jacket had cost him a fortune and that the force had better cough up for a replacement. He knew he had to find a way into the house. The kitchen door was no good. He couldn't get to that without Slater seeing, even if a sudden, miraculous cloud covered the moon. He knew there was a front door with a storm porch, on the side of the house that faced the garden, and decided to make for that. When he reached the orchard he stood up. He was round the corner of the house and out of Slater's line of view. But he knew he had to be quick. Slater might notice at any time that he was no longer in the car. He pushed his way past the washing and through a tangle of overgrown shrubs.

The door of the storm porch was unlocked. It was stiff, as if it had warped and was seldom used, but it gave way at last to Hunter's tugging. The inner door had panes of bubbled glass and it was impossible to see inside. Hunter stood still for a moment, trying to hear if the conversation between Ramsay and Slater was going on, but Ramsay had lowered his voice so much that he could not tell. Perhaps Slater had come downstairs and was waiting on the other side of the door, with the shotgun in his hand. He turned the handle and pushed. The door was locked.

Swearing under his breath, he looked about him for a hiding place for a spare key. The front of the house was in shadow, and though his eyes had become accustomed to the gloom, he could make out nothing in detail. He felt along the window ledge. His fingers found nothing but a thick layer of dust. There was a filthy doormat on the floor of the porch but no key underneath it. He retreated into the garden.

On each side of the porch was a large terra-cotta pot, which in Cissie Bowles's day might have held a flowering plant. Now each contained soil and a few dried-up weeds.

Hunter lifted each pot and felt underneath. Nothing. He scrabbled around in the dry soil and in the first pot he tried there was a large key. He cleaned off the muck and returned to the path. The key was rusty, but it fitted.

"Open, you bugger," he muttered, thinking that all he needed now was for the door to be bolted on the inside.

The key turned remarkably easily. He put his shoulder against the door, turned the handle, and pushed it slowly open.

At first it seemed pitch-black inside. He could hear a clock ticking, Slater's voice insistent but indistinct upstairs. Then he saw he was standing in a wide hall. Stairs, with a banister to one side, led away from him. He hesitated. Sod the heroics, he thought. Let's get Lily out and let the cavalry deal with the lunatic upstairs. But he was pleased to think that for her he *would* be the cavalry.

He felt his way around the downstairs rooms. There was a lounge, crammed with furniture, a dining room, damp and cold as a cellar with a huge mahogany table but no chairs, the kitchen, which was flooded with moonlight. No sign of Lily. The bastard's got her upstairs, he thought, and felt a rush of adrenaline.

He stood in the hall listening, but he could only hear Slater, relentless as a politician, going on and on about never having been understood.

Perhaps she's dead, he thought. He stared up the stairs, testing each tread with his foot before putting his weight on it, listening after each step for some sound from Lily. A cry or a movement from one of the other upstairs rooms.

There was nothing.

At the top of the stairs he stopped. Sean's voice was very clear now, still ranting.

"She believed in them, you know," he said. "She believed they could make everything better. I knew she was fooling herself. Some things you can't heal. Not just by talking."

Slater was in the bedroom over the kitchen. It, too, would have the moon shining directly in through the window. The door was slightly ajar and white light spilled out onto the landing.

Hunter moved softly along the landing, looking in the other rooms for Lily. There was a big square bathroom with a gurgling cistern, bedrooms with unsavoury beds and threadbare carpets, a huge commode like a throne. As he pushed open one door quietly there was a rustling of movement, but it was only a family of mice scattering to the holes in the skirting board. So Lily must be in the room with Slater, he thought. Why, then, was she so quiet?

"We've got a suicide pact, you know." Slater's voice came suddenly. "You won't take either of us alive."

The door to Slater's room was panelled, with a dark and peeling varnish. Hunter pushed it open a crack further. He could see Slater's back. The man was almost hanging out of the window, shouting to Ramsay, waving the shotgun to make his point. Hunter thought he might overbalance and go tumbling into the farmyard below.

Lily was standing in the corner beside Cissie's high lumpy bed, with her back to the wall. She looked at Hunter. He gestured her to walk towards him, but she did not move. She was wearing her nightdress, a long, white calico shift with a shawl thrown over the top. Hunter saw then that this was no victim waiting to be rescued. She did not seem frightened. She was watching Slater sadly, waiting for him to run out of steam. She thought he was making a fool of himself, but she was prepared to indulge him. For a while.

Sean turned back into the room. Still he could not see Hunter.

"I mean it," he said. "I'd rather kill you than let you talk to that pig. He was tricking you. Can't you see?"

Lily moved slowly away from the wall.

"Go on, then," she said.

"What?" he shouted. "Are you mad?"

"Kill me, then," she said firmly, "if that's what you want. I don't care one way or the other."

She walked towards him. Her bare feet made marks on the

228

dusty floor. They were long and bony and they reminded Hunter of a bird's feet.

Slater raised the shotgun towards her. In the farmyard below Ramsay was becoming anxious. They heard him calling, "Sean! What's going on, Sean? Why don't you come back and talk to me?"

Frustrated and helpless, Hunter stood very still. He knew that any movement might panic Slater into firing. Lily walked right up to him, so the barrel of the shotgun touched her chest.

"Love," he said. "I only did it for you."

"I know," she said. "I know."

"I thought you'd realised," he said.

She lifted the barrel of the shotgun so it pointed towards the ceiling, then she took it from his hands, cradling it carefully in her arms like a baby."

"I thought you'd be pleased," he said.

She turned and threw the gun onto the bed.

"Come on," she said. "Come on." She hugged him to her, so his head was on her shoulder, and looked over him at Hunter, who came into the room and emptied the gun. They did not move, even when Hunter went over to the window and shouted out to Ramsay: "It's all right, boss. It's all over."

Later, back at the police station, Ramsay asked:

"How did you manage that, then? The Indiana Jones trick. Disarming your man with a single blow."

Hunter paused. For a moment there was a temptation to lie. It would have been a much better story if he'd been more than an onlooker. He still felt cheated that there'd been no chance for action after all that buildup.

"It wasn't me," he said. "It was Lily. She persuaded him to give himself up."

"Ah yes," Ramsay said. "Lily Jackman."

33

It was almost dawn when they sat round in the incident room listening to Ramsay tell the story. Bleary-eyed and crumpled, they were too tired to interrupt and they were surprised that he found the energy to keep going. He wanted to explain it, he said, though they thought that motive wasn't really important, not now that the case was over. They should be celebrating.

"It was quite simple," Ramsay said. "Obvious really, once you realised that the story about Faye Cooper was just a distraction. Slater sent the anonymous letter to confuse us. And because he's always resented the Abbots and the time Lily spent with them. He moved James McDougal's body for the same reason. To make us think that the murder had something to do with Faye. . . ." His voice dropped, so they could hardly hear. "And I suppose it did have a lot to do with the girl, in a way."

He paused and took a breath, not to make a drama out of it, because by now they all knew at least the basics of what had happened, but because he wanted the facts straight in his mind before he started.

"Lily Jackman killed Ernie Bowles on that Saturday night," he said. "She was on her own in the caravan after she'd finished work. Slater, as we know, had wandered off and bumped into his hippy friends. He was stoned out of his brain and sleeping it off in their van. Perhaps that explains some of his feelings of guilt, something of what happened later.

"Lily wanted to make tea, but there was no water in the caravan. She took the plastic container to the farmyard to fill it up from the outside tap just as Ernie Bowles arrived back at Laverock Farm from Otterbridge.

"We know what state of mind he was in. He'd arranged to meet a woman through a dating agency and Jane Symons wasn't at all the sort of person he'd planned. He'd expected sex, and that obviously wasn't going to happen. And then she'd had the nerve to leave him in the restaurant when they were still halfway through the meal. Ernie was disappointed, angry, frustrated. He wanted to lash out at someone. We know he'd had a fair lot to drink. We know, too, that he'd been sniffing round Lily Jackman for a long while. So when he saw her, in the light of the headlamps, probably not wearing a great deal, bending over the tap in the yard, he thought Christmas had come early.

"Perhaps he didn't intend more than a bit of a grope. He put his arm around her, tried to give her a kiss, hoping to rescue something from the evening. She pushed him away, and that's when he really did get mad. He'd been rejected once that evening and it wasn't going to happen again. He pulled her struggling into the kitchen. It was quite clear to Lily that he intended to rape her. But he was drunk, unsteady, and unfit. She was taller than him. Strong enough to lift the sacks of flour and grain in the health-food shop. And she was desperate. She got her hands around his throat and she strangled him."

He paused again and looked round at them. They idled across their desks, heads in their hands, but he had their full attention.

"You see why I say there are similarities with the Faye Cooper case. Daniel Abbot attempted an assault on Faye, but she didn't fight back. She'd been told by Magda Pocock that she had to take responsibility for whatever happened to her, so she blamed herself. Lily Jackman *did* fight back and committed murder."

231

"That wasn't murder," Sally Wedderburn said. "Not the way you've described it. That was self-defence."

"Why didn't she call us in, then?" Rob Newell asked. "If she'd called us at the time, explained, the most serious likely charge would have been manslaughter."

"She panicked," Ramsay said. "You must remember that she'd had dealings with the police before and she hadn't found them particularly sympathetic. She believed the New Age travellers' mythology. She thought we were all corrupt and brutal, that we wouldn't take her story seriously. It's not really surprising that she went back to the caravan and tried to pretend that it had never happened. Later she came to discover that one or two of us are human after all. She had decided to trust us and confess. That's what provoked Slater's little outburst tonight. By then he had a vested interest in keeping her quiet. Besides implicating him in murder, it would have made her independent of him again. He wanted to feel that she needed him."

He stopped and took a sip of almost cold coffee from his mug.

They wished he would get to the point, wondered what he was rambling about.

"It was a mistake to convince ourselves that the murders had all been committed by the same person." He looked across the room like a teacher in a lecture theatre. "I'm sure you've all worked out why Slater killed the McDougals."

There was no response. They were too tired to play his games.

"What did Lily do on the Sunday?" he demanded. "Come on. Think."

"She had lunch with the Abbots," Sally Wedderburn said. "And then she went to Magda Pocock's Insight Group."

"Where she worked in a pair with Val McDougal," Ramsay said. "And that's another parallel with the Faye Cooper investigation. Faye went to a Voice Dialogue session at Juniper Hall. She found it impossible to hide her anxieties and guilt from Magda, who was working as her therapist. Lily had spent all Saturday night alone in the caravan worrying

232

about what she'd done. I don't think she'd even confided in Sean Slater at that point. In the emotional atmosphere of Magda's group I think she'd have found it impossible to keep it to herself. Perhaps using one of the other voices, through Voice Dialogue, she told Val exactly what had happened."

"Why didn't Mrs. McDougal tell the police, then?" Hunter said. "Someone tells you they've committed murder you get in touch with the police. She might have been into all that New Age crap, but she was a teacher, a respectable woman."

"I don't think she was sure it had actually happened," Ramsay said. "Bowles's body wasn't discovered until Monday. Perhaps she thought it was an outrageous fantasy. Even if she did believe Lily, do you really think she would have turned her in? I think she would have seen that as a sort of betrayal. Everyone involved in Magda's group would have assumed that what they said there was confidential. I can imagine her going back to Lily, urging her to give herself up, but in the end leaving the responsibility to her. Of course she never did contact Lily again because on Monday night, just as news of Bowles's death was coming out, Slater killed her."

Outside, the sky was getting lighter and there was a burst of birdsong. Hunter sat on his usual perch on the windowsill and looked out over the playground. Ramsay continued.

"Lily confided in Slater on Sunday afternoon, as they walked home from the group. He went to meet her. She told him that she'd strangled Ernie Bowles and that Mrs. McDougal knew the whole story. In the morning they pretended to find the body in the farmhouse kitchen and we were called in. She says she didn't know Slater had murdered Val. Not at first. Perhaps she guessed what he'd done, but she didn't want to admit it to herself. She preferred to imagine her murder as a convenient coincidence. It was only after James's death that she realised she'd have to do something."

"Slater killed Val McDougal just to protect the girl?" Newell said.

Ramsay nodded. "That's what he's admitted. Lily was baby-sitting for the Abbots. There was no one at Long Edge Farm because the Richardsons had a do at the agricultural college. Sean knew about that—there were posters up all over the town. Anyway, he was prepared to take a chance. We know that he's got a record for car theft and there would have been other vehicles left outside the holiday cottages. He drove the Fiesta into Otterbridge and parked it in front of the McDougals' house. He wasn't concerned about anyone seeing the car. He didn't think it would be possible to trace it back to him. I'm not sure what he would have done if the family had been there. He would probably just have driven away. But the house was empty, so he waited. He went into the garden and found the nylon rope. When Val McDougal came back to her house, he was ready for her. . . .

"He had parked the Fiesta at Long Edge Farm and had walked to the caravan before Lily was home from baby-sitting. I think if she'd ever asked him if he'd murdered Val, he'd have told her. But she didn't ask. Later he typed the anonymous letter which sent us chasing after the story of Faye Cooper. He'd heard all about Faye, of course, from Lily. The letter was franked in Newcastle because he gave it to a feed rep to post. That was just a coincidence."

"I don't understand why he didn't just leave it at that," Newell said. "Why did he go after the boy? James didn't know that Lily had killed Bowles."

"But Slater couldn't be sure of that, could he? There was always a risk that Val had passed on Lily's story. They were close, after all. Everyone said that. More like friends than mother and son. And then he knew that Win Abbot planned to visit the boy. It would be an opportunity for James to pass on his suspicions, hints perhaps that Val had given. Sean convinced himself that Lily was in danger again. He was quite unbalanced, of course, more infatuated every day; it was as if he wanted to prove to Lily just how devoted he was.

"This time he didn't bother to steal a car. He took the Land Rover instead. He was quite reckless and drove down Mittingford High Street, giving our inebriated farmer a shock on the way. Do we know yet where he parked in Otterbridge?"

"Yes, sir." It was Newell, full of himself. He'd carried out the boss's instructions and got a result. What does he want? Hunter thought. A pat on the head? "An old chap who works part-time as a gardener saw the Land Rover. It was in a little cul-de-sac just round the corner from the McDougals."

"Sean followed James for most of the way by foot," Ramsay said. "Until he realised where he was heading and he came back for the Land Rover. When he got to the cemetery, it was empty except for James, sitting on a bench, dozing. It couldn't have been easier for him. . . ."

Ramsay's voice trailed off. For the first time that evening he, too, was feeling tired. They looked at him, wondering if he had finished, hoping they could go to their beds, but he continued:

"When I went to see him later that night he was working in the garden at Laverock Farm. He made a joke about not having made much progress for a whole day's work. I should have realised then that he hadn't spent all day in the garden. Lily made the connection. I think that's when she found she couldn't delude herself any longer."

"By then, though, there wasn't only herself to consider. She couldn't admit to having strangled Ernie Bowles without telling us about the others. She wanted the killing to stop, but she thought she owed Sean more than that. Before we arrived at Laverock Farm tonight, she told Slater she intended giving herself up. She was going to come into the station this morning and explain everything to Hunter here. For some reason she trusted him. She gave Slater the night to run away. Instead he found Ernie Bowles's gun and started talking suicide pacts. Perhaps that's what he really wanted all along.

The team ambled out of the station and up the road to the pub for a celebratory breakfast and plenty of coffee. It was almost seven, but the sun was bright. It would be another warm day. Ramsay and Hunter were left on their own in the incident room.

"Do you want to see her?" Ramsay asked. "Before she goes off to Otterbridge?"

Hunter did not answer directly. "What will they charge her with?" he said. "Murder or manslaughter?"

Ramsay shrugged. "That's up to the CPS."

Hunter remembered the straight-backed woman with the dark eyes he'd seen in Cissie Bowles's bedroom.

"Na!" he said. "She won't want to talk to me."

Like Sean, he thought, he wasn't really into independent women.